Eileen Dunlop was born at Alloa, and educated in Alloa and Edinburgh. She has lived all her life in Scotland, and all her books have Scottish themes and backgrounds. Her other novels are *A Flute in Mayferry Street, Fox Farm, The Maze Stone, Clementina,* and *The House on the Hill.* Eileen Dunlop and her husband, Antony Kamm, have written several information books about Scotland, and compiled collections of Scottish verse. Her recreations are reading, gardening and going to the theatre.

For my father and mother

EILEEN DUNLOP

Robinsheugh

Richard Drew Publishing
Glasgow

First published 1975
by Oxford University Press

This edition first published 1987 by

Richard Drew Publishing Limited
6 Clairmont Gardens, Glasgow G3 7LW
Scotland

The publisher acknowledges the financial assistance of the Scottish
Arts Council in the publication of this book.

British Library Cataloguing in Publication Data

Dunlop, Eileen
    Robinsheugh. — (Swallow).
    I. Title II. Series
    823'.914[F] PR6054.U52

    ISBN 0-86267-194-9

Set in Chinchilla by John Swain & Son, Glasgow
Printed and bound in Great Britain by
Cox & Wyman Ltd., of Reading

Journey

As the north-bound train swayed slowly out of King's Cross Station, and her mother's face, anxiously smiling, receded into a featureless dot far down the platform, Elizabeth allowed her own brightly frozen smile to dissolve, and huddled back in her corner seat, knowing that for the next six lonely hours she had nothing to do but read magazines, eat sandwiches, and brood over the unfairness of everything. Her face was aching with the effort of smiling carelessly, and every few minutes she felt the hot discomfort of tears stinging behind her eyes, but whether she wept in grief, because she would not see her father and mother again for three months, or in anger, because she was being sent away to Scotland to stay with Kate, or in frustration, because no one would even try to see her point of view, she could not have said.

As the train gathered speed up the line, and the yellow brick suburbs of London fell back relentlessly, street by street into the past, Elizabeth stared moodily out of the window, and thought about the misery of the present. It wasn't as if she had objected to her parents' going to America without her. At twelve and a half you don't make a fuss because your mother is going to leave you for a few weeks, especially if you have a grandmother as loving and indulgent as Elizabeth's, who is longing to look after you. Elizabeth was sure she could not have behaved more reasonably.

'Of course you must go, Mother. It's a marvellous opportunity, and you and Father really do need a holiday. You mustn't worry about me at all. I'll be perfectly all right with Granny.'

And her parents had said how grown up and sensible she had become, and how proud of her they were, and had told everyone. That had been last week. Then suddenly, just when everything had been settled, and all the packing was done, Elizabeth's grandmother had to go into hospital for an operation, and they all realised that she would not be able to look after Elizabeth after all. Which was very unfortunate, and of course Elizabeth had been properly sorry, but deep down in the secret place where no one else could see, she was also exultant, because she knew that there was no one else in London with whom her father and mother would be willing to leave her, and for a whole day she had happily assumed that now they had no alternative but to take her with them when they left for New York four days later. That was before she heard her mother talking on the telephone to Kate.

'Kate, darling, I'm at my wits' end. I just don't know what to do with her. If you could take her off my hands, I'd be so grateful....'

Sitting all alone in the train, Elizabeth flushed as she recalled her own rage and humiliation. At my wits' end. Take her off my hands. She had heard Kate's voice, cool and incisive, very far away, say something she could not quite catch, then her mother's voice again, insulting in its relief, 'Oh, Kate, you are kind. I really don't know how to thank you. I know she won't get in your way. Yes, Saturday — we'll pack her off first thing.'

There was more, but Elizabeth did not wait to hear it. In a red, blinding hood of rage she went out to the back door, and sat on the step, seething with anger and disappointment. So after all, she was not to go to America. There would be no New York and California to boast about when she went back to school next term. She was to be packed off, farmed out, disposed of, to anyone who would take her off her mother's hands. And anyone was Kate, Kate who was a Doctor of Philosophy and an Oxford don, and never knew what day of the week it was. Kate, who always had her nose in a book, and liked people in history better than people now. Kate who was Elizabeth's aunt, and had no idea how a proper aunt should behave. It was insufferable. It was not fair.

The burble of telephone talk, punctuated by bursts of private merriment, went on for ages. Elizabeth hated their exclusive, grown-up chatter, with its laughter which left her out. After a while, she heard her mother ring off, and come into the kitchen, humming a contented little tune. There was a clattering as she began to put the supper dishes into the sink, ready for washing up.

'Elizabeth, are you there? Come in and close the door now, it's getting chilly.'

Elizabeth got up slowly from the step. Although past experience told her it would be futile, she would make one attempt to change her mother's mind. Perhaps if she really understood how hopeless it was, she would listen, even at the last minute. Elizabeth went into the kitchen, shut the door, and leaned against it.

2

'Mother,' she said hastily, addressing Mrs Martin's broad back as she stood at the sink, 'don't make me go to Kate. Think of something else, please.'

Her mother glanced round at her, eyebrows lifting.

'Oh, you were listening, were you?' she asked, putting Elizabeth in the wrong. Elizabeth blushed, and felt angrier than ever.

'I overheard,' she said with dignity. 'I wasn't listening. And I don't want to go.'

She watched her mother trying not to look exasperated, and resented her having to make the effort.

'Oh, Elizabeth, you've been so good about everything till now. Please don't spoil it.'

'That was when I was going to Granny's,' pointed out Elizabeth. 'Now it's different. I don't want to go to Kate.'

Mrs Martin sat down on a chair, and looked helplessly into her daughter's stubborn face.

'Darling, try to be reasonable. What else can we do? I know you're disappointed, but no one can help illness. Granny's very disappointed too. It's very kind of Kate to offer to take you at such short notice —'

'She didn't offer. You asked her. I heard you.'

'Well, yes, but —'

'I don't want to go,' repeated Elizabeth, as if repeating it were going to make any difference. 'You could take me to America with you.'

She saw her mother's carefully fixed veil of patience slip a trifle.

'Elizabeth, for heaven's sake. If we could have afforded to take you with us, do you suppose we'd be having all this fuss trying to find somewhere for you to stay while we're gone? Now you're just being silly. And anyway, I don't understand what's the matter with you. I always thought you and Kate got on so well together. Think of the fun you used to have with her when you were little.'

Elizabeth glared stonily.

'That was then,' she said. 'It's not the same now. Now, she doesn't even like me.'

'Doesn't like you?' Mrs Martin stared at her in perplexity. 'What nonsense is this? What on earth makes you think she doesn't like you?'

'I know she doesn't. When we were all at Granny's at

Christmas, she didn't speak to me once. Not once, in five days.'

She said it with emphasis, stressing the enormity of such bad manners. But as she would have expected, Mrs Martin brushed the matter aside with the loving indulgence which for some reason all the grown ups in the family showed towards Kate. It made Elizabeth crosser then ever, especially when she considered what her mother would have said if she had been so rude as not to speak to anyone for five days. But if you were Kate, you could get off with anything, apparently.

'Oh, I wouldn't worry about that,' Mrs Martin was saying. 'Actually I don't think she spoke to anybody much at Christmas. She had a dreadful cold, and I think Christmas is a bit of a trial to her. She isn't really the kind of person who enjoys wearing a paper hat and playing party games. You know how she always cheers up enormously on the day when she's going back to Oxford.'

'You always make excuses for her,' said Elizabeth bitterly.

'Well, she's my sister, and I'm fond of her. And she is different from other people. And,' continued Mrs Martin in a tone which Elizabeth knew well meant that patience was wearing thin, 'if I have to go away and leave you for three months, I'd certainly rather leave you with Kate than with anyone else. And you're wrong if you think she doesn't want you, because she does. She's spending the summer at a lovely house in Scotland, called Robinsheugh — she says it's a marvellous place, and you'll love it. . . .'

And that, Elizabeth reflected, as the train hurtled on through the flat summer fields of Huntingdonshire, shimmering pale and vibrating under the fierce July sky, had been the final blow. It would have been bad enough living with Kate in Oxford, but there at least there would have been shops and the cinema to help relieve the terrible boredom of life in a scholar's household, but instead Kate had to be staying for the summer in Scotland, poking about in the library of some old house, reading ancient diaries and letters, and no doubt forgetting when it was lunch time, or tea time, or time to go to bed. And meantime there would be nothing for Elizabeth to do except look out at sheep and endless acres of heather. She had never been to Scotland before, but she knew there was heather, with sheep, because she had seen them on picture postcards. She had thought there were wild Highland cows too, with menacing horns and shaggy brown coats, but her mother thought that they were to be found much

4

farther north; the place where Kate was staying was in the south of Scotland, not far from the English border. She remarked on this so often that Elizabeth began to wonder if she thought being near the English border would make her feel more at home.

The last few days with her parents were such a strain that Elizabeth would have been happy to get away, had it not been that Kate was waiting at the other end of the line. She had not protested again. It was useless, obviously, because as far as her mother was concerned, Kate could do no wrong, and as far as her father was concerned, her mother could do no wrong. So she pretended she didn't care, and this upset Mrs Martin, who tried to hide her anxiety by being too bright, too kind, too affectionate. It was much more trying than if she had simply been brisk and matter-of-fact, as she usually was. Eventually Elizabeth had thought that she would go mad if she heard just one more time that she was going to have the most marvellous summer of her life, alone in the wilderness with Kate Jenkins, who could not boil an egg, and did not speak to people for five days at a stretch.

The train left York. Elizabeth ate her sandwiches and tried not to think about Kate, but could find nothing else to think about. It was true, as her mother had pointed out, that when she was little she had had endless fun with Kate, who used to come often to stay when she had a holiday from the University. She had very clear memories of the Kate of those days, who took Elizabeth to the Zoo, and gave her rides in the basket of her bicycle, and was always finding something to laugh about. She had taught Elizabeth to play a mouth organ, and told her stories, and for a long time had been the most exciting person in Elizabeth's life, whose visits were longed for through weeks of days crossed off on the calendar, and whose departure brought tears only forgotten in the joy of opening the magical parcels she always left behind her.

What change of heart separated these laughing, dancing days from that disastrous Christmas holiday when Kate had wandered around the house, shivering and cross, complaining about the noise the children made and wishing that Christmas could be abolished by law, Elizabeth did not know. She could not even remember when it was that Kate had stopped coming regularly on visits; it seemed a very long time, but perhaps it was only about three years, perhaps around the time when she got such an important job at Oxford that she said she could not afford the time to take holidays any more. She always remembered to send presents, and now that she had plenty of money these were more extravagant than ever. But Elizabeth would have given all the cameras and tape recorders and transistor radios in the world to have again the Kate who sang silly songs in the bath, and sneaked baited mouse traps into the dustbin when Granny wasn't looking, because she said it was quite disgraceful behaviour to murder guests in one's house, even if they were uninvited.

It was then that Elizabeth began to notice how hopeless Kate was, how untidy, how forgetful, how vague in her manner, how unlike what a proper aunt should be. She did not try to hide her contempt for Kate's unfashionable clothes and studious habits, and the clever books she wrote, and when sometimes she saw Kate looking at her with a hurt, puzzled expression in her grey eyes, she would not allow herself to feel sorry, but excused herself, saying, 'If she were nicer to me, I would be nicer to her.' And so the gulf between them grew, and widened till neither of them made the least effort to bridge it. To Elizabeth, the most astonishing thing was that her mother apparently had not even noticed that a gulf existed. She was beginning to see, however, that people only noticed the things which could be noticed without too much inconvenience to themselves.

The train hurried relentlessly into the north. Elizabeth ordered herself firmly to stop thinking about Kate, because of course all this retelling of an old story made her feel worse, and to help herself do so she set her mind to imagining that she was going to Scotland to stay with another aunt, a make-believe aunt of the kind she would really have liked Kate to be. An aunt called — Elizabeth hunted for a suitable name — called Aunt Rosina, who would be waiting for her at the station in Edinburgh, expectantly on tiptoe on the platform, scanning the carriage windows eagerly for a first sight of Elizabeth. She would be delighted to see her, and would come running up to her, and hug her, and say, 'Elizabeth, darling, how lovely to see you. I've been longing for you to come. And how nice you look. You always have such pretty clothes. . . .' But it would not be like that.

It was not like that.

When at last the train came to a juddering halt in the huge underground cavern that was Waverley Station, and all the people on their feet were almost thrown over on top of one another, Elizabeth caught sight of Kate, waiting on the platform. She was leaning idly against a station barrow, watching two sparrows fighting over a soiled crust of bread, and paying not the least attention to the arrival of the train. Half the buttons on her faded linen frock were undone, and her rather beautiful fair hair, escaping from an unsuccessful knot on top of her head, was cascading in wild tendrils around her thin, clever face. Not until Elizabeth had heaved her suitcase out onto the platform, and gone back to collect her duffle bag and coat, did Kate apparently wake up to the fact that she had arrived. Then she tore herself away from her sparrows, and strolled over to greet her niece.

'Well, Miss Martin,' she said, ruffling up Elizabeth's hair with a casual hand. 'Your train's late. Were you held up?'

'No,' snapped Elizabeth, hastily smoothing down her hair again, and forgetting Aunt Rosina in her annoyance. She was hot and tired and cross, and she was just opening her mouth to say something rude when, inconveniently, she remembered a promise she had been forced to make to her mother the night before, that she would at least try to be pleasant to Kate. Because none of this was Kate's fault, et cetera, et cetera, of course, of course. So she swallowed her vexation as well as she could, and said quite mildly, 'At least, I don't think so. I didn't notice.'

But Kate was not really listening. She was looking down at Elizabeth's suitcase, with an amused expression around her mouth.

'Another suitcase?' she asked teasingly. 'Your trunk arrived yesterday. We thought you had come to stay for a year.'

'This is just an overnight bag, in case the trunk hadn't arrived,' explained Elizabeth seriously.

Kate looked at her incredulously, and gave a soft squeal of laughter, as if she had said something very witty. She picked up the suitcase, staggering under the weight, and Elizabeth eyed her dubiously, uncertain whether she was fooling, or whether the case really was too heavy for her. She had heard her mother say more than once that Kate was not strong.

'I could take it,' she offered.

'No, of course not, it's quite all right. You bring your duffle bag, whatever that may contain, and have your ticket ready. You do have it, don't you?'

'Yes,' said Elizabeth, fishing it out of her pocket. She gave it up with some reluctance, although it would have been of no more use to her. It was not a return ticket, because she was to home with Kate, by car, at the end of the summer. That day seemed years away.

'Then hurry up,' said Kate, reverting to her usual coolness. 'It's nearly four o'clock, and I want to get out of Edinburgh before the rush hour.'

Robinsheugh

Unlike most of the grown-ups Elizabeth knew, especially those who were not used to children, Kate never fell into the chattering, nervous small-talk of those who feel that silence is an embarrassing void which they must work feverishly to fill, sensing that if they do not, a child may in some obscure but important respect find them inadequate. Kate did not care whether Elizabeth, or any one else, found her inadequate. She was at home in silence. So as they drove out of the subterranean gloom of the station into the hot glare of the afternoon city, and passed into the streaming traffic between pavements trampled by slow, weary multitudes in summer clothing, she did not ask Elizabeth how her parents were, or when they left for America, or if she had seen Uncle Kenneth lately, or what the weather was like in London, as any of her other relations would have done, but drove slowly behind a bus, and used the quiet for thoughts of her own. She did dutifully point out Edinburgh Castle, which it would have been difficult to miss anyway, and also the National Library of Scotland and the University, which she probably thought were the two most important buildings in the city, but she did not try to cushion Elizabeth's arrival in friendliness, to make her feel more at home in the strangeness of this sudden new place. Elizabeth glanced sidelong at her pale, abstracted face, and her heart sank down into her feet. This was how it had been at Christmas, and this was how it was going to be. The ripple of laughter at the station, which had momentarily raised her hopes, had only called up briefly the ghost of a Kate long gone.

Soon the crowded streets of shops faded out among large, substantial stone houses, set down ponderously in well-tended gardens, then further on still the uneven fringes of the city frayed out into green fields spattered over with housing developments and untidy villages under the steep green rise of the Pentlands. Beyond Penicuik, the country suddenly opened out under a clear sky, and Elizabeth saw for the first time the expected tracts of wild moorland, stretching away on either side of the road, through marshy hollows ringed with reeds and patches of rough heather and clover, into grassy uplands freckled with grazing sheep. Here and there isolated knots of trees rose tall among the grass, but the bareness of the scene intimidated the city-bred Elizabeth; there was not a single human dwelling in sight.

But this was a land of sudden contrasts, and next moment the car was plunging headlong into a lushly wooded valley, where a river scurried along on the other side of a mossy stone wall, and trees overhung the road so that the sun dappled their path with a moving, dancing, changing pattern of black and gold. It was a beautiful day, but Elizabeth was too sad to enjoy it. Only seven hours after leaving London, she was already homesick for grey pavements and red brick houses, and the trains that thundered endlessly past the end of Cranbury Avenue.

They left the main road abruptly, turning down a side road which was really no more than a lane, skirted by high banks of grass and clover, and crested on either side by rambling, dark green hedges spotted with the pink and white of the wild rose.

'Are we nearly there?' asked Elizabeth.

She must have sounded tired, because Kate came suddenly out of her reverie and turned her head briefly towards her.

'About another fifteen miles,' she said, 'but we'll get along quite quickly now. There's not much traffic on these country roads. Are you hungry?'

'A bit,' said Elizabeth. 'I had some sandwiches on the train.'

'That's not very much,' said Kate. 'I should have asked you in Edinburgh, but I forgot. But never mind — Gerry will probably have our supper ready when we get home.'

'Who's Gerry?' enquired Elizabeth.

'Oh, of course, you don't know. Gerry Temple — she's one of my students. She is spending the summer with me, supposedly to help me with my research, and do the cooking, but as things have worked out, I do practically all the research, and she does all the cooking. Which is probably just as well, or we wouldn't eat at all. I didn't realise that cooking took up so much time. However, now that you're here, things should be easier. We can research, and you can cook.'

Elizabeth looked at her nervously, hoping that this was meant to be a joke, but the long-nosed profile did not seem to be laughing at all.

'I can't cook,' she announced wildly.

A faint smile crept up the corners of Kate's mouth.

'Well, I didn't really suppose you could,' she said. 'I expect we had better leave things the way they are, and hope that you can find other ways of amusing yourself.'

No more was said, and Elizabeth assured herself that of course it must have been a joke, because not even Kate could have expected her to cook, but every time she glanced at Kate's impassive face she wondered unhappily whether she had so soon disappointed her and the unknown Gerry. It was terrible not to know when a person was joking and when she was not. After a while, because she could not bear the silence any longer, she broke it.

'Is Robinsheugh a nice place?' she asked tentatively.

Kate seemed to hesitate for a moment, then she said, 'I think it's the most beautiful house I've ever seen in in my life.'

'Do we live in it?'

Kate laughed wryly.

'Well, no, not exactly,' she replied. 'To be precise, we live in a cottage behind it. You know that old hymn that says, "The rich man in his castle, the poor man at his gate —" We're the poor man at his gate.'

'Who's the rich man?'

'His name is Sir Gilbert Melville. He isn't there at the moment — he lives in London most of the time, but he has taken a great interest in the work I'm doing, and let me have the cottage for the summer so that I can study his family papers, which are kept at Robinsheugh.'

'What exactly are you doing?' asked Elizabeth, less because she wanted to know than to keep the silence at bay.

'I'm collecting material for a biography of Sir Giles Melville, who was the Laird of Robinsheugh towards the end of the eighteenth century.'

'Oh,' said Elizabeth. 'Did he do anything special?'

Kate seemed again to consider her answer before she gave it.

'It really depends on what you mean,' she said. 'He was a fairly successful statesman, and was British Ambassador for a time to several Courts in Europe. Then of course he knew a lot of people who were far more famous and important than he was, and he wrote his opinions of them in his diary, which makes fascinating reading. But he was more than just a diarist and a minor public figure — he was a poet and a scholar, and a man of great personal courage. A good friend and a just enemy. Perhaps in the end of the day he didn't *do* anything so very special, compared with some people, but he *was* something special and that matters much more.'

There was a sudden, unexpected tenderness in her voice which made Elizabeth look at her curiously.

'You like him a lot, don't you?' she said.

'Yes, I like him a lot.'

More than me, thought Elizabeth sadly. More than Mother, or Granny, or Uncle Kenneth, or any of the living people she meets every day. She likes people in history better than people now. She watched Kate thinking about Giles Melville, her angular face softened by affection, and wondered what it was like to care so much about somebody who had lived not even in the last century, but in the one before that. It was not something she thought she would ever understand.

But in any case she did not have long to consider the matter, for without warning Kate swung the car off the road down a narrow, rutted lane between lines of tall beech trees. They flew over a small, hump-backed bridge and bounced down beyond it so that Elizabeth's stomach seemed to be catapulted into her throat; she heard the crunchy spurt of gravel under the wheels as the car shot through between two tall, ornately carved gate-posts, and ground to a halt in the middle of a semi-circular carriage drive, surrounded by a low wall of creamy stone. Robinsheugh.

To the end of her days, Elizabeth would never forget her first sight of the house of Robinsheugh, lying asleep in its hollow among the hills, in the clear air of a late July afternoon. It was a tall, tranquil, golden house, with corbelled turrets and rows of small-paned windows, deeply sunk into the walls, and crowned by a steeply pitched roof of green slate, where peaked dormer windows, like witches in hoods, seemed to balance precariously, chatting in the sunshine. It had all the assurance of great age which is still confident of its beauty, and always afterwards, when she remembered that day, Elizabeth thought of a feeling of intense and mysterious happiness, out of place at a time when she was not happy at all. She got out of the car and stood for a moment outside the shadow of the walls, looking up at the mellow stone façade and drinking in the sweet, untroubled beauty of the place, and, as she looked, it came to her mind that only happy people could have lived in such a lovely house, for surely here no pain or trouble had ever intruded. She too thought it was the most beautiful house she had ever seen. Then a cloud out of nowhere covered the sun, and the walls darkened.

Elizabeth turned back to where Kate was with difficulty

heaving the suitcase out of the boot of the car, and her fleeting delight in the house was forgotten in the strain of arrival, the uncertainty and confusion of new faces, new rooms, new sensations. At the back of the great house, and in its shadow, but tucked away out of sight of the carriage-way and gardens, was a cluster of lesser buildings, built round a cobbled yard; stables, harness rooms, a dove-cote, several cottages. Two of these rather cramped dwellings, occupying the whole of one side of the square, had been joined together to make one long, low house, built like the rest of the same yellow stone as the main house, and roofed like it with greenish slates. It had a regular pattern of small windows facing in towards the yard, and a green door at one end. The door stood ajar, and as Kate led Elizabeth through an archway and across the cobbles towards it, there was a flash of colour as a girl emerged and waved to them from the doorstep.

'I thought you were lost,' she called cheerfully.

'The train was late,' replied Kate, 'and I drove carefully because you told me to.' She added, 'Elizabeth, Gerry,' by way of introduction, and went past Gerry into the house, leaving them both on the doorstep. Gerry grinned at Elizabeth. She was a small, dark girl with long black hair and shining brown eyes like a friendly fieldmouse's, looking out from a sallow, bright little face. She was a lot older than Elizabeth, but very much younger than Kate, who must, Elizabeth reckoned, be well over thirty. She was wearing blue denim jeans and a very pink T-shirt, and she was certainly the most cheering sight Elizabeth had seen that day. But before they had time to exchange any conversation, Kate's voice called from within, 'Gerry, there's another trunk. I left it beside the car. Give Elizabeth a hand to bring it in, will you?'

Gerry made an enquiring face at Elizabeth, who blushed, and said, 'It's only a suitcase. Not very big.'

'Come on, then,' said Gerry. 'Let's go and fetch it.'

Gerry at least knew how to treat a newly arrived guest, thought Elizabeth, as they went back across the yard and round the corner of the house to the car. She asked Elizabeth about her journey, and said that supper would soon be ready, and if she thought the suitcase was too big, at least she was polite enough not to say so. They took turns in carrying it back to the cottage, and when they got there, Gerry let Elizabeth go in first. 'After you,' she said.

Stepping from the porch into the kitchen, direct from the

blinding light outside, Elizabeth could at first see nothing at all, but as she frowned the sunshine out of her eyes, she saw that she was standing in a large, square, low-roofed room with a stone-flagged floor and a fire burning low in an old-fashioned kitchen range which stretched along one wall. The furniture was miscellaneous; an enormous table occupying the centre of the room, a quantity of wooden chairs in various stages of dis-integration, a high-backed dresser with rows of assorted cups and plates along shelves, and rather incongruously, a large white refrigerator standing in the angle between the range and the kitchen sink. The darkness was genuine, and not merely the contrast of indoors with the summer day outside. The only light entering the room filtered through a filigree of dark green leaves, rising among explosions of red geranium from brown earthenware pots set on the sills of three tiny windows, two at the front of the house, one at the back.

Despite the fire, the place had the cool dimness of a sea cave. It was quite unlike any other room Elizabeth had ever been in, and why it should remind her of Kate's sitting-room at Oxford, she could not at first imagine. But then it came to her that of course it was because of the books. There were books everywhere, and every flat surface in the room was overlaid by printed matter of one sort or another. One end of the table was piled high with books, notebooks, letters, pencils, pens, folders and bundles of typescript. More books were on the floor, on chairs, wedged in between the flower pots on the window-sills, while sheafs of paper protruded from pots and jars and kettles on the dresser and the chimney-piece and the shelves on either side of the fire. So it was in Oxford; the chaos was indescribable, and Elizabeth hated it. Her fingers itched to begin tidying it up. But Kate, who was stretched out resting in an old leather armchair by the fire, read either her thoughts or her expression with accuracy.

'And if you are thinking,' she remarked in her cool, clipped voice, 'how nice it would be to put everything in order, forget it. I won't be tidied up after. I hope that is clearly understood.'

Elizabeth said 'Yes, Kate,' meekly, and Gerry, who had turned aside to stir something in a pot on the range, interjected, 'Don't do it, Elizabeth. I tried it once, and the fireworks were quite spectacular.'

'You have never seen me angry,' said Kate, in a tone which somehow managed to sound both pleasant and ominous at the same time. She took Elizabeth up to her room, leading her from

14

the kitchen down a long, uncarpeted passage which smelt of summer and wax polish, and up a steep narrow staircase to the bedroom floor. This consisted of another long passage running along the centre of the house, with rooms opening off on either side. Kate's own room was at the end of the passage, and therefore above the kitchen; Elizabeth's was next door to it, with a window overlooking the yard.

'I'm afraid it's rather small,' said Kate, not sounding apologetic at all, 'but it's all we could get together in the time, as we don't have the use of all the rooms. The bathroom is next door. I'll call you when supper is ready.'

And with that she departed, closing the door behind her, leaving Elizabeth alone.

Elizabeth listened to the sound of her feet clattering away down the passage, and descending the stair erratically, jumping steps in a way that Elizabeth thought must be highly dangerous at her age. Then she sat down on a stool in the middle of the floor, and looked around the room that was to be hers for the next three months. A quarter of a year, she said, torturing herself, and London seemed further off than ever. Kate was right in saying that the room was small. It was not much more than a large cupboard, with whitewashed walls and a bare, varnished floor.

The furniture would have been sparse in a room of normal size, but here it gave the impression of terrible overcrowding. There was a camp bed, a large, old-fashioned chest of drawers, a small armchair with a faded tapestry seat, the stool Elizabeth was sitting on, and in front of the window, the trunk which had come from London the previous day, containing her books and games and almost every stitch of clothing she possessed. The subtraction from the floor-space caused by the suitcase which Kate had patiently carried upstairs for her meant that there was barely room to turn round without falling over one thing or bumping into another. It was all so different from her pretty pink and white room at home that she wanted to cry again, but then she thought that at least it was a place of her own; she had brought ballet posters for the walls and her collection of china animals for the chest of drawers, and there was a view from the tiny window of the beautiful house of Robinsheugh and a river through a gap in some trees. She reflected that it would have been really dreadful if there had been no room at all available for her, and she had had to sleep with Kate. The days when that would have been a delightful prospect were long since over. But the next minute she realised that of course it would never have happened, anyway. Nothing would have been allowed to violate Kate's scholarly solitude; had there been no other room, she would have had to sleep with Gerry.

She decided to wash now, and unpack later, because a strong cooking smell suggested that supper would not be long. So she found her sponge bag and a towel in her suitcase, went into the bathroom, washed her hands and face, and came back to her bedroom to brush her hair and put on a clean dress. It was then that she noticed the flowers, orange and gold marigolds in a little brown pot, smiling up at her from the window-sill. She supposed that Kate must have put them there to welcome her, and Elizabeth suddenly felt absurdly pleased, far more pleased than anyone ought to feel on account of a jar of marigolds. But it was the one thing she needed, just one small gesture on Kate's part to make her feel welcome in this strange house. Through all her sadness, a small spark of hope was struck; perhaps despite all the years of change, Kate had not completely forgotten what she and Elizabeth had once meant to each other. Just then she heard a voice calling, 'Elizabeth! Supper,' and after she had looked in the bathroom mirror to make sure that she was tidy, and put a string of beads round her neck, she went downstairs, and walked up the passage to the kitchen.

Gerry had spread a cloth at the clear end of the table (Elizabeth was soon to learn that this table was divided by unwritten law into Study End and Cooking End) and three places were laid. Kate was already seated at the table, wearing her spectacles and abstractedly spooning soup into her mouth, her head poked forward into a book which she had propped open between the coffee pot and the milk jug. Elizabeth looked at her in horror, but then she remembered that Kate had always done this, anywhere she could get away with it, and that meant everywhere except at Granny's. Even Kate had to do as she was told at Granny's, and if Granny said there was to be no reading at the table, then Katherine Jenkins, Doctor of Philosophy, might grumble, but she did not read at the table. But this was her own house, and there was no one to check her bad manners. Gerry was standing by the fire, dishing Elizabeth's soup from a pot on the hob. She said, 'Sit down beside Dr Jenkins, Elizabeth. I shan't be a minute.'

Elizabeth sat down, and looked along at Kate to see how she would react to this unexpected use of her title. Of course she knew that Kate was a Dr Jenkins, had been a Dr Jenkins for many

16

years, but she had never in her life before met anyone who would dream of calling her that. It was something you wrote on envelopes, not a name you would actually call a person, not Kate at any rate. It sounded so odd. She wondered why Kate did not tell Gerry to stop it at once, and call her Kate like everybody else. But Kate did not even seem to notice. She ate and read with absorption, and when Gerry removed her soup bowl and put a plate of meat and vegetables in front of her, she merely murmured a word of thanks, groped for her knife and fork, and went on reading.

Elizabeth was hungry, the food was good, and Gerry was obviously pleased to have someone to talk to. It should have been a pleasant meal, but then, 'I can't get used to it,' said Gerry to Elizabeth, smiling at her across the table. 'You're so like Dr Jenkins it's incredible. You could be her daughter.'

It was the wrong thing to say. Elizabeth went scarlet.

'I'm not,' she said crossly. 'I'm not, and I couldn't. I'm not like her in the least.'

She heard the rudeness in her own voice, and knew from Gerry's startled expression that she heard it too. If Kate heard it, she made no sign, and the situation might have been saved if Gerry had let the matter drop. But unwisely she pressed her point, appealing to Kate for support.

'But you are,' she insisted. 'You're terribly like her. Isn't she, Dr Jenkins?'

She had of course to ask twice, and then a third time when she had at last attracted Kate's unwilling attention, and Elizabeth, who was sure that Kate was being provoking on purpose, was almost ready to weep with mortification. Eventually Kate looked up, and glanced at Elizabeth's red face, gravely and without much interest.

'No,' she said, 'not really,' and returned to her book.

Tears of anger trembled on the edges of Elizabeth's eyelids, and it was with difficulty that she forced them back. Deep down, she knew that she did look like Kate; they shared the same fair hair and grey eyes, although Elizabeth noted thankfully that her own nose was shorter. Still, if she had to imagine her pretty, pink-cheeked face as it might be when she was old, she supposed it might be something like Kate's. But it was not something she wanted to think about. She did not want to be old, still less did she want to look like Kate. Yet now, when she realised for the first time that Kate did not want to admit the likeness either, she was not only angry, but hurt as well. It was all so confusing that she only knew she could not sit there for one more minute, with indifference on one hand and puzzled embarrassment on the other. She had to get out. With one sharp movement she kicked back her chair.

'I don't want any more supper,' she said abruptly. 'I'm going to bed.'

'Yes, do,' said Kate calmly. 'You'll feel better in the morning.'

Gerry said nothing at all. Blinded by tears unshed, Elizabeth made her way out of the kitchen, and went miserably upstairs. It was only half past seven.

Imprisoned by her own choice in her bare little cell of a room, with no escape until morning, Elizabeth sat on the stool and snivelled for a while into her handkerchief. What had happened downstairs had upset her dreadfully, and just when everything had been going so well, and Gerry was being so friendly. But now Gerry was embarrassed, which was not surprising, but then she could not possibly know yet how unpleasant Kate could be to Elizabeth. If she did, she would understand why Elizabeth did not want to look like Kate. Of course, there was the possibility that Kate was unpleasant to Gerry too, indeed it seemed so if she raged at her for tidying up that dreadful kitchen, and insulted her by reading at the table. And if they were really friendly, surely Gerry would call her Kate, not Dr Jenkins. You would not call a friend Dr Jenkins. This thought cheered Elizabeth a little, because she very much wanted Gerry as an ally and friend.

After a while, she wiped her eyes and began to unpack, lifting her clothes and books out of the trunk with a lingering, tactile pleasure, deriving what comfort she could from their accustomed look and texture. They seemed to provide her with a lifeline, stretching back through this interminable, trying day to that safe, homely London life that was hers this morning and now seemed a million years away. She put her books and games on one end of the chest of drawers, laid out her china animals at the other, and put her teddy bear on the bed. Five years had passed since Elizabeth had stopped taking her teddy bear to bed, and she had been so ashamed of wanting to bring him that she had hidden him up the front of her jersey, and slipped him into the trunk when her mother's back was turned. But now she was glad that he was here with her; the familiarity of his threadbare body, worn to tatters by seven years of rough loving, was very consoling.

What to do about the clothes was a problem, because there was no wardrobe, and even the chest of drawers, which was enormous, would not hold everything. She took it all out of the trunk, and laid piles of dresses, jerseys, cardigans, nightdresses, socks, petticoats, knickers, shoes, trousers, tights, on the bed, on the floor, on the chair, on the stool, and stared at them hopelessly. She was kneeling in the midst of the confusion, wondering what to do, when she heard footsteps outside, the door opened, and Kate was standing there with a plate of lemon pudding in one hand, and on her face an expression of utter astonishment. Elizabeth waited for some mocking comment, but Kate merely said, 'If you were to clear a square foot of space, I could come in.'

Suspiciously Elizabeth cleared a space between the door and the bed, and Kate squeezed in. She sat down on the end of the bed, and said, 'I brought your pudding. I didn't really notice, but Gerry said you hardly ate anything.'

Elizabeth did not know whether to be mollified or not. She took the plate and put it beside her on the floor.

'Eat it,' said Kate. 'Now, please.'

Her command was comforting. It was what Elizabeth was used to. She took up the spoon and began to eat.

Kate looked round again at the vast piles of clothes, and she said, 'Put as much as you can in the chest of drawers, and I'll ask Gerry to give you some coat-hangers tomorrow. You can hang your dresses in the cupboard beside the bathroom.' She paused, then added, 'On second thoughts, you had better ask her yourself. You know how forgetful I am.'

'Yes,' said Elizabeth. 'I mean, yes, I'll ask her.'

'I know what you mean,' said Kate.

Elizabeth ate her pudding and watched Kate, and Kate watched Elizabeth, and they had nothing to say to each other, and yet it mattered to Elizabeth, who was so far from all that was familiar, that Kate should have come. It pleased her as the marigolds had pleased her earlier in the day.

'Kate, may I read in bed?' she asked, hoping for the reassurance of another direct order. But she was disappointed. As far as Kate was concerned, she could read in bed all night if she wanted to. It would seem to her a perfectly natural thing to do.

'You may do exactly as you wish,' she said firmly, and Elizabeth quailed in the insecurity of so great a freedom.

As soon as the pudding was finished, Kate put out her hand for the plate.

'I must go,' she said, getting to her feet. 'I have so much work to do.'

She picked her way through clothing to the door, then turned with her hand on the doorknob.

'I'd leave all this till tomorrow, and get to bed, if I were you,' she said, quite kindly. 'You've had a long day, and you must be dead beat. You can finish it in the morning.'

'Yes,' said Elizabeth, 'all right.'

Kate nodded, and was about to close the door, when on an impulse Elizabeth called her back.

'Kate.'

'Yes?'

'Thank you for the flowers.'

But even before the words were properly out of her mouth, Kate's blank expression told her she had once more made a mistake.

'Flowers?' she said.

'Marigolds,' said Elizabeth miserably. 'On the window-sill.'

Kate's short-sighted eyes sought out the little brown pot.

'Ah, yes,' she said. 'Very pretty. It must have been Gerry. Sorry.'

And she closed the door and went away.

Elizabeth sat quite still for moment. Then she swept all her belongings off the rickety camp bed, and, tearing off the clothes she was wearing, threw them all over the room. She put on her nightdress, and climbed into the sleeping-bag, dragging the blankets round her in a tight, unhappy knot. And clutching her teddy desperately to her chest, in the frail, silver half-darkness of the summer night, she cried herself to sleep.

3

Solitude

Elizabeth had never in her whole life been as lonely as she was that first week at Robinsheugh, and what made her loneliness doubly bitter was that with a companion Robinsheugh would have been the most delightful place on earth. She could not help thinking what fun she could have had if she had been able to bring her friend Susan with her, or even her cousin, David Jenkins, and imagining the picnics they would have had, and fishing trips, and expeditions into the hills. Reality was very different; the days dragged past on heavy feet, and in her solitary explorations she found no pleasure because there was no one to share with her the colour and warmth and startling beauty of these perfect summer days.

Every day she went out alone, and soon the roads and woods and meadows around Robinsheugh were as familiar to her as the streets of Highgate where she had lived all her life. She quickly discovered that the countryside in this part of the Scottish Borderland was as different from her imaginings as anything could possibly be. Although in fact it was surrounded by great, hidden marches of open moorland, such as they had passed through on their way from Edinburgh, the house of Robinsheugh, and the little village which bore its name, and was situated half a mile further up the road, lay in the bottom of a tree-girt valley among softly rounded hills, with a river running through the midst. The hills were bearded low down with bristles of regularly planted fir trees, which grew thickly half-way up, then halted in a clean line, exposing the thinly yellow, rock-encrusted summits to the shifting cloud reflections of the summer sky. The river was called the Wishwater; it passed Robinsheugh so closely that Elizabeth could hear it chuckling softly over its stones as she lay in bed at night, and about a mile farther on, between steep banks stippled with Pink Campion and Herb Robert, its laughter ceased, as it flowed out deep and solemn to meet the Tweed.

The village was a poor affair as the English Elizabeth understood a village. It was little more than a parcel of shabby dwellings, cottages of stone and whitewash huddling where the hillside petered out into the valley floor. They had little by way of garden, only a few stunted trees with their ears laid back to the heathery slope, and here and there a straggling rose-bed with some unkempt bushes hastily reverting to briars. There was a tiny grey school, a Celtic Cross for a War Memorial, enclosed by a green wire fence, a shop, a telephone kiosk, and up a stony track, some distance from the cottages, a weathered grey church without a steeple, clinging to the hill in the middle of a bleak, walled graveyard. It was not, Elizabeth thought, a comfortable village. Its one street was always deserted, and it seemed uneasy, suspicious of the sunshine, as if it would be more at home in the greyness of wind and rain which its sturdy walls were built to withstand.

She longed on these walks for someone with whom she could share her thoughts, who would rejoice with her when she found a baby hedgehog, and mourn with her when she saw a poor dead chaffinch in the hedgerow, but Kate was busy with the past, and Gerry was busy with the present, and everyone else she knew was far away. And no matter how far afield she rambled, eventually her watch told her that it was time to return to the cottage in the courtyard, but before she did, she had one important thing to do. It soon became a habit, an odd kind of comfort which she absorbed without understanding how or why. On her return from her walk, before she made her way back to Gerry's kitchen, she would go round to the front of Robinsheugh, and stand where she had stood on the day of her arrival, gazing up at the soaring walls and lightly floating turrets, loving its elegant beauty, and experiencing something she could not put into words, but which seemed to her to be a kind of magic. She would walk round and round it, looking at it from every side, until there was not a stone, a line, a window, a turret which was not printed on her mind. Last thing at night, before she got into bed, she looked at its sharply-cut silhouette, stamped onto the deep blue of the evening sky. It was a compensation, in a life which at the moment had very few.

Elizabeth scarcely ever saw Kate at all. Her routine was fixed, and nothing was allowed to interfere with it, short, said Gerry cheerfully, of the end of the world. Long before Elizabeth came downstairs in the morning, she had departed for the great house, and her work on Giles Melville's diaries and letters, and apart from a half-hour break for coffee at one o'clock, she was there till seven in the evening, when she returned, white-faced and exhausted, to eat her supper and read still more at the table. Afterwards, while Gerry and Elizabeth washed up, she would sit at the Study End of the table, writing up notes for an hour or more, before going upstairs to her room, where the clattering of her typewriter through the wall sometimes kept Elizabeth awake till three o'clock in the morning.

There were days, Elizabeth reckoned, when Kate scarcely opened her mouth to speak to a living soul from the time she got up till she went to bed. Every evening she telephoned to London to enquire after her mother's progress in hospital, and usually she told Elizabeth what the news was, but apart from that she rarely spoke to her at all. Nor did she talk much to Gerry, except occasionally to discuss with her something she had discovered in the Melville papers, and in which Gerry was supposed to be interested, because she was a student of history when she was not being a cook. Of the light, trivial chatter which makes most people's lives amusing, she had absolutely none, and Elizabeth, who was chatty by nature, found it very depressing. Gerry, surprisingly, did not seem to mind at all. Her attitude towards Kate reminded Elizabeth of her mother's, a mixture of admiration and anxiety and affection — for it did not take Elizabeth long to see that Gerry was very fond of Kate; she was always trying to cook things which she thought would tempt her appetite, and she worried openly about her systematic overwork, although she was far too respectful to try to bully her as Mrs Martin would certainly have done.

'Why do you call her Dr Jenkins?' Elizabeth had asked on the first morning, as she sat at the kitchen table, watching Gerry prepare vegetables for a salad. 'Why don't you call her Kate, like everybody else?'

Gerry looked surprised, then she laughed.

'That would hardly do,' she explained. 'You see, it would seem to be cheeky if I did. She is a Ph.D. and a Fellow of my College, and second-year undergraduates do not call such beings Kate.'

'Is she important, then?' asked Elizabeth disbelievingly. Kate's supposed importance was something of a family joke.

'In her world, which happens to be mine at the moment, yes,' said Gerry.

Elizabeth's hopes of Gerry as a companion and ally had also been disappointed. It was not that Gerry had been in any way unfriendly, but she too was busy, cooking in the mornings, helping Kate with her research in the afternoons, returning to the cottage at five o'clock to prepare the evening meal, and having all the tidying up to do afterwards, so that she really had very little time to spare for amusing Elizabeth. In any case, one thing she seemed to have in common with Kate was the belief that no intelligent person should need to be amused. If you had the use of your legs, and an adequate supply of books, you should be able to amuse yourself very pleasantly.

So Elizabeth was forced into a world of solitude, which she had no wish to inhabit, and which was quite against her nature, but which closed in around her because of the circumstances of her new life. She too fell into a routine. She rose late, not because she was lazy, but because there was nothing to get up for, and in any case she had usually been kept awake half the night before. Gerry never complained, however late she came, but cooked for her when she did, and when she had finished, and helped Gerry to wash up, she went out to wander through the fields and woods. In the afternoons, when the house was empty, she sat in the kitchen with a book on her lap, reading a little, and wondering where her parents were, and what Susan was doing, and how long it would take for three months to pass. Since the only answer to that was three months, it was not very helpful. And then she would fall to dreaming, in the armchair by the fire, about Robinsheugh, and wonder what they were like, these long-ago people whom Kate loved so much, and whose house by the Wishwater still stood in its beauty long years after they were all dead. And slowly she gathered courage to ask Kate the question which only fear of a curt refusal had prevented her asking the very first day she came.

The Friday after her arrival, the weather broke. Grey clouds marched low and sullen over the hills, turning the leaves and grass to a darker, brooding green. Then the rain came, at first small, drizzly summer rain, making a cloak of tiny silver droplets for trees and grass, and wrapping the hilltops in scarves of restless, waving mist. Later in the day, the wind rose, and by the time when Kate came running across the courtyard at seven o'clock, holding her flapping waterproof over her head like a tent, the rain was jumping off the cobble-stones in angry spurts, and the gale was lashing water in wild flurries against the window panes.

'Back to normal,' said Kate to Gerry, shaking herself so that the splashes flew everywhere, not a few landing on Elizabeth as she sat by the table. She removed herself to a safer distance, and asked, 'Is it often like this, then?'

'All the time,' said Gerry crossly. 'At least, we've been here since June and we've had — how many good weeks, Dr Jenkins?'

'Two, I think,' said Kate. 'And that day we went to Edinburgh. That was a lovely day, and we spent it all in museums.'

'And restaurants,' said Gerry with a happy sigh. 'It was marvellous.'

Elizabeth saw Kate give her a glance of unexpected sympathy.

'I'm sorry,' she said, sounding for once as if she meant it. 'I know it can't be much fun for you, stuck here in the wilds without your Peter, and no company except mine, which is no company at all. Maybe I shouldn't have brought you.'

'Don't be foolish, Dr Jenkins,' said Gerry, going red. 'That wasn't what I meant at all. I'm perfectly happy, and we were all agreed that Peter would be more likely to pass his exams without me around to distract him.'

'There is no doubt whatsoever about that,' agreed Kate dryly. She looked at Gerry for a moment, then she said, 'I'll tell you what. We'll have to go home by London to drop off Elizabeth, so after we've deposited her, we'll have a night out in the West End. We'll go to the theatre first — you can choose — then I'll take you anywhere you like for supper. No expense spared. How would that do?'

She looked at Gerry with a kind of innocent hopefulness, and Gerry began to laugh, which made Kate laugh too.

'If we live that long,' said Gerry, 'we'll have cause for celebration.'

The tactlessness of this conversation, carried on in front of her as if she were not there, reduced Elizabeth to a state of silent, shaking, helpless fury. She had been deposited here by people who couldn't wait to be off enjoying themselves, and now already it seemed that the people here couldn't wait to deposit her back where she had come from, so that they could be off enjoying themselves. And what was worse, this private sympathetic conversation made it perfectly obvious how friendly Gerry and Kate really were, despite the difference in their age and status, and the fact that they hardly ever spoke to each other. A friendship that did not depend on chat was something she could not understand, but more than ever now she could see that she was the outsider, the one who had nothing in common with either of the other two. They at least had Oxford and Giles Melville. She was so angry that all through supper she determined that she would never speak to them again, but just as she finished drying the last spoon, and saw Kate, carrying her books and her coffee, preparing to leave the kitchen and go upstairs, she remembered that she would have to speak to Kate, because she had something very important to ask her, something which could not be delayed. So she swallowed her pique, and taking a deep breath, followed her aunt out into the passage.

'Kate, may I ask you something?'

'Of course, Elizabeth.'

'It's about the house — Robinsheugh, I mean.' She paused, nervously.

'What about it?' asked Kate, quite encouragingly.

'Well, I've been wondering — do you suppose I could see inside it?'

She tensed herself, waiting for Kate to say no, it was private, it wasn't possible. But Kate said without even hesitating to consider her answer, 'Heavens, yes, of course you could. I'd have suggested it, if I had thought you'd be interested. In fact, I can't see any reason why you shouldn't go in as often as you like, provided you're careful, and don't touch anything. What day is this?'

'Friday,' said Elizabeth, so delighted that she forgot to feel her usual irritation at this recurrent question.

'All right. I'll take you over tomorrow after lunch, and show you how to get in and out, and what rooms we're allowed to go into. After that, you may go in and out as you please.'

It had all been so easy that Elizabeth could not believe her good luck. Anticipation sustained her all through a restless, windy night, and a morning when it was too wet to go out of doors, and Gerry, taking seriously her complaint of having nothing to do, gave her an enormous mound of vegetables to clean for soup. Then, at half past twelve, Gerry discovered that she had no lentils left, and since the rain had gone off, she asked Elizabeth to go up to the shop at Robinsheugh to buy some, and also some other things she had forgotten to buy the last time she was in Kelso.

So Elizabeth put on her waterproof and her Wellingtons, and set off with a basket, fairly dancing along between squirming rivulets of rain water, swollen by dank drippings from overhanging branches and the sodden grasses along the verges on either side of the road. Water trembled everywhere, on hedges, and flowers, on grass, and trees, embroidering with silver

26

beads the spider's web in the hedgerow. The Wishwater's placid gurgling had taken a louder tone, and as she walked along under the flat grey sky, wrinkling up her nose at pale earthworms in puddles and fat black snails along the margins of the grass, Elizabeth thought it was the wettest day she could ever remember. Wet to look at, wet to smell, wet to hear, and wet to touch. But she did not care, not even when a beech tree chose to shake itself just when she was passing underneath, and most of the water seemed to find its way down her neck. Nothing mattered, because two hours from now, she would be inside Robinsheugh.

It took about three quarters of an hour to walk to the village and back, but Elizabeth felt no need to hurry. Kate never came over to the cottage for her coffee till after one, nor returned till about twenty to two; her movements were as regular as clockwork, and you could have set your watch by them. So there was plenty of time. She walked back most of the way along the top of the grass banking, jumping the field drains and hitting the hedge with a stick for the pleasure of seeing the hanging pear-drops of water leap, sniffing the scented air and altogether feeling happier than she had done since she knew she was coming to this place to live.

Gerry had the light on in the kitchen, and Elizabeth could see it from the road as she hopped along between the beeches and crossed the courtyard with her basket. She stopped to take off her boots in the tiny entrance porch, and then went into the kitchen. The first thing she noticed was that Kate was not sitting by the table as usual, drinking her coffee and reading the newspaper. She was not in the room at all, and Gerry was standing by the fire with a hot water bottle in her hand, and a worried expression on her face, waiting for the kettle to boil. Without being told, Elizabeth knew. No Robinsheugh. With a sick, tight feeling across her stomach, she put the basket on the table, and said dully, 'Where is she?'

Gerry glanced at her, her bright eyes clouded with misgiving.

'I made her go to bed,' she said, her voice begging Elizabeth to share her anxiety. 'She has the most dreadful headache, it's quite pitiful to see her.'

Of course Elizabeth knew she should try to look concerned, to say she was sorry. But even while she wanted to behave well, disappointment made her behave badly.

'She was supposed to be taking me over to the house this

27

afternoon,' she said sullenly, and turned away quickly from Gerry's reproachful eyes.

'Then you''ll have to wait till another time, won't you?' Gerry said, and Elizabeth was aware that she was making a great effort to stop herself saying something much less agreeable. 'She isn't being ill to annoy you, you know.'

'I didn't say she was. All I said was —'

'Yes, yes,' said Gerry wearily, 'I heard what you said.'

She lifted the kettle off the fire and began to fill the hot water bottle.

'I don't know what to do,' she went on, and Elizabeth knew she was only talking to her because she had no one else to talk to. 'She keeps having these terrible headaches, and she won't see a doctor, and if she doesn't stop this crazy overworking, it won't be Oxford she'll be going back to in October, it will be a nursing home. And I know she's worrying about something, but she won't tell me what it is.'

'She's always working. She likes it,' said Elizabeth. She did not mean to be unkind, but then a little twinge of nastiness made her add, almost in spite of herself, 'It's the only thing she's good at.'

Gerry screwed on the top of the hot water bottle, and turned it upside down to make sure there were no drips. She gave Elizabeth a long, serious look, and seemed for a moment to be on the verge of saying something important, but then she changed her mind. As if she wanted to give her a last chance to redeem herself, she held out the hot water bottle, and said, 'I think you should take this up to her, and ask if she would like a cup of tea.'

And although she knew that it was an appeal to the kind and the good in her and perhaps in a way an opportunity which would not come again, Elizabeth would not give in. She drew back, and shook her head, and failed the test. Without another word, Gerry turned on her heel and walked out of the kitchen, leaving her truly alone.

4

The Silver Looking-Glass

After Gerry had gone, Elizabeth stood by the table, listening to her feet receding down the passage, and struggling with anger and shame and disappointment too terrible for tears. She knew that she must not be in the kitchen when Gerry came downstairs again, so as soon as she heard her moving about in Kate's room overhead, she went stealthily upstairs in her stockinged feet and shut herself in her own room. Through the wall she could hear the muted murmuring of Gerry's voice as she tried to make Kate comfortable, and through all her other misery Elizabeth felt a quick, sharp stab of jealousy, for Kate might have a sore head, but she also had a good friend. Then the door of Kate's room opened, and was closed again very quietly, and Gerry went off on tiptoe downstairs, leaving silence in her wake.

Elizabeth sat down on her bed, covered her flaming face with her hands, and wished that she were dead. She knew that she had behaved disgracefully, she knew it was not Kate's fault that she had a headache, and that it must be a really terrible headache to make her leave Giles Melville for her bed, she knew that Gerry's disgust was justified, but that did not stop her immediately starting to make excuses for herself. Kate had made her a promise, and had broken it. Kate never paid any attention to her, so why should she pay any attention to Kate? Kate was always letting her down. It was Kate's fault that Elizabeth had been shown up in a bad light, and that now Gerry didn't like her either. Kate was to blame. The knowledge that she was being thoroughly unfair did not improve her temper in the least.

Elizabeth looked out of the window, and contemplated running away. The trouble was, she had no idea where to run to. It must be miles to the nearest bus stop, and in any case she had only fifteen pence in her purse, since she had foolishly handed over the rest of her pocket-money to Gerry for safe keeping. She could hardly go to Gerry and ask to have her money back, so that she could run away. Besides, it was wet and nasty outside, and Elizabeth was not really made of the stuff of successful runners-away. So she rejected that idea, and then she had a much better one. She would write to Uncle Kenneth, and tell him how unhappy she was, and how badly she was being treated, and ask him to come to Scotland and take her away. He was her best hope, because Kate annoyed him too. She was his sister, and they were always fighting about something. They were always making up too, but Elizabeth found it more convenient to forget that for the moment. In any case, the only other person she could write to was Granny, and there would be no point in that. She was just out of hospital, for one thing, and for another she would never believe a word Elizabeth said. Granny might be fond of Elizabeth, but Kate, as everyone knew, was the apple of her eye.

So Elizabeth climbed off her bed, and went over to the chest of drawers, to fetch out her writing-case, which she had put in the top drawer on top of a pile of clothes. All the drawers had been packed far too tightly, and when Elizabeth tried to pull the top one open, it came out about four inches and stuck, because the writing-case had sprung up inside above the top of the drawer. She slid her fingers inside to dislodge it, but as she poked and wiggled about trying to get a hold on the slippery leather, she accidentally pushed it in the wrong direction, so that it slipped over the back of the drawer and fell down, hitting the floor of the chest with a muffled thud. Exasperated, Elizabeth banged the top drawer shut, and, kneeling down, drew out the bottom one, lifting it clear so that she could put in her hand among the dust and darkness and grope for the writing-case with shrinking, fastidous fingers which loathed their task. Spiders, said her imagination, bats, cobwebs, mice.

But it was none of these she touched first, nor yet the writing-case. It was something else, something cold and hard and carved under her hand. Curiously she drew it forth, and examined it with interest, but with no great excitement, no inner feeling that what she held was of any particular importance. It was a small, dirty round looking-glass, set in a tarnished frame of silver, with a handle embossed with a design of fruits and flowers. On the back of the frame, set among swirling scrolls of delicate engraving, were the entwined initials, 'E.M.' Even this coincidence did not rouse her; she was not in the mood. However, it was an incident to break the monotony of things, so after she had looked at the glass for a moment, because the room was dark she got up and took it to the window, the better to examine its beautiful tracery. Casually she rubbed its dusty surface on her sleeve, then as one does almost instinctively with a looking-glass, she held it up to look at herself. A moment passed before she realised that what she was seeing was not her own face.

Elizabeth could never afterwards describe, even to herself, what it was she thought happened with that glass, but it seemed to her then that in an instant the outline of the glass seemed to expand, then float away, and she thought she was standing in the doorway of a room, looking inwards on a scene so far removed from her in time and season that though she watched it, she was totally aloof from it. It was like looking at a lighted Christmas Crib in a church, a tableau which suddenly melted into a scene on stage as the figures moved, acting a play that was not a play for no audience that ever existed.

It was evening, in a wide, white-walled room, where the dancing firelight from an open hearth patterned the ceiling with flickerings of rose, and cast enormous shadows across the polished wooden floor. Daylight was fading fast, and the last rays of a pallid sun, sliding into the room through small, deep-set windows, sent a weak shaft of light across three little wooden beds which stood along one wall, each with a coloured counterpane turned back to reveal a neat line of sheet beneath the pillow. In the centre of the room stood a table with a white cloth, and the remains of a meal laid out in dishes and cups of wood, and some of a dull, silvery metal. There were wooden chairs too, stools, a vast cupboard against the wall, a spinning-wheel . . . all these Elizabeth saw, but it was to the fire that her hungry eyes were drawn.

In a low chair beside the hearth, a young woman was sitting. She had dark hair, and a pretty, gentle, brown-eyed face, with cheeks like the bloom on a pink rose. She was wearing a long dress of black and red striped wool, with a white scarf crossed over her breast and knotted behind. Over her dress she wore a white apron, and on her head a frilled cap of muslin, decorated and tied with green ribbon. On her lap she was holding a little child of about three years old, in a long white gown, his sleepy head in the crook of her arm, while at her feet a red-haired girl of about Elizabeth's age, also in white, leaned comfortably against her knee. Two sounds floated into Elizabeth's ears; the thin, sleepy whimper of an unseen baby, deep in a carved wooden cradle at the young woman's side, and the rhythmic tapping of her shoe against the rocker of the cradle as she swayed him into sleep. Elizabeth looked and looked, as if she could never stop looking, and then, full and sweet and clear down all the years that separated their evening from her day, she heard the woman sing,

> O can ye sew cushions, and can ye sew sheets?
> And can ye sing balaloo when the bairn greets?
> And hee and ba birdie, and hee and ba lamb?
> And hee and ba birdie, my bonnie wee lamb.
>
> I biggit a cradle upon the tree top,
> And aye, as the wind blew, my cradle did rock.
> O hush a ba baby, O balilliloo!
> And hee and ba birdie, my bonnie wee doo.

The pure, unearthly voice died away into silence, the little boy slept, the baby's cry was stilled. And in that moment, as Elizabeth stood with the glass in her hand, a mist seemed suddenly to arise on its face, its frame was redefined, the vision faded; somewhere, in their house or hers, a clock began to strike the hour.

Elizabeth laid the looking-glass on the window-sill, and rubbed her eyes with the back of her hand. She realised that she was shivering, but not with cold. She stood quietly for a moment longer, looking at the chest of drawers, the drawer still lying in the middle of the floor, the dirty silver looking-glass face downward on the varnished wood. Then she took one hasty step backwards, as if from the edge of a cliff. Through the open window she could hear the tender, shuddering note of a pigeon in the cottage eaves, and farther off, the swollen gabble of the Wishwater hurrying to the Tweed. She heard a car engine, far up the road, drawing closer as Mr Lindsay, the gamekeeper and their neighbour across the yard, drove his van home from Kelso. Elizabeth saw him get out of the van, a bulky figure in an oilskin coat, and heard the door slam behind him as he prepared to make a dash across the cobbles to get out of the rain. The prosaic, everyday substantiality of his appearance steadied her; she turned, retrieved her writing-case, and put the drawer back in its place. She shut the window, aware now of the cold, and lifting the looking-glass, but without allowing herself to look at it, she put it away in a top drawer, burying it carefully among her jerseys. Then she closed the drawer and sat down on the bed.

It was, of course, an impossibility, something which simply could not happen. Elizabeth told herself this over and over, slowly and seriously, as often as she had to to convince herself that it was an impossibility, something which could not possibly happen. That was what an impossibility was. So if it could not happen, she had dreamed it, she had imagined it, because everyone knows that when you look in a mirror what you see is yourself, and behind you what is behind you, only all the other way round. In one sense what you see is real, in another it is the opposite of what is real. But whatever you see, you can't get through to it, unless you are Alice, and although that was a good story, and Elizabeth had enjoyed it, it was after all only a story. And even then, when Alice looked in the glass, she saw the reflection of the room she was in, not, as Elizabeth had seen, a completely different room. Only of course, she had not seen it, because it was a dream. She had dreamed of that peaceful group by the fire, in their clothes of long ago, of the beautiful girl, the baby in its cradle, the loving children at her knee. They had all looked so happy and warm and contented, and the song had so strangely stirred her heart.

Elizabeth wondered if one could really dream a song, a song one had never heard before, and full of words one did not understand. She could not remember ever having dreamed a song before, and this one sang itself so tunefully in her mind,

> O can ye sew cushions, and can ye sew sheets?
> And can ye sing balaloo when the bairn greets?

It was a Scottish song, then, because 'bairn' was the Scots word for child; Mrs Fergus, who came in three mornings a week to do the washing and polish the floors, referred to her grandchildren in Kelso as 'the bairns'. So the beautiful young woman was Scottish, and the children. . . . Only of course there was no young woman, no children. They did not exist, they were the floating unreality of her dream.

Elizabeth had no idea how long she sat there, trying to convince herself that she had not seen what she had seen, but it must have been a very long time, because eventually she was roused by the sound of Kate's bedroom door opening, and she heard Kate go into the bathroom and run the tap. Then she came out again, and instead of returning to her room, went downstairs to the kitchen. Everything was quiet again for a time, and Elizabeth realised how cold and stiff she had become. Reminding herself that she could not stay in her room for the rest of her life, and hoping, though without much conviction, that Gerry might have forgotten their disagreement earlier in the day, she got up, took her book, and followed Kate downstairs.

The light was on in the kitchen, and Gerry was moving about quietly, laying the table for supper. Kate was sitting in the armchair by the fire, curled up in a knot of misery, with a cup and saucer in her lap. She was as white as a sheet, and Elizabeth could tell from the rigid, unnatural way she held her head that she was still in pain. Neither she nor Gerry paid any attention to Elizabeth's arrival, so she went into a far corner of the room, and sat down with her book, pretending to read. Gerry went to the dresser to fetch cutlery from the drawer, and on her return stopped by Kate's chair.

'For heaven's sake, Dr Jenkins,' she said, her voice raw with anxiety, 'go back to bed. I'll bring you up some soup when it's ready. You look absolutely dreadful.'

This candour made Kate smile a little, but she put down her cup, and said with evident relief, 'If you're sure you don't mind, I think I shall. Don't worry, Gerry, I'll be all right presently.'

'Don't worry,' repeated Gerry incredulously, her voice running up the scale and leaving the words quavering on the air.

Wearily Kate pulled herself to her feet, and crossed the kitchen to the door. As she passed Elizabeth, she paused, as if noticing her for the first time.

'Elizabeth, I'm so sorry,' she said. 'Do forgive me. I'll take you tomorrow morning, first thing. I promise.'

And before Elizabeth had time to think of an answer, she was gone. Then Elizabeth felt deeply ashamed, but she did not feel any more kindly to Kate for shaming her.

5

The Door Opens

When Elizabeth went up to bed that night, she debated with herself whether or not she should peep into the looking-glass again, just to reassure herself that what she had seen was only a dream. It wasn't that she was afraid to look, she told herself, because of course she knew she had only been dreaming, but nonetheless she undressed, bathed, put on her nightdress and got into bed without opening the drawer and taking out the little silver glass. She would wait, she decided, and look in the morning, because she was tired, and wanted to get to sleep.

Elizabeth did sleep soundly that night, perhaps because for once there was no typewriter rattling next door, keeping her awake, and certainly no dream she could afterwards remember disturbed her rest. And in the morning, the day was new, and when she hurried down to breakfast it was to find that Gerry had gone to Church, and Kate was sitting by the window, in a splintered shaft of sunlight, drinking her coffee and waiting to take her over to Robinsheugh. Elizabeth gulped her cornflakes, and made herself a sandwich with toast and two of the blackened sausages which Gerry had left in the frying-pan. Kate looked at it with faint revulsion, but all she said was, 'Take your time. It has been there for four hundred years, and it will be there in ten minutes.'

'I'm ready,' said Elizabeth, through a mouthful of sausage.

'All right,' said Kate, surprised and laughing a little, but for once Elizabeth was too eager to notice whether she was being laughed at or not. She managed to hide her impatience while Kate scrabbled among the litter at the Study End, collecting the books and papers which she needed to take with her, and spent ages searching for her spectacles, which she eventually found in her cardigan pocket. But at long last she was ready, and they set off across the yard, blown along by a stiff breeze which bent the crests of the beech trees and threatened to whip more storm clouds across a bright but thin blue sky. It was a watery kind of morning.

'Is your head better?' asked Elizabeth gruffly, as she scuttled along to keep pace with Kate's long stride.

'Yes, quite better, thank you,' said Kate, in a tone which without being ungracious still managed to put a full stop to the matter. 'Now look,' she continued, 'we go in by this back door, being back-door people. I have a key, and I open it when I come over in the morning, and lock it when I finish work in the evening. So you can come in at any time during the day. Only don't be here after seven in the evening, or you may find yourself locked in.'

'When you found out I was missing, you'd come and let me out,' said Elizabeth.

'That might not be for quite some time,' said Kate. 'You are the one who says I am absent-minded.'

'I could shout,' persisted Elizabeth, who could turn the most innocent conversation into an argument, if she could find someone willing to argue with her. Kate was not.

'Please yourself,' she replied. 'But remember that it's unlikely anyone will hear you through walls that are nine feet thick.'

The thought of such walls silenced Elizabeth. She waited for Kate to unlock the heavy, studded wooden door at the bottom of a semi-circular tower which protruded from the back of the house, and followed her into a narrow stone passage. It felt damp, and bitterly cold. Elizabeth shivered.

'Yes, it is cold,' said Kate, noticing. 'No sunshine, and not much heating in this part of the house. It's much warmer at the front, because that faces south, like our cottage windows. I must just run upstairs and leave my books — you can come too, and we'll start at the top of the house.'

So Elizabeth followed her up a narrow staircase, which wound giddily upwards, spiralling through rounded walls of creamy stone, and lighted by tiny windows set too high up in the walls to provide any view. In any case, Elizabeth soon realised that it was wise to pay attention to one's feet, because many of the treads were worn to a dangerous unevenness, and more than once she caught her toe and stumbled. Every fifty steps, more or less — Elizabeth counted — the stair opened out onto a square landing, with a window, and doors opening from it; on each landing one of the doors led into a short, low-roofed passage, then the stair began again. Elizabeth counted four landings and two hundred and fifty-seven steps before she reeled breathlessly after Kate through a final door, finding herself in a tiny circular room, filled with light flooding inwards from a window which was on a level with the treetops. It was Kate's workroom.

Elizabeth leaned against the roughly plastered wall, trying to recover her wind, and looked curiously round about her. There was very little furniture; a table, surprisingly tidy, with pens and pencils in a cocoa tin, piles of clean paper and piles of paper covered with Kate's spindly black handwriting. There were two chairs, one for Kate and one for Gerry, and a large leather chest, brass-bound and exciting, like a pirate's treasure chest, with the lid thrown back to reveal drifts of yellowed paper and parchment, tied into packages and bundles with faded ribbon and string. There were books too, leather-covered diaries, old ledgers and receipt books, all mixed up among the papers in the striped silk interior of the box.

'What is it?' asked Elizabeth.

'The Melville family papers,' replied Kate, dropping her books onto the table. 'Three hundred years of them, in fact.'

Elizabeth stared.

'But you're never having to read them all?' she cried in horror.

'No, but we're having to sift through them all to find what we can use, which takes ages. They've never been properly classified, and Gerry is getting very shirty about the whole thing. Gerry will never have the patience to be an historian.'

Elizabeth was not in the least interested in Gerry's capabilities as an historian. She eyed the trunk and its contents dubiously.

'You'll never get through all that in three months, will you?' she enquired.

'I hope to finish by the end of September,' said Kate. 'This is the third summer I've spent here, and I plan that it shall be the last.'

It was much later that Elizabeth remembered this remark, and thought that there had been an undertone in it which suggested something different from normal weariness of a task which had lasted through three summers. At the time, she felt only some surprise that Kate should have been coming to Robinsheugh for so long, because she had never heard its name mentioned before. But then, Kate never talked about her work; Elizabeth had no idea what she did, except in a general way, that she taught history at Oxford, and wrote books about people that no one had ever heard of. Giles Melville, for instance.

She went to look out of the window. The distance to the ground made her feel dizzy, and she stepped back hastily.

'You shouldn't be writing in a room like this,' she remarked to Kate, 'you should be spinning.'

'Spinning?' said Kate, who was farther from her fairy tales than Elizabeth was. 'Oh, yes, I see what you mean. I don't think I'd be very good at it — I'm hopeless with my hands. But since you mention it, there is a spinning-wheel in the room next door — it seems to be a kind of lumber room where they've pushed away a lot of things not grand enough for downstairs. You can have a look at it as we go through. We have to, to get into the main part of the house.'

She led Elizabeth through a little door which opened out of the wall of the work room, into another room, square this time, but otherwise very similar to the tower room. It was, as she said, filled with the sort of bits and pieces that accumulate in every house over the years, things no one will ever want again, but which are never thrown away, old chairs, travelling boxes, a cobwebby old 'cello, piles of musty books, some family albums. But there was no doubt that much of the lumber in this room was far more exotic and exciting than any which Elizabeth, or Kate for that matter, would have had in their attics at home. Besides the spinning-wheel, there were wax fruits and flowers under dingy glass domes, stuffed birds, model ships, military uniforms, a tailor's dummy wearing a faded grey crinoline. And a cradle, all dusty and in need of polish, its lovely oak carving chipped and filthy with neglect. Elizabeth stared at it, her stomach lurching with the shock of recognition. She would have passed the spinning-wheel, but there was no doubt in her mind where she had seen that cradle before. In that instant, she seemed to hear again the steady tapping of shoe against rocker, and a clear singing voice,

> I biggit a cradle upon the tree top,
> And aye, as the wind blew, my cradle did rock . . .

'I've always thought it was such a pity,' Kate's voice remarked, interrupting her thoughts. 'It's such a beautiful thing, and so genuinely ancient, it really ought to be restored, and put where people can enjoy looking at it. I've never in my life seen a finer one.'

'How old is it?' asked Elizabeth, trying to sound casual, although her head was whirling, and she felt sure that Kate must notice her agitation. But Kate was looking at the cradle, running loving, regretful fingers over its disfigured side.

'One can't say for certain,' she said, 'but cradles like this one were in use both in Scotland and England in the sixteenth century. Of course they were handed down in families, and became treasured heirlooms. This one might have been in use well into Victorian times. I must mention it to Sir Gilbert — he really should do something about it.'

She turned away then, and Elizabeth, pulling herself together with an effort, went after her through a door on the far side of the room, which led into the house proper. She was taut and vibrating with expectation, although exactly what it was she expected she would have found hard to put into words.

It was a tall, rambling, unexpected house, full of dark passages and sudden flights of steps; the waxed wood floors, which occasionally turned to stone half-way across a room, were uneven, and the ceilings of varying heights, even where the floors of the rooms were on the same level. This, Kate said, was because the house had been begun in the 1500's simply as a fortified tower, and later owners had enlarged and improved it by tacking bits on as and when they could afford it. That was why it lacked the design and symmetry of a house built all of a piece, but it was also, Kate thought, what gave it its charm of surprise. The most ambitious improvements, she went on, had been made by Giles Melville's father in the 1760's, when for the first time the Scots were able to move away from the idea of a house as a stronghold, because the defeat of the Jacobites at Culloden had at last put an end to the danger of civil war. They were beginning to make their homes beautiful and comfortable as they had never been before, and here in the Lowlands they were for the first time having the opportunity to buy fine furniture, and lay out lovely gardens, without the fear that they would be destroyed by marauding raiders from across the Border. The eighteenth century, Kate said, was the Golden Age in Scotland.

She spoke, as she always did, in a cool kind of voice which made you feel she found it all more interesting than thrilling, but that day, for the first time, Elizabeth sensed beneath her detached, moderate manner a deep, loving concern for the things she spoke of, no less intense for being firmly kept in place. It was what previously she had called liking people in history better than people now, but here she began to see, in a confused kind of way, that it was something really far more complicated than this. It was not only that Kate was at ease and at home in the past, it had something to do with her not being at ease and at home in the present. And that being so, Elizabeth wondered, as she half-listened to her aunt's polite, patient commentary, whether she too was aware of the strangeness of this house, the sense of something alive, dreaming perhaps, but with its eyes open and its ears cocked, waiting. . . .

No one lived in these white-walled rooms, with their damask curtains, old rich carpets and graceful furniture; the Melville family, when they were in residence, lived in private rooms in the most recent wing of the house, and the apartments through which Kate and Elizabeth now walked, like ghosts out of their time, were left to the caretakers, and the tourists who came in droves on the five Sundays in the year when the house was open in aid of charity. And yet they did not feel at all abandoned and forlorn, as if they had given up expecting the people to return who had left them long ago. On the contrary, they felt as if they were expecting them to return any minute. . . . But Elizabeth did not confide any of her thoughts to Kate, for fear of being misunderstood.

She wandered in Kate's wake through bedrooms and dressing-rooms and drawing-rooms, none of them so very much bigger than the rooms in her own home. It was not the size of these rooms which made them imposing, it was a grandeur of age, a confidence born simply of having been there longer than anything else. And although Elizabeth was already going back to her belief that what she had seen in the looking-glass was a dream, despite the evidence of the cradle, she could not help looking all the time for more objects she recognised. There were none. She examined black-lacquered tables and elegant chairs with tapestry seats, a beautiful little spinet and graceful satinwood chests of drawers, but nothing which fitted into the homely scene she had witnessed in her dream.

The last room was the most impressive; it was the dining-room, and had once been the Great Hall of the original keep. It would then have had walls of stone, Kate said, but in the eighteenth century these had been covered with wood panelling, and the floor covered with carpet, which in those times was a great luxury. Six windows, following each other down the south-facing wall, were hung with dark green curtains, while on the opposite wall was a vast, open hearth swept cold and clean. A long mahogany table — Victorian, said Elizabeth's guide without enthusiasm — with neat rows of chairs, ran almost the whole length of the room, overhung by three crystal chandeliers suspended from the lofty ceiling on chains, and flanked at either end by a matching sideboard and serving table.

'I'd love to see this room empty,' said Kate wistfully.

But for Elizabeth, what made this room different, and in a way unnerving, was that every available square foot of wall was covered by a portrait. Surrounded by thin borders of the panelling, they hung in tidy rows, paintings in oils enclosed in massive, ornately gilded frames. Some of them were so enormous that they stretched almost from roof to floor, and were in a true sense larger than life. They stood there stiffly, bewigged and beruffed, men and women in old-fashioned, uncomfortable clothes, glaring at the intruders with all the insolent self-confidence of those who are already safe in history. Elizabeth was suddenly overawed by the haughty stare of their sightless, painted eyes.

'Who are they?' she enquired of Kate in a whisper, in case they might be listening and think her bold.

'Melvilles,' said Kate carelessly. She was perhaps too familiar with history to be overawed by it. 'They start down here with the first Sir Giles, who was given the lands of Robinsheugh and Bieldhall by King James VI, as a reward for disposing discreetly of a couple of His Majesty's enemies.'

Elizabeth glanced up at an alarmingly fierce red face, surrounded by a gigantic white ruff. She looked away hastily from the choleric glare of his small eyes.

'Is your Giles here?' she asked.

'Yes, down here. He was painted by Romney on a visit to London while he was Ambassador to the Court of Spain. It's really the best portrait in the collection.'

She indicated it with her long forefinger, and Elizabeth looked up into the melancholy dark eyes of a man in middle life, dressed in blue breeches, white silk stockings, and a dark velvet coat, so very velvety that it was hard to believe it was really made of paint. George Romney had painted Giles Melville after the fashion of the time, emerging from a wooded, leafy background, carrying a riding whip in his hand and with his dogs at his heels; but it was neither the background nor the details of the painting which commanded Elizabeth's attention at this first encounter, it was the face. She could not stop looking at the face, at the pale skin and clear features, the sad eyes the colour of dark wallflower, the firm mouth, half humorous and half scornful, the soft, light brown hair drawn back in a straight line from a tall forehead; all seemed to penetrate Elizabeth's memory so that if she never saw

Giles Melville again, she would remember every line of his face till the day she died. Though why it was that for a fleeting moment she thought that his face was in some way familiar, she did not know. Feeling that something was expected of her, she said, 'He's marvellous,' knowing as she said it how inadequate the word was to express the presence and haunting power of this man of long ago. And Kate, who had expected nothing, said, 'Yes, I think he was,' and Elizabeth noticed that it was she herself who had put Giles Melville in the present tense, and Kate who had firmly put him back where he belonged. She left Kate looking at Giles, and wandered down the room, until her eye was drawn to a large, rectangular canvas above the chimneypiece, gilt-framed and laid horizontally to the wall.

'Why, look,' she called to Kate, 'here he is again.'

On several occasions when Giles Melville's name had been mentioned, Elizabeth had fancied a hesitation, a certain reluctance on Kate's part to discuss him. Now, as Kate came slowly down the room towards her, she sensed it again. There was an unwillingness to look at the picture closely, a brevity quite at odds with her previous, detailed explanations.

'It's a family group,' she said. 'Giles Melville and his wife and children. They are sitting down among the trees by the Wishwater. You can see the house in the background.'

But she might as well not have spoken at all, for Elizabeth was not listening. Her gaze had passed from Giles Melville and his satin-gowned wife, sitting uncomfortably in the midst of a familiar landscape stiffened into paint, with the house of Robinsheugh small across the fields, to the children grouped at their feet. There were four of them; a tiny baby in a long white robe and frilly bonnet, scarcely able to sit up on the grass, a little fair-headed boy in a long frock like a girl's, with a green velvet sash, a long lad in a brown suit and a white shirt, who looked very like his father, and sitting on the grassy bank at her mother's feet, playing with a kitten, a red-haired girl of nine or ten, in a yellow silk dress with long blue ribbons. But she was paying no more heed to Elizabeth now than she had yesterday, when Elizabeth strayed to the door of her nursery with the looking-glass in her hand.

'Who are they?' asked Elizabeth hoarsely.

'Sir Giles and Lady Melville, of course,' said Kate unhelpfully. 'The tall boy is their eldest son, Robert, and the others are their younger children.'

There were a thousand questions which Elizabeth wanted to ask, and she could not put a single one of them into words. She just went on staring at Giles Melville's children, while her mind spun round, and her heart hammered painfully in her chest. Just then, Kate suddenly lost interest. She fidgeted for a moment, then she glanced at her watch, and said, 'Lord, look at the time. I must go and do some work. Explore a bit more on your own if you want to. You'll soon find your way around.'

And just as Elizabeth was opening her mouth to ask the names of the other children, she was gone.

Elizabeth spent the afternoon walking by the banks of the Wishwater, her thoughts rushing and tumbling along like the swollen river at her feet. Kate's reluctance to talk about the picture she had forgotten; she was not unused to strange behaviour from Kate. In any case, that was as nothing compared with the strangeness of other things. Because for the first time, she was really making herself face the possibility that what she had seen in the glass was not a dream, at least not in the sense we usually mean when we talk of dreaming. The children she had seen in that room with white walls really existed, two hundred years ago, and they had been Giles Melville's children. And if she had dreamed them, she knew it had been a most unlikely dream, because until she came to Robinsheugh she had never heard of Giles Melville, and until this morning had not even known that he had children. As for the young woman Elizabeth had seen in the nursery, she was not their mother; Lady Melville was much statelier, and had blue eyes, and the same red hair as her daughter. And Elizabeth remembered too, as she stood on the little bridge over the Wishwater, staring down into the foaming brown flood, that she had not seen Robert in the nursery, but that there were three beds along the wall, and only two occupants. It was then that she knew that whatever might happen, she must look again into that glass which was burning a hole in her mind, she must look for Robert. . . . She would look at bedtime. And having made that decision she walked home, feeling suddenly calm, and hardly afraid at all.

6

The Third Bed

As soon as supper was over that evening, Elizabeth said she was feeling tired, excused herself, and went upstairs to her room. It was doubtful, she realised, whether either of the other two even noticed her departure. Kate was busy with her notes, and Gerry was writing a letter; Gerry at least gave her a muttered, abstracted 'Good night'. But for once Elizabeth did not waste time brooding over this. Knowing now that she was going to do something which had to be done, she undressed, washed, and put on the long white cotton nightdress which had been her parting gift from her father, and which she loved because she knew she looked pretty in it. Then she went over in her bare feet to the chest of drawers, opened the top drawer, and felt among the layers of soft wool for the looking-glass. Her fingers grasped the cold metal of the handle, she pulled it out, and without allowing herself even to glance at it, carried it over to the bed. She climbed in, hearing the now familiar squeaking and creaking of wood and canvas as she wormed her way down into the sleeping-bag. Only then did she raise the glass in front of her eyes.

The effect was instantaneous. The frame drew back, her surroundings melted into a grey vacuity, she was no longer lying flat on her back, but once again was standing, glass in hand, at the door of the room where the children of Giles Melville were going to bed two centuries ago. Nothing had changed; the cradle still rocked endlessly, to and fro, to and fro, the little boy slept, the little girl sat leaning her head sleepily against a comfortable knee. It seemed that for Elizabeth, a day and a night had passed, for them, no time at all. And as she stood there, watching, a rush of longing overwhelmed her, to leave this cold house where no one wanted her, or even noticed her, and to be one of that happy, loving group by the fire.

At the very instant when the wish filled her mind, the woman in the white cap looked up, and Elizabeth saw recognition smiling in her eyes. She was discovered. She tried to step back, but it seemed that a wall was behind her, and she heard a clear voice in her ears, 'Come you here to me, Elizabeth. You must not stand there in the cold. Come to the fire, child, and get warm.' So because she saw that now she was substantial to their eyes' belief, as they to hers, Elizabeth stepped forward; she felt the cold hardness of polished wood under her bare feet, and the warmth of the fire on her face as she drew near, then a firm, kind hand stretched out, and pulled her down on the rug beside the hearth.

'Now sit you down, Elizabeth, and content yourself. It is far too cold to be running about the house on bare feet, and what will your Mamma say if she catches you?'

Elizabeth found no words to reply, but the little girl on the other side of the striped woollen knee piped up on her behalf, 'You will be whipped, Elizabeth, she said so last time, did she not, Grizel?'

Alarm mingled with Elizabeth's astonishment, but the clear laughter of the young woman called Grizel calmed her fear.

''Twas but a threat to make Elizabeth obey,' she said, putting an affectionate arm round Elizabeth's shoulders — 'For all the world as if she had known me for years,' thought Elizabeth — 'Mamma would not whip you. Now sit over, Lucy, till I put this sleepy-head in his cot.'

Elizabeth watched as she stood up, and with her long skirt standing out around her, carried the child to one of the little beds by the wall, and laid him down, tucking the covers warmly around him.

'Good night, little James,' she said, kissing his golden head. Then she straightened her back, and came slowly back to her seat.

'Now, ladies, your combs,' she said, 'for you are next to bed. No, Lucy, there is no use girning. The hour is late, and Willie Winkie is coming. Fetch the combs, please.'

Lucy closed her mouth, which had been open to complain, and obediently rose to her feet. Elizabeth watched her cross the room to the huge dark cupboard against the wall, open it, and take out two brown bone combs with silver edgings. It crossed her mind that it was fortunate she had not been bidden to fetch the combs, since she would not have had the first notion where to look. She watched while Grizel combed Lucy's long red hair, and tied it back with a length of blue ribbon which she took from a basket on the floor at her side. Then Lucy was scampering across the floor to bed, and it was Elizabeth's turn. She sat on the floor at Grizel's feet, and the comb passed through her hair, slowly, soothingly, over and over; Elizabeth grew sleepy, and the soft voice was like honey dripping in her ears.

'What bonnie hair, Elizabeth, what bonnie hair, like spun gold in the firelight. I'll swear it's the bonniest hair I ever did see. Now, what colour will I tie it with tonight? Green, I think, for the fairies' colour. Do you fancy green?'

Elizabeth nodded dumbly. The heat of the fire, the rhythmic stroking of the comb, the sweet, murmurous voice, all were making her so sleepy that she could scarcely keep her eyes open. Then again, that silver laughter round her head.

'Bless me, child! Still holding the looking-glass Master Robin sent you. I'll wager you think more of that glass than you do of anything in the world.'

Elizabeth looked down, and saw that her fingers were indeed still knotted around the handle of the looking-glass — only now she had to look twice to convince herself that it really was the same glass. For instead of being the dull, dingy object she had discovered — was it only yesterday? — in the chest of drawers, it was apparently new. Its glass sparkled with a sharp brilliance, while the bright silver handle and beautifully wrought frame shone and winked and twinkled in the orange firelight.

'And I suppose you will be sleeping with it under your pillow again tonight?'

It was then that Elizabeth heard her own voice in that room for the first time, and she thought it sounded like her voice, and the words certainly came from her lips, but to the astonishment of her mind.

'I like to,' she said. 'You know I do, Grizel. It reminds me of Robin, and makes me feel he is nearer. I shall sleep with it under my pillow every night until he comes home.'

Then before she even had time to contradict herself, she too was being pushed across the floor to bed. She snuggled down among the softness of feathers and the smoothness of cool linen sheets. She pushed her looking-glass under her pillow, but kept her fingers tightly around the handle. Good night, Grizel, good night, Lucy . . . she was floating out onto the billowing sea of sleep. Grizel's lips brushed her forehead. . . . Good night, Elizabeth. . . .

Elizabeth woke in her camp bed with something sharp sticking into her side. Drowsily she put down her hand, and pushed it away. It was bright daylight, and in a drifting half-wakefulness she could hear Kate moving about in her room next door, getting herself ready for the day. Downstairs, the kitchen clock chimed seven; Gerry's door opened and shut, Kate's door opened and shut, and in the stir of their tapping feet and morning voices, Elizabeth sat up in bed, wide awake in an instant. A glance round the room confirmed her whereabouts. Her books, her china animals, her Royal Ballet posters were all there as they had been when she got into bed last night, outside her window she heard the rattle of milk cans as Mr Fergus, the dairy man, made his way round the cottages in the yard. There was Gerry's voice, crisply English against his slow Lowland tongue, 'Good morning, three pints, please. Yes, isn't it a lovely day?'

The commonplace was everywhere.

Long afterwards, when she was far enough away from the events of that summer to consider them clearly, Elizabeth wondered why for so long she had clung obstinately to her theory that the things which were happening to her were a dream. It seemed such an unimaginative solution, and certainly did not at all describe the experience, which was not in the least dream-like. She came to the conclusion then that she did so because she knew that, once she had admitted to herself the possibility that she was not simply dreaming, the alternative she had to face was so stupendous and dangerous that her mind naturally fought a long and stubborn battle to reject it. So it was that on this sunny summer morning, lying in bed among the sights and sounds of twentieth-century Robinsheugh, her first feeling was one of relief, because if you begin in bed, and end in bed, you may reasonably suppose that any occurrences in between are of a dream-like nature. Or so Elizabeth assured herself, and in that way took a step back from the attitude of the previous afternoon, when briefly she had been prepared to open herself to the chance that what was happening was something outside what is usually meant by a dream.

Yet she knew too, that she could not simply dismiss the matter; there were too many questions unanswered. Was it usual, for instance, to dream about exactly the same situation twice? Was it usual to dream about people one had never heard of, and then see their portraits in a room one had never before entered? Elizabeth did not know the answers to these questions; prior to this time, she had never dreamed very much at all. It had all been so distinct, that vision of Grizel and Lucy and James, and the going to bed in the firelight. It had been so warm and loving, and intimate in a way that was not dream-like at all. It had been — Elizabeth could not think of the word she wanted. Then it came to her. It had all been so substantial. There was none of that floating, airy, unreal sensation which somehow accompanies the most convincing of dreams.

Turning on her side, Elizabeth curled herself up, drawing the blanket more closely around her, and let her memory loose on that fleeting visit to the nursery of the Melvilles. That was the oddest thing about it, of course. To her it was a visit, but to the occupants of that room it had not apparently been a special event at all. They had not recognised her with awe, as a visitant from another time and place, as she would have expected. Instead, she seemed to be part of their everyday life. They had known her, had known her name. Not a flicker of surprise had greeted her arrival from another world. There had been a bed ready for her, the bed she had supposed was Robert's bed. No, not Robert. Robin. Grizel had called him Robin. She had forgotten all about Robin, and that was strange, because she remembered that she had looked in the glass a second time because it was Robin she wanted to see. Where was he? Elizabeth pondered this for a moment, then some words of Grizel's floated back into her head.

'Still holding the looking-glass Master Robin sent you. I'll wager you think more of that glass than you do of anything in the world.'

And she had said — what was it she had said?

'It reminds me of Robin, and makes me feel he is nearer. I shall sleep with it under my pillow every night until he comes home.'

Now why, Elizabeth Martin asked herself, as she lay in a shaft of slanting morning sunshine with her blue blanket pulled up to her chin, would she say that? She who did not know Robin Melville, and could not possibly be expected to know where he was? She wondered about this for a long time, before an answer came to her, and when it did, it came to her in a most peculiar way. For she felt it was being somehow fed into her mind from without, by a reasoning which was not hers, and over which she had no control. And more sinister still was the extraordinary awareness she had that in some way the mind which received it was only half hers. Of course, said a voice in her head, she should know where Robin was. The knowledge of his whereabouts hung about the skirts of her memory, as at waking the lost aspect of the dream-world hovers tantalisingly just beyond the power of recall. In Elizabeth Melville's world, I knew where my brother Robin was, because I was Elizabeth Melville.

Elizabeth got up quickly then, scrambling out of her sleeping-bag in a hurry, because the burden of her thoughts had suddenly become too much to bear. How she had come to think such a thing she did not know, did not want to know. Just when she had been trying to reason everything out so carefully, that voice out of nowhere, I was Elizabeth Melville. She washed, and put on her clothes. I am Elizabeth Martin. There was no Elizabeth Melville. In the picture in the dining-room, she had seen Robin, James and Lucy, and in the nursery she had heard the baby, deep in his hooded cradle. There was no Elizabeth Melville. She shook out the sleeping-bag, as she did every morning, and with a slither and a thud, an object fell out onto the canvas mattress of the bed. Elizabeth stooped to pick it up, realising as she did so that of course this was what had been sticking into her side when she awoke. It was the looking-glass, which she had been holding last night when she went to bed. And now she had another shock, one which made her suddenly sink down upon the side of the bed, because her knees went weak. For the glass, which had been so dirty and dull, till in the firelight she had seen it restored, lay in her hands as clean and sparkling as the day it was new, polished to a perfection which with days of labour Elizabeth could never have achieved. And when she looked in it, it reflected nothing but her own face, very wide-eyed and surprised, and her tousled morning hair, tied with a piece of narrow green ribbon.

Elizabeth stared at herself for a long time, then she took the ribbon out of her hair, rolled it up, and put it away in a drawer with the looking-glass, burying them deeply among the jerseys as if she were afraid someone would find them. This was silly, because she knew that neither Gerry nor Kate would have dreamed of touching her things, but the desire for secrecy was heavy upon her. Then she closed the drawer, brushed her hair, and descended to the kitchen.

7

Another Elizabeth

When Elizabeth walked into the kitchen, she found Gerry alone, sitting by the table, reading a letter from her boy friend, Peter. Peter wrote to Gerry nearly every day; if he did not, she went around in a panic, wondering whether he had had an accident, or been evicted from his lodgings, or, worst of all, had found another girl friend. Kate appeared to find this vastly amusing, but Elizabeth did not. She could so easily imagine how Gerry felt, and she thought it was just like Kate, who had no boy friend that Elizabeth had ever heard of, to make fun of Gerry, who had, and she could not understand why Gerry did not seem to mind. It seemed to Elizabeth that Kate and people like her took the easy way out; it was safer and easier to love Giles Melville than it was to love Peter Barrett, because Giles Melville, being dead, was much less likely to surprise you. At least so Elizabeth reasoned, not knowing that Kate would have disagreed with her on a variety of counts. Kate and Elizabeth never discussed such interesting questions, which was a loss to both of them.

Elizabeth too received letters every day, and picture postcards with United States stamps on them. She supposed that she got so many because her father and mother had bad consciences about leaving her with Kate. In this she was mistaken. They did not have bad consciences, and she would have got them anyway. Kate too received an occasional letter from America, or from her mother in London, but most of her mail consisted of official-looking typewritten envelopes, re-addressed from her college in Oxford. Elizabeth thought they all looked very boring.

There was a letter from her parents lying by her plate now, with a red and blue striped border, and important, brightly coloured stamps. It was just the sort of letter she used to long for at home, when she never had any mail of her own, but sadly, now that she got one practically every day, she had lost interest. The element of surprise was gone. She put it in her pocket to read later; she knew already what was in it. There would be a description of the places they had visited, and the people they had met, an assurance that they were safe and well, and missing her, and always at the end, the anxious hope that she was happy, and getting on well with Kate. She made a point of not telling Kate that they sent their love to her, which she knew was petty and mean, but she could not bring herself to do it. She was not, she told herself, on these terms with Kate.

'Well, well, well,' said Gerry cheerfully, folding up her letter and putting it away in its envelope behind the kitchen clock, 'you're bright and early this morning. Now what would you like for breakfast? You can have anything you like, as long as it's an egg.'

Her joky tone encouraged Elizabeth. Gerry had been very cool since the day of Kate's headache.

'That will be fine,' she said. 'Has Kate gone to work already?'

'Actually, no,' said Gerry, standing on tiptoe to reach down a pan from a high shelf, and catching it neatly just before it hit her on the head. 'She has gone to Edinburgh for the day.'

Elizabeth had too much on her mind at the moment to feel her usual annoyance at whatever Kate did or did not do, but because it was second nature to her now to feel aggrieved, she said, 'Whatever for?' in tones which suggested that she was furious.

Gerry dropped an egg into the pan.

'She has some books to return to the University Library, and she's meeting someone from the Museum of Antiquities for lunch. At least that's what she says. It may be she just wants to get away from us for a while.'

Elizabeth could not decide whether this was supposed to be funny or not.

'She didn't tell me,' she said.

'She didn't remember till one o'clock this morning,' said Gerry, grinning at a private memory. 'She came flying into my room in her nightie to ask what day it was. All of a dither, she was. Anyway, what has it got to do with you?'

'Nothing,' said Elizabeth, capitulating before war began. There was no sense in risking another quarrel, and she knew Gerry well enough by now to realise that here was another of the company who thought Kate Jenkins could do no wrong. So all she said was, 'I wanted to ask her something, but maybe you can tell me.'

'I shall, if I can,' agreed Gerry, turning over the egg timer. 'What is it you want to know?'

'It's about the Melvilles,' Elizabeth was beginning, when Gerry interrupted her with a loud groan.

'Oh, please,' she wailed, 'don't tell me you're going to start talking about the Melvilles now. Don't you think I get enough of that from Dr Jenkins? If you saw that trunk full of papers — '

'I have,' said Elizabeth crossly; then, in the hope of driving a small wedge of misunderstanding between two friends, she added, 'Kate says you'll never have the patience to be an historian.'

Gerry laughed without a trace of rancour or annoyance.

'That's what she says to me, every day in life,' she said. 'And of course she's right. Goodness knows, I don't want to be an historian, and spend all my life in an Oxford College. I only came because I needed a job for the summer with a roof over my head, and we were all agreed she needs someone to look after her.'

'We?'

'Her students. I mean, you can't let someone loose on her own who doesn't know what day of the week it is, or how to fry a slice of bacon. Here's your egg.'

Elizabeth looked at Gerry with a mixture of puzzlement and irritation. She could hear in her voice the same kind of friendly indulgence she was used to hearing in the voices of the grown ups in her own family when they talked about Kate. As if somehow the rules which applied to other people's behaviour should not apply to hers, as if she were somehow special. It made Elizabeth cross, because for the life of her she could not see what was special about Kate.

'Well, she should know how to fry bacon at her age,' she snapped, decapitating her egg with an angry spoon.

'Oh, it hasn't anything to do with age,' replied Gerry tolerantly. 'It's just the way she is.' She chuckled, and added, 'She probably knows how to make possets and a syllabub, and how to stuff a sheep's head.' Then she caught Elizabeth's eye, and said hastily, 'What was it you wanted to know about the Melvilles?'

'I wanted to know,' said Elizabeth, with a sense of relief at having got to the point at last, 'what Giles Melville's children were called.'

'Oh, yes, I can tell you that,' said Gerry. 'No problem. As a matter of fact, we were working only yesterday on some letters he wrote to them when he was abroad, as ambassador, you know. They're rather amusing. Well now, there was Robert, he was the eldest son. They called him Robin. The other two boys were called James and Alexander. Then there were two girls, Louisa and Elizabeth.'

Elizabeth tried to keep calm, while the kitchen went round

and round. When it began to settle, she ran her tongue round her dry mouth, and said, 'Are you sure there were two girls?' hoping that Gerry would not notice the thickness in her voice.

Gerry at first thought she noticed something, but could not think what she had noticed, so then supposed she hadn't. 'Why, yes, certainly,' she replied, adding automatically, 'Why do you want to know, Elizabeth?'

Elizabeth fell back on the stock answer of children faced with this question. 'I just wondered,' she said. 'I was looking at their portrait in the dining-room, over at the house, and I just wondered. But there was only one girl in the portrait, Gerry.'

'Was there?' said Gerry, getting up and beginning to clear the table. 'I've never really looked at the portraits closely. Dr Jenkins says they're not up to much. Still, I suppose I should, when I can find the time. Anyway, there were two girls, Elizabeth. Now,' she went on, dismissing the matter, 'how would you like to pop up to the shop at Robinsheugh and get a couple of pies for our lunch? I thought if we had something simple today, I could get a bit of extra work done on the papers, while Dr Jenkins is away, then maybe she'll be pleased with Gerry the historian, for a change.'

For once, Elizabeth walked the road to Robinsheugh unheeding of its beauty. The grass was freshly green after the rainy weather, and clover, vetch and Queen of the Meadow stirred in a warm little breeze, displaying their wild loveliness to anyone with eyes who happened to pass by. But today Elizabeth, who was usually their most devoted admirer, was as blind to their quiet glory as she was deaf to the busy chirping of small fowl in the hawthorns, and the further, lonelier, two-beat call of the shy wood-dove in the leaves.

There was an Elizabeth Melville. Elizabeth trailed slowly along the earthy margin of the road, looking down at her feet, watching them step out and in, out and in. There was an Elizabeth Melville. Gerry had been quite definite about it, and there was no reason to question her accuracy. She was, after all, a reluctant expert on matters relating to the Melville family. But if this were so, from Elizabeth's point of view the problems were daunting, and to most of the questions which now were chasing each other round in her head, she could scarcely even begin to give answers. So much was mysterious. On her visit to the nursery, she had found three children, Lucy, whose name was really Louisa, James, and a baby, who must be Alexander. There was no Elizabeth until she arrived, and was mistaken for this

53

other, unseen Elizabeth. Which was quite extraordinary, for how could anyone mistake her own sister for someone else, unless — Elizabeth's mind formed the words uneasily — unless they were identical. As for that, of course it was impossible to speculate, because — and this was the next great mystery — Elizabeth Melville did not appear in the family portrait. She did not appear in the portrait, she did not appear in the nursery — how did one explain such elusiveness? Where was she while Elizabeth Martin was filling her place, sleeping in her bed?

Elizabeth knew she could not answer any of these questions, and she did not waste time at the moment in trying to, but turned her mind instead to the matter of the looking-glass. It had been Elizabeth Melville's looking-glass, that much was certain. The fact that she shared Elizabeth Martin's initials was surely coincidental, and how the glass came to be in her chest of drawers in Kate's cottage was another question which was not going to be answered by thinking about it. It was so, and that was all. What was much more interesting, in a frightening sort of way, was the apparent power of the glass to make things seem other than they were, to let the beholder see, even participate in, things that happened long ago in another age . . . but no amount of pondering was going to tell Elizabeth whether it had the power to induce dreams only, or whether it was possessed of some other, stronger charm. In any case, she decided, it did not matter, because she was not having anything more to do with it. It could stay where it was, along with that alarming piece of green ribbon, until the end of the holidays, when she would hide it away somewhere, for some future occupant of the cottage to find. Elizabeth certainly was not going to look in it again. It was far too dangerous, and she did not like danger. She was a quiet, ordinary person, she told herself, who liked a quiet, ordinary life.

She went to the shop, bought two pies and an iced lolly, and so returned home.

A week passed, and the hushed, monotonous life of Kate Jenkins's household continued in its humdrum regularity, regardless of the very singular irregularities seething below its well-ordered surface. Gerry cooked and wrote letters to Peter. Kate worked on her manuscripts and had headaches in silence. Elizabeth spent her days wandering around a countryside which was beginning to lose even its first charm of unfamiliarity, or sat alone in her room, playing Ludo against herself with four sets of counters, or Patience, a game whose very name she loathed. She spent one afternoon in the empty room of Robinsheugh, searching in vain for a room she could recognise as the Melville nursery. There was none. It was bitter to find that the house she had so loved and longed to enter now roused in her only feelings of uneasiness, and she did not go back again. In any case, she soon got to a point where it irked her to be out of the cottage at all; this was on account of the looking-glass.

Her attitude had nothing to do with her judgment and common sense, that she knew. The fact was, the thing was haunting her. At every instant she was aware of its presence in the chest of drawers. There was not a second of wakefulness when it was not in her thoughts, teasing and stinging and troubling her mind. Sometimes, by dint of concentrating very hard on something else, she was able to push it away from her, but the second she dropped her guard, back it came, bright and burning, turning like a wheel in the forefront of her consciousness. It was not that at the beginning she felt any desire to touch it, she just could not stop thinking about it. Then she began to worry about its safety. She knew this was absurd, because she was the only person who knew it was there, and no one was likely to stumble on it by accident, because no one in the house would ever look in any of her drawers or boxes without asking her permission. They were not that kind of people. Nonetheless, she could not shake off the feeling that her secret might be discovered and even although she had no intention of looking in the glass again, still she was sure, without knowing why, that discovery would be disastrous. So she found herself making excuses, at all hours of the day, even during meals, to go up to her room, simply so that she could open the drawer and poke furtively among her jerseys, just to reassure herself that the looking-glass was still there. However she did not take it out, and it was not until eight days after her first visit to the Melville nursery that she was seriously tempted to meddle with it again.

It was a Monday evening, after a day of steady rain, when it had been impossible to go outside, and Elizabeth, driven by that terrible compulsion that had nothing to do with reason, had spent the whole day running upstairs at short intervals to make sure that her glass was safe. Her own folly in this made her irritable, and by supper time she was almost screaming with boredom and frustration. This was half the reason why she tried to pick a quarrel with Kate; the other half was that she had now got to the stage where she would have preferred the fury induced by a row to the hurt of being constantly ignored.

As usual, Kate spent the whole of supper time with her nose in a book. Elizabeth, who had been taught that this was bad-mannered, often suspected that it was done so that Kate was spared the boring necessity of making conversation with her and Gerry, and it irritated her anew every time she sat down at the table, the more so because nothing she could have said would have made the slightest difference. On this evening, however, towards the end of the meal, Kate did surface for a moment to congratulate Gerry on the excellence of her caramel pudding, which was one of her favourites. Whether Gerry was a satisfactory historian or not, she was certainly a splendid cook. Kate then began to tell Gerry about a pudding which Giles Melville's wife had served at a dinner party in the last years of the eighteenth century. She had found a book of recipes in the chest, she said, and had wasted much valuable time reading it.

'The pudding was called Whippit Sillabubs,' she said, 'and if I could afford it, I'd let you make it every night, because it sounds delicious. You should take a mutchkin of thick cream, and add half a mutchkin of white wine and the rind and juice of a lemon, and some sugar. Then you whisk it well, skimming off the top while you're whisking it, and put it through a sieve. When it's really thick, you pour glasses of red or white wine, and float the mixture on top. Then you eat it with a teaspoon.'

'It sounds very potent,' said Gerry, winking at Elizabeth with an I-told-you-so expression on her face. 'Maybe it's just as well you can't afford it. How much is a mutchkin?'

'A pint,' said Kate, losing interest. She put on her glasses, and peered at the page to find the place where she had left off reading.

Normally Elizabeth would have found this funny, and particularly would have enjoyed the inclusive friendliness of Gerry's wink, for once sharing a joke with her in a private sort of way. But Elizabeth was not in the mood for jokes.

'It seems to me,' she said snappishly to Kate, 'that there's not much point in knowing how they made pudding in the eighteenth century if you can't even make a decent cup of coffee now. That's the trouble with you, you're all talk.'

This was so ridiculous that Gerry laughed right out loud, and Kate smiled at her in spontaneous delight.

'That isn't an accusation often brought against me,' she said, with a kind of relishing amusement which made Elizabeth angrier than ever, especially since she saw that she had only succeeded in uniting the other two against her once again. She tried to think of something really hurtful to say, but it came out sounding feeble and foolish.

'You can laugh if you like,' she said rudely, 'but it doesn't alter the fact that you can't do the simplest thing without making a mess of it.'

'Perfectly true,' agreed Kate mildly. 'I am a theoretician, not a practitioner. Now eat your pudding, Elizabeth, and stop trying to provoke me. It's too tiresome.'

The cool, languid, grown-up voice, using words she did not understand, and making her seem childish and silly, reduced Elizabeth to the kind of rage where even if she wanted to, she could not have spoken another word without choking. But afterwards, when she was alone in her bed, her anger seemed to fall away from her, leaving only the desolate, piercing sadness of misunderstanding between people who once loved each other, and now try to hurt each other in an attempt to ease their own pain.

Voices from her own past returned to her:

'Darling Kate, don't go back to Oxford. I don't want you to go back, ever. Let's run away together where no one will ever find us.'

'I'd like that too, Elly. Where shall we run away to?'

'To India, Kate, to Egypt, to the Moon.'

'To Eldorado, Cathay, Samarkand. . . .'.

So long ago, so far away, so sad beyond tears.

It was then that she fell to thinking again about Grizel and the little Melvilles, and the happiness of that firelit room where she had been wanted, and loved, and admired. She forgot about danger and not wanting to be Elizabeth Melville, and once more, as on that night a week ago, longing overwhelmed her. Quickly she slipped out of bed, and went to fetch the glass.

8

A Day Beyond Time

It was the thin, weak wail of Alexander's crying that woke Elizabeth, and in the pale light of the early morning she pushed herself up on her elbow and looked around the nursery. The fire, which must have been banked up with peats the night before, was burning low on the hearth, the dull redness of its reflected glow on ceiling and wall now paling in the growing whiteness of the dawn. On Elizabeth's right, little James lay fast asleep, his head a golden ball on the pillow, his round cheeks flushed and soft. On her left, a hump in the bed suggested Lucy; she had pulled the bed-clothes right over her head, and was not visible at all. Elizabeth wondered if she would suffocate. The baby's desolate cry rose to an angry howling, and out of the shadows Elizabeth saw Grizel appear, a tall figure in white, with dark hair loose about her shoulders, and approach the cradle. She stooped and lifted the child in her arms, and carried him back to her bed, which Elizabeth could now see, in the increasing light, defined against the far wall of the room. It seemed to be surrounded by a frame, like a door's. She watched Grizel get back in, holding the baby firmly against her breast, murmuring to him in a low, crooning voice. His weeping dropped to a fretful whimper, then into silence.

Elizabeth lay down again, reflecting on the comfort of a good feather mattress, as compared with the Spartan hardness of an ex-Army camp bed, but in spite of the warmth and softness, she did not fall asleep. She slipped her hand under her pillow to make sure that her looking-glass was safe, and once she had satisfied herself on that point, she curled herself up under the covers and thought how peaceful and happy she felt, not afraid in the least. Somewhere, far away at the back of her mind, a tiny whisper of caution pointed out that she really ought to be afraid, but she had no difficulty in silencing it. It was as if she had left all her doubts and fears and anxieties behind her in the world she had come from, and here found a peace of mind she had been yearning for without even knowing what it was she lacked. She did not — and this was what afterwards would seem to her most peculiar — even worry about how she was going to return. She supposed, without really bothering to think about it all, that the looking-glass which had the power to bring her here also had the power to take her back. It did not occur to her that this was something which still had to be proved or disproved.

Suddenly outside the window, a cock crew, shrill and eager and full of zest; almost simultaneously a clock chimed seven, and in an instant the whole house awoke. Elizabeth saw Grizel lay Alexander among her pillows, and slip out of bed, reaching up her arms to loose the ties of her nightgown. Immediately she closed her eyes, because she was far too well brought up to spy on a stranger dressing. She could hear voices outside the nursery now; doors opened and shut, feet clattered on stone stairs. Elizabeth drew up her knees, and hugged herself for joy, for the silent house of Robinsheugh had come alive, and she was in it. It went through her mind that Kate would have envied her.

Recollected afterwards, the events of that day, stretching endlessly beyond time as she understood it, were so confusing and strange that she wondered she did not make mistakes and betray herself. From the moment when Grizel, dressed now in her striped frock and white apron, came to wake her, every moment was full of interest and surprise, and danger too, because Elizabeth had no idea at all of how she should behave, or what was expected of her. Sensibly, she copied Lucy. When Lucy, who hated getting up, stood sleepy and groaning beside her bed, took off her nightgown and stretched for a flannel petticoat laid out on a chair nearby, Elizabeth did the same, for she had a flannel petticoat laid out too. A dress of blue wool, similar to Grizel's, but shorter, with a white muslin scarf, went on top, and there were brown woollen stockings, which came up to the knee and were held up by garters. Elizabeth hated these because they felt scratchy and insecure, but the shoes delighted her. They were square-toed, and had high heels of red leather, and little ornamental rosettes of red ribbon. She put them on gleefully, pushing out her feet one at a time to admire them, but alas, long before the end of the day they were pinching her toes cruelly, and she longed to kick them off, and have relief. When she was dressed, she went to Grizel to have her hair combed, and teased into long, curly ringlets over her shoulders, and while Lucy was having the same done to hers, she went back to the bed to fetch her looking-glass, which she put in a convenient pocket of her dust-gown; this was a rough calico pinafore of a cream colour which both she and Lucy wore to protect their frocks. She saw Grizel shake her head and smile at her, but it was such an understanding, affectionate smile, so unlike Kate Jenkins's expression of mockery, that she did not mind at all, but smiled back, thinking that surely she would find out today where Robin was, and when he was coming home.

Elizabeth expected breakfast, and indeed would have been glad of it, but here apparently the order of the day was different. As soon as they had finished the ritual of dressing, Grizel said, 'Fetch the books from the press, Lucy,' and Lucy went to the same cupboard from which earlier she had brought the combs, and brought out two books bound in black leather, similar to some in the chest in Kate's workroom, and two small pamphlets in covers of yellow paper. She gave one of each to Elizabeth, with such an expression of disgust on her small, pointed face that Elizabeth felt quite alarmed, wondering whether she were the cause of her disgust. She soon realised that this was not so.

'Now bring your creepies to the window, where you can see,' said Grizel. ''Tis wasteful to light the cruisie in the morning.'

Elizabeth glanced up at the wall, where an iron lamp with a round saucer for oil and a long wick, was hanging from a nail. A cruisie, she supposed. But a creepie? Again Lucy unwittingly came to her rescue. From a corner she was dragging out a three-legged wooden stool and Elizabeth ran to do the same. 'A press, a cruisie, a creepie,' she said to herself. It was like learning a foreign language.

While Grizel was tending the fire, and making the yellow flames leap again, Elizabeth sat down, and opened the book which Lucy had given her. Somewhat to her disappointment, she discovered that it was an Old Testament. She had been hoping for something quite unfamiliar, but as she glanced down at the first page, she realised that there was something unusual about the book. It was the print. She had looked at it for some time before she worked out that most of the letters 'S' were printed as letters 'F', which meant that 'God said, let the earth bring forth grass, the herb yielding seed and the fruit tree yielding fruit after his kind, whose seed is in itself, upon the earth: and it was so', was printed here as 'God faid, let the earth bring forth grafs, the herb yielding feed and the fruit tree yielding fruit after his kind, whofe feed is in itfelf, upon the earth: and it was fo'.

Elizabeth found this a little perplexing at first, and she was glad of a moment's quiet so that she could get used to it. But she was a very good reader, and she soon worked out the rules of what was only an old style of printing. If small 's' came at the beginning or in the middle of a word, it was written as 'f'. If it was the last letter in the word, it remained 's'. Capital 'S' remained capital 'S'. She got this sorted out while Grizel was fetching Alexander from her bed. He was awake now, but quiet, and Grizel sat down on her chair by the fire, dandling him on her knee. Elizabeth would have liked to go over and look at him properly, but she saw that that would have to be left till later, because Grizel was saying, 'Now, my young ladies, we must hasten on before Master James awakes and disturbs our peace. Where was it we finished yesterday, Lucy?'

'The end of Deuteronomy, chapter five,' said Lucy gloomily. 'Grizel, why cannot we read an interesting story for a change?'

'Now, now, Lucy. You know fine it is Mr Cockburn who chooses our readings, and we who have to obey him. He knows more of such things than we do. You would not want to grow up a heathen, now, would you?'

Lucy looked as if she would have been very happy to grow up a heathen, if only she could have been spared the necessity of reading the book of Deuteronomy now, but she said no more, and began to thumb through her Bible to find the place. Elizabeth was not at all sure where Deuteronomy was in the Books of the Bible, but once again she was lucky; when she opened the book at random, she saw that it was at Deuteronomy chapter twenty-eight, so it was easy to turn back from there. She followed the lines with her forefinger as Lucy's high, childish voice began to read.

'Now these are the commandments, the statutes and the judgments, which the Lord your God commanded to teach you, that ye might do them in the land whither ye go to possess it: that thou mightest fear the Lord thy God, to keep all his statutes and commandments, which I command thee, thou and thy son, and thy son's son, all the days of thy life. . . .'

She read as if she had not the faintest understanding of what she was reading, as indeed she had not, and her shrill monotone went on and on until Elizabeth felt she could not bear it another moment. At last Grizel told her to stop, and, 'Now you, Elizabeth,' she said.

Elizabeth glanced up, and saw Grizel's dark eyes smiling at her encouragingly, so she began, 'And thou shalt do that which is good and right in the sight of the Lord: that it may be well with thee, and that thou mayest go in and possess the good land which the Lord sware unto thy fathers. . . .' She knew she was reading beautifully, and she felt elated with success. Elizabeth Melville herself could do no better, she said to herself, than Elizabeth Martin pretending to be Elizabeth Melville. For today there was no doubt in her mind about who she was, or what she was doing. She was Elizabeth Martin, pretending to be Elizabeth Melville, and if these people thought that she was Elizabeth Melville, that was their affair, and not something she could do anything about. Even when she turned to the fly-leaf of her book, during one of Lucy's stints of reading, and read there, written in round, childish letters, 'Elizabeth Frances Melville, the Year of Our Lord 1776', she felt no more than mild interest. Her mind was making no attempt to wrestle with what she should have known was the central question, the real mystery; if they thought that she was Elizabeth Melville, and she knew that she was Elizabeth Martin, where was Elizabeth Melville? Instead, she sat there feeling pleased with herself, telling herself easily that of course it was all a part of the wonderful magic of the looking-glass, which had brought her here out of her own world, and when she was tired of pretending, would naturally work backwards and take her home. The childish folly of her attitude did not for a moment strike her, nor did the silliness of her use of the word 'naturally'; whatever else the working of the glass was, it certainly was not natural.

However she did not have much time to think about anything; she found she was having to keep her wits about her for the matters in hand. There was so much that she did not know, so many new things to be got through without any help. It was rather like arriving at a new school in the middle of a term, and not being allowed to ask anyone where the cloakroom was, or which seat one might take in the dining-room. Elizabeth simply had to watch Lucy, keep as quiet as she could, and try to memorise everything as she saw it happen.

After about an hour of reading, when Elizabeth's back was aching, and she had several times been told by Grizel to keep it straight, and her head up, they were allowed to put their Bibles away. Elizabeth hoped that this might be the end of lessons meantime, but she was disappointed. Grizel told them to take their Catechisms, and following Lucy again, Elizabeth opened the little yellow booklet at the first page. She had no idea what a Catechism was, and after she had read the long explanation of the title page, she was no wiser than when she began.

THE SHORTER CATECHISM
agreed upon by
THE ASSEMBLY OF DIVINES
at WESTMINSTER with the assistance
of COMMISSIONERS FROM THE CHURCH OF SCOTLAND
and approved anno 1648, by the General Assembly of the
Church of Scotland to be a Directory for catechising such as are
of weaker capacity
WITH REFERENCES TO THE PROOFS FROM THE
SCRIPTURE

Elizabeth read this fearsome introduction several times, then turned over the pages in some alarm. She discovered that the book consisted of a quite incomprehensible series of questions and answers, which she vaguely understood had something to do with the Bible. A hasty reading of the first two dismayed her even more, because she saw that the questions were almost as impossible to understand as the answers, and it was with a sinking feeling that she realised she was expected to learn them by heart. Then Grizel was speaking again.

'Today,' she said firmly, but not without sympathy, 'you are to learn the answers to questions eighteen and nineteen. I shall dress James, and when I have finished, you will repeat them to me.'

Lucy looked at Elizabeth, and made a face so hideous that Elizabeth wanted to laugh out loud, but she sensed that this would not be a proper time for laughter, so she composed her face, and settled down to get by heart the answer to the question, 'Wherein consists the sinfulness of that estate whereinto man fell?'

It was not easy, because James, once he was out of bed, and the sleep rubbed out of his eyes with fat pink fists, was charging about the room in his nightgown, pretending to be a horse and a coach and a coachman and passengers all at the same time. He shouted to the horse and cracked an imaginary whip, and lost a wheel and rolled over in the ditch, he was a lady screaming and a gentleman shouting, and the horse whinnying and shaking its mane. The noise was awful, and Elizabeth, who found the little boy enchanting, was torn between the desire to watch him and the pressing need to get by heart, 'The sinfulness of the estate whereinto man fell consists in the guilt of Adam's first sin' (and five more lines after that). She was further distracted by the arrival of a bare-footed maidservant, a pale, sandy-haired girl in a rough brown dress and a coarse apron, whose job it was to sweep the floor, make the beds and prepare the breakfast, which meant making porridge in a big pot like a witch's cauldron, which was slung over a hook above the fire. Elizabeth heard Grizel call her Alison, but she learned no more about her at this time, because she did her work and departed without ever once opening her mouth. Other details kept catching her attention. Grizel's bed, for instance — she noticed that she had been right in thinking that it was surrounded by a frame like a door's. The bed was in fact set into a recess or cupboard in the wall, and after Alison had tidied it, and straightened up the bed-clothes, she drew folding doors, like shutters, across it, so that it looked for all the world like the door into another room, and no one would have guessed there was a bed hidden behind it.

'Elizabeth,' said Grizel, 'you are not thinking hard, are you?'

'Sorry,' muttered Elizabeth, and dropped her eyes to the book.

When the porridge was almost ready, Grizel caught coachman James as he came galloping past her, and with much panting on her part, and much squawking and struggling on his, succeeded in getting him out of his nightgown and into a flannel petticoat and a long brown garment rather like a dressing-gown, with a collar and buttons from throat to foot. Then she left him to play again, and came to where Elizabeth and Lucy were still sitting captive on their creepies, with their Catechisms in their hands.

''Twas not long enough,' said Lucy plaintively. 'They are such large questions, Grizel.'

Grizel smiled at her sympathetically.

'They are that, my lamb,' she said. 'Too large for small heads, I fear. But Mr Cockburn will be coming to catechise you next week, and we must try to please him if we can. Now, see if you can answer, "Wherein consists the sinfulness of that estate whereinto man fell?" '

'Um,' said Lucy, twisting miserably on her stool. 'Er, yes. The sinfulness of that estate whereinto man fell consists in the want of — no, er — consists in the — um — in the guilt of man's first sin — er, I mean Adam's first sin, the want of original righteousness — is that right so far?'

Grizel nodded.

'The want of original righteousness — oh, dear — and, and — '

'And the corruption,' prompted Grizel.

'Of course, and the corruption of his whole nature, er, um.'

Elizabeth would have thought it was funny if her turn had not been coming next. She listened to Lucy stuttering her way through the answer, and thought that the really awkward thing about pretending to be somebody else was that you could not ask questions without betraying yourself. She could not, for instance, ask, 'Who is Mr Cockburn?' any more than she could ask, 'Where is Robin?' or 'What is the date?' or 'Where are our mother and father?' She could only keep her mouth shut, and her eyes and her ears open, and make sure that she did not get separated from her looking-glass.

Her own performance in the Catechism was even less inspired than Lucy's; she had very little experience of learning things by heart, and Grizel was shaking her head sorrowfully as she told them to put their books away and come to the table. 'I fear we must spend longer on the questions,' she said, 'or we shall be disgraced when Mr Cockburn comes. I am surprised at you, Elizabeth.' Elizabeth wondered why she should be singled out for a special black mark, and she felt guilty, because it was the nearest approach to a reproof that she had heard from these gentle lips. But the next moment she was telling herself it was silly to feel ashamed, because after all, it might matter to Elizabeth Melville whether she was disgraced in front of Mr Cockburn, but it had nothing to do with Elizabeth Martin. She followed Lucy to the table, and took her place.

If her mother, or Gerry Temple, had set before her the breakfast she was now obliged to eat, Elizabeth would have refused indignantly to touch it. It consisted of a thick oatmeal porridge and thin milk, served in a wooden bowl, and followed by some hard, dry oatcake with a scraping of rancid butter. She ate it, because she was afraid to refuse it, but she hated it, and she was surprised to see the others eating their share with obvious enjoyment. James, particularly, seemed to love his porridge, which he scooped up with his fingers, and got more on his cheeks and on the tablecloth than he did in his mouth. Lucy did most of the talking at the table, and Elizabeth soon realised that it was from her that she was most likely to learn the things she wanted to know about the Melville family. Already, before breakfast was over, she had discovered that Mr Galt was their dancing master, and Mr Boston their music master, that they learned French with Miss Latouche on Fridays, and that Papa would not allow Lucy to have drawing lessons, because he said she had no talent for it, and that to produce drawings without talent was a waste of time and money. Apparently Lucy did not agree that she was without talent; she made it plain that she thought she was very talented indeed, and she would again plead with Papa, she said, either by letter or when he next came home from Paris. Elizabeth stored all this information away for future use; she was a little anxious about the possible arrival of Miss Latouche. She had only been learning French for a year, and she doubted very much whether she could hold a conversation with a real Frenchwoman. With a name like Latouche, she must be French.

'What day is this?' she asked, and thought she sounded exactly like Kate Jenkins.

Lucy looked at Grizel and laughed, as if this were a well-worn joke.

'It is Tuesday, of course,' she said. 'Why is it you can never remember the days of the week?'

'I can,' said Elizabeth, annoyed. 'I just forgot.'

'You're always forgetting,' said Lucy, and although the injustice of this angered Elizabeth, when she had time to consider the matter, she realised that it might prove quite convenient if Elizabeth Melville had a reputation for forgetfulness.

There were more imminent dangers than Miss Latouche, however.

'Now then, Elizabeth,' said Grizel, when breakfast was over, and Alison had reappeared to clear it away, 'it is your turn to practise first upon the spinet today, while Lucy sews her seams. Fetch your music, and I will come downstairs with you and see to the fire in the drawing-room. I do not wish you to catch a cold.'

It was the first time Elizabeth had had to do something on her own. She cast an anxious look around the room, and realised that the cupboard which contained books and combs probably contained music too. So rather nervously she moved towards it, and opened the heavy oaken door. Obviously the nursery press contained everything. Neatly arranged on its deep shelves were piles of linen, jars of flour and oatmeal, bunches of dried herbs, books, dishes, cutlery, baby clothes, tapers, loaves, black bottles — all the plenishing of a little self-contained household. And there, in the middle of the bottom shelf, next to the combs and the box of ribbons, were two manuscript music books, stuffed with loose sheets, one marked 'E.F.M.' and the other, 'L.A.M.' With a sigh of relief, Elizabeth took hers, and said, 'I'm ready, Grizel.'

Clutching her sheaf of music, she followed Grizel out of the nursery, and down a long stone passage, her panic tempered only by curiosity to see what lay outside this room, where she had been since she arrived. At the end of the passage they passed through a door on to one of the landings she had crossed with Kate when they climbed the spiral staircase on that Sunday morning, which seemed so long ago. At the bottom of this stair, thought Elizabeth, is the door to the world outside. What if I should run down, and open it, and run out into the courtyard — what should I find? When would it be? Could I run on, across the courtyard, and find Gerry peeling potatoes in the kitchen, and listening to Radio One, or is this really a century and a half before even Kate was born? Such enormous questions, so impossible to answer. She followed Grizel down one flight of steps, and into a room leading from the landing below.

Elizabeth had only visited Robinsheugh twice, once with Kate and once on her own. It was not often enough to familiarise herself fully with the geography of so large and random a house, and now she had no idea where she was, at the top of it or at the bottom. She saw that she was standing in a room which seemed familiar and yet unfamiliar at the same time. This, she saw at once, was because she had seen a lot of the furniture before, but perhaps differently placed, and mixed in with other pieces which were not here now. She recognised a black lacquered table — Kate had said that lacquered furniture had been very fashionable in the eighteenth century, when it was called japan — some chairs, a rosewood cabinet, inlaid with a design of flowers, a walnut bookcase, a firescreen, and of course the lovely little wing-shaped spinet, over which Elizabeth had drawn secret, appreciative fingers, because she loved music . . . and fortunately she was very musical. She had been learning the piano since she was six, had passed all her examinations with Honours, and apart from Kate was the most accomplished pianist in the family. She had complained about the lack of a piano at Robinsheugh, but Kate, her mind on something else, had merely said, yes, wasn't it a pity, she missed it too. Elizabeth had longed to touch the smooth keys of the spinet, to bring music out of it, yet now, as she slid herself on to the long stool and laid out the unfamiliar music in front of her, it came to her that she scarcely even knew what sort of sound it was going to make. She was afraid that Grizel would stay with her, an unwanted audience for her mistakes, but Grizel had work awaiting her in the nursery, and as soon as she had attended to the fire of logs which was burning on the hearth, she turned to go.

'I shall send Lucy at twelve,' she said. 'See you work hard till then, and hurry upstairs, my love. We have all the stitching to do over that I unpicked for you last night.'

This sounded ominous, but Elizabeth was learning to take things one at a time. She waited till the clatter of Grizel's stiff-soled shoes had died away on the stair, then she slipped off her stool, and ran to the window. She measured with her eye the distance to the forecourt, and reckoned that she was on the second floor, in the room above the dining-room that used to be the Great Hall. Then she scanned the view for clues. For if it were the twentieth century outside, she thought, she would be able to see cars on the road, and telegraph poles, and perhaps one of the cottage women returning down the drive from the shop at Robinsheugh. That would be proof enough to solve at least one problem. But then she noticed that from this side of the house, the road was not visible at all; it was hidden by the estate wall and the dense growth of trees in the driveway and around the perimeter of the park. As for the telegraph poles, they might be there, hidden by the trees, but then again, they might not. And since Elizabeth had no way of knowing whether the trees she knew at Robinsheugh had also been there in Elizabeth Melville's day, the landscape she saw from the drawing-room window told her nothing at all. She turned back to the spinet.

The music consisted of keyboard works by Scarlatti, Pasquini, and J. S. Bach. The notation was more or less what she was used to, and there was nothing, Elizabeth thought, that she could not have attempted on the piano. So she took a deep breath, and started to play. It took some time to get used to the fact that when she struck a key, the note sounded and ceased immediately. She remembered having been told at school that the spinet and the harpsichord had strings inside them which were plucked by quills, instead of strings struck by hammers, as a piano had. Because of this, she could understand, the notes did not resound and linger as they did when she played the piano; once she began to grasp the different technique of fingering, she managed to coax a tune out of the little instrument and felt reasonably pleased with her own efforts. All the same, knowing nothing of Elizabeth Melville's standard of playing, she was glad there was no one there to hear her. She had no idea how long she sat there, and no one came to disturb her. Beyond the door, she could hear feet ascending and descending the stair, and occasionally voices calling, but it did not occur to her to go and investigate. It was as if her movements were determined by some force outside herself, and she did as she was bidden, no more, no less. A clock struck noon, and Lucy arrived, clutching her own sheaf of music. She skipped into the room on her little high heels, her red curls bouncing around her shoulders.

'James has been wicked again,' she announced gleefully. 'He took a bag of flour out of the press and emptied it on his head, then he pulled the pussy's tail, and made her yowl, and then he threw your muslin cap on the fire.' She said it all with such satisfaction that Elizabeth could not help laughing.

'Is my cap burned?' she asked.

'To a cinder,' said Lucy happily. 'It was that one you hate, that you had from Grandmamma last Hogmanay — the one that makes you look like the Duchess of Queensberry.'

Elizabeth sensed that this was another family joke at her expense, so she made a face at Lucy and said, 'That's all right, then. I'm glad it's gone.' She gathered up her music and made for the door, but before she opened it, she turned round, and said, 'What happened to James?'

Lucy was sitting on the stool, peering at her music and flexing her fingers above the keyboard as she had seen Mr Boston do.

'Nothing,' she said. 'Grizel says he is too young to understand his wrong-doing. Mamma would have whipped him. So would I.'

And Elizabeth, as she left the room in a frenzied and inaccurate burst of Scarlatti, had no doubt that she would.

Long before the day was over, Elizabeth was exhausted. She felt that she had never worked so hard in her life. The hours at the spinet were followed by two more spent hemming a shirt, a task which bored Elizabeth to tears, and which she performed so badly that Grizel had to keep taking the work out of her hands and unpicking it. If anyone else had done this, she would have been angry and rude, but Grizel was so kind and patient that Elizabeth forgave her, and tried to improve her dirty, stuttering stitches. But, 'I fear you will make a poor housewife, Elizabeth,' said Grizel, shaking her head.

It rather surprised Elizabeth that she should be expected to be a housewife at all. She knew that Giles Melville was a rich and important man, and she supposed that as his daughters she — or rather the other Elizabeth — and Lucy must be people of some consequence too, and surely, she thought, when they were grown up, they would have servants to do for them such lowly tasks as hemming shirts? But of course that was another of those questions to which she could not ask an answer.

At four o'clock, a dinner of salt beef and a cabbage-like vegetable called kale was served; Elizabeth thought it was terrible, especially the beef, which was so salty and fat that she could scarcely swallow it. Whatever Lady Melville provided for her guests at supper parties, she reflected, the food in her children's nursery was deplorable, and she remembered Gerry's cooking with thankfulness. After dinner, the girls again read from their Bibles and learned their Catechisms, then at last, when night was drawing on, and the cruisies were lighted on the walls, Grizel at last told them to 'go and play themselves'.

Elizabeth was too tired to do anything of the sort. Politely refusing an offer from the indefatigable Lucy of a game of hopscotch, she went over to the table, where Grizel was sitting, mending one of James's petticoats.

'Grizel,' she said, venturing at last the question she had been longing to ask all day, 'please may I hold Alexander?'

'Of course you may, my lamb,' said Grizel. 'This is the time you always hold him. Sit you down in my chair by the fire, then, and I will lift him in a minute.'

So Elizabeth sat down, and Grizel lifted the baby out of his cradle, and laid him in her lap. She put careful arms round his little body, stiff with many layers of frilled cotton, and looked down into the rosy, brown-eyed little face, surrounded by a froth of lace bonnet, and smelled his sweet-sour baby smell, and she had a moment of sheer happiness, because after years of looking longingly at other people's babies in their prams, she was actually holding one for the first time in her life. She put her finger into his tiny fist, and felt the bite of his elfin nails; he made little contented chuckling noises and bubbles at his little round mouth. Presently James, tired out after a day of unending rumpus, came and leaned against the arm of the chair, and Elizabeth put her fingers in the gold silk of his hair, and thought how lovely it was to be the sister of two such perfect little boys.

Of course it did not last long enough. All too soon Grizel got up, folded her mending, and said it was time for bed. While she undressed the two little ones, and got them into their nightgowns, Elizabeth and Lucy also undressed, before the fire, and put on their nightgowns, Elizabeth's the same she had worn to come into this room — she could not remember how long ago. Then there was the combing again, slow and gentle in the fireglow, soothing her tiredness and bringing her peace.

'Tell us a story, Grizel,' said Lucy from the other side of the striped skirt.

Elizabeth pricked up her ears hopefully, but Grizel laughed and shook her head.

'Not tonight, lamb. 'Tis too late for stories.'

Disappointment.

'A song, then?' said Lucy, who was not easily put off, ever.

'Well, perhaps we can make time for a song,' agreed Grizel indulgently.

Was there ever a nurse like Grizel, mused Elizabeth, so kind, so patient, so lenient, so loving? Her last recollection that night was of mingling her voice with Grizel's clear notes, and the shrill piping of Lucy and James, in a song the Melville children all learned in their earliest years. . . .

I had a wee cock, and I loved it well,
I fed my cock on yonder hill;
My cock, lily-cock, lily-cock coo,
Everyone loves their cock, why should I not love my cock
    too?

I had a wee dog and I loved it well,
I fed my dog on yonder hill;
My dog bouffie-bouffie,
My cock, lily-cock, lily-cock coo,
Everyone loves their cock, why should I not love my cock
    too?

I had a wee pig, and I loved it well,
I fed my pig on yonder hill;
My pig squeakie-squeakie,
My dog bouffie-bouffie,
My cock, lily-cock, lily-cock coo,
Everyone loves their cock, why should I not love my cock
    too?

9

How Many Miles To Babylon?

The following afternoon, when Kate and Gerry were at work on the manuscripts in the tower room, and she was as usual alone, Elizabeth went down to the banks of the Wishwater, and found a place among the trees where she could sit and throw stones into the brown stream, and think things over in peace and quiet. She took the looking-glass with her; obviously it was the most sensible thing to do, and she did not know why she had not thought of it a week ago, to keep it about her person, where she could feel it through the material of her blazer pocket, and know that it was safe. Although whether it was going to be of any more use to her, she had no way of knowing.

Ever since she had wakened that morning, knowing by the familiar creaking of wood and canvas where she was, even before she opened her eyes, she had been peeping into the glass at intervals, testing it out, expecting every time to be transported back into that incredible world which she had had no desire to leave so suddenly. But all she had seen was her own face, looking nervous and furtive at first, but then only cross, and crosser still as the morning wore on, and she found that no amount of looking was having any effect at all.

So two things at least were obvious. First, the glass was capricious. It did not work to order. Second, she might need it to get into the Melville world, but she did not need it to get out again. That seemed to be something over which she had no control at all. Twice now, she had gone to sleep in the great house, and had wakened up in the cottage, and on neither occasion had she willed it so. Rather, she had been snatched unwillingly out of an experience she was enjoying, and deposited back unconsenting into her humdrum, boring everyday life. Of course she wanted to be able to return to her everyday life; she had no desire to exchange it for Elizabeth Meville's life, with its salt beef and its Catechisms, in any but the most temporary way, and it was in a sense a relief to find that she could make the transition back so easily, and with so little fuss. For Elizabeth was not a fool, and although in the Melville world of yesterday enchantment had made light of danger, in the light of common,

72

twentieth-century day she could see very clearly that far more important than knowing how to get into the Melville world was knowing that one could get out of it again. And if one knew that one simply fell asleep in the nursery feather bed, and woke up in Gerry's second-best sleeping bag, it was a weight off one's mind, to say the least of it. The annoying thing was that she did not seem to have any control over what happened, or when. Elizabeth was the sort of person of whom it is said that they want the best of all possible worlds, and in this case it was a particularly apt comment, because she did indeed want the best both of Elizabeth Melville's world and her own. And it irked her that she could not control her coming and going, that the decisions of adventure were not hers to make. For then it would be perfect in every way; she could choose what time she spent in each of her lives, picking out the best bits of both, and escaping the rest. Unfortunately it did not seem to be as simple as that.

Elizabeth skimmed a couple of flat stones expertly across a still pool, and turned her thoughts to the question of how the looking-glass operated. She had a tidy mind, and the idea that the glass revealed its secrets fortuitously, without any rules to govern its behaviour, was one which offended her. Perhaps, she thought, the looking-glass only revealed the past at night, or, at any rate, perhaps one could only pass into the firelit world at night, for although she had first seen the nursery and its inhabitants in the afternoon, it had been night there, and she remembered that both of her actual visits had been made in her nightgown.

> How many miles to Babylon?
> Three score and ten.
> Can I get there by candle-light?
> Yes, and back again.
> If your heels are nimble and light,
> You may get there by candle-light.

But however nimble your heels were, Elizabeth knew that you could never calculate such a journey as hers in miles, nor in years, even. It was beyond such reckoning. What was it they said of stars? Millions of light-years away. Comprehending such things was like counting grains of sand, a feat so immense that one's mind broke at the thought, one's concentration collapsed under the strain of it. And it seemed to Elizabeth that what was happening to her was no less extravagant, no less dangerous in its demand upon her understanding. For as she saw it now, there were two possibilities, the third, that it was all a simple dream, being now rejected. The first was that she had truly travelled back in time, that now had really become then. But if that were so, what had happened to all the years in between? Did it mean that the centuries between Elizabeth Melville, aged twelve, and Elizabeth Martin, aged twelve, had been for the period of her absence wiped out? That the years which were the future to Elizabeth Melville, and the past to Elizabeth Martin had got lost somewhere between the lifetime of one, and the lifetime of the other? And did that mean that Kate and Gerry and Mother and Father and all the millions of other people alive now, had temporarily ceased to exist? The second possibility — and of the two it seemed to Elizabeth the more likely, though scarcely less astounding — was that in the house of Robinsheugh, in some mysterious and inexplicable way, the eighteenth century co-existed with the twentieth, that they were both going on at the same time, although with a different time-scale. The problems involved in such a notion made Elizabeth's head ache, but she thought it could go some way towards explaining the dilemma of where yesterday was, and why she had been away for a whole day, and Kate and Gerry had not even noticed that she was gone. This aspect of the affair puzzled her sorely.

She had looked in the glass on Monday night, and she had been with the Melvilles all day Tuesday — she was sure of this because of her conversation with Lucy about Miss Latouche — and when she got up this morning she had been afraid that there would be the most dreadful row, because she had been away a whole day without an explanation. Elizabeth was always complaining that Kate did not notice her, but she did not for a moment imagine that Kate was quite so vague as not to observe her total disappearance. Anyway, there was Gerry, who was sharp enough. It had even occurred to her while she was dressing that they might have called the police. But as she came gingerly into the kitchen, it was just in time to hear the announcer say clearly from Gerry's transistor, 'This is the eight o'clock news for Tuesday, the second of August. . . .' And Gerry, who was filling the teapot from the kettle on the hob, merely turned her head and nodded a frosty good morning, as if she had never been away at all. After a short truce, she and Gerry were apparently on bad terms again, following the incident at table the night before last —

or was it last night?

It was all very confusing, but after long thought Elizabeth came to the conclusion that the Tuesday she had spent with the Melvilles could not have been the Tuesday of Kate and Gerry; apart from the evidence of the B.B.C., who presumably knew what day of the week it was, surely a whole day of absence would not have been allowed to pass without comment, and most of it pretty furious, she could imagine. And so she must suppose that the Melvilles' Tuesday did not exist in twentieth-century time, and that although it seemed to her that she had been gone for many hours, to those she left behind her truancy had not been noticeable at all. For her, there had been two Tuesdays, yesterday and today, but for Gerry and Kate, yesterday had been Monday, and Elizabeth had simply gone to bed, and got out of it nine hours later as usual. And Elizabeth was quick to see that if this were so, it might be strange, but it was also convenient — assuming that there were any more visits still to come — because however absent-minded and easy-going Kate might appear, she was responsible to the Martins for Elizabeth's safety, and Elizabeth was well aware that should she disappear for even a few hours without permission, the result would be very unpleasant indeed. It also meant, and this was very important, that there was no possibility that what had happened to Rip Van Winkle would happen to her, that she would come back thinking that she had been gone only a short time, to discover that she had been gone for years, and that everyone had forgotten her. That would be truly dreadful, and if there were any such danger, she would go back again. But if, as it now seemed, she could go, and be quite sure that she would be returned safely in the night, well then, surely there could be no harm, and she did so want to see Robin, when he came home for the holidays from school in England. And the odd thing was that as she scrambled up the grassy bank, pulling herself upwards by rough handfuls of sedge and clover, she did not even notice that she had thought anything odd at all.

Elizabeth walked back across the fields into the view which the painter had caught fast for ever in his family portrait of the Melvilles. It was still very much the same; although now fences and gates were more in evidence, the turreted house and the trees and the hills beyond were all there as they had been when Giles Melville and his family sat for the painter in their uncomfortable Sunday clothes by the Wishwater, under the pale blue enamel of the sky. Elizabeth climbed a five-barred gate, because it was easier than opening it, checked to make sure that her looking-glass was safe, and set off along the little path of beaten earth which skirted the backs of the cottages in the yard, and met up with the carriage drive just below the point where it fanned out into a roundel before the front door of Robinsheugh.

As she walked along, she looked up at the house, which seemed as always to spring lightly up from the ground, not at all as if it consisted of thousands of tons of stone and lime and slate and timber, but as if it were some airy, insubstantial thing, all white light and velvet shadow, its turrets and chimneys floating away as the wisps of summer cloud passed behind them. And Elizabeth loved it, as she had ever since the day she first saw it, and she thought how lucky Lucy and Elizabeth Melville were to be born and brought up in it, instead of in a red-brick, semi-detached villa in Highgate. Yet even so, and despite the fact that Kate had said she could go in whenever she liked, Elizabeth had great difficulty in persuading herself that she should do so. It was always like this now; she loved the house as much as ever, but every time she approached it she felt stiff all over with uneasiness. And in the end, it was only an overpowering curiosity to see again, on Elizabeth Martin's Tuesday, the rooms she had lived in on Elizabeth Melville's Tuesday, that overcame her reluctance to enter by the door of a place which she knew to have another, stranger entrance. So she followed the gravel walk round the east side of the house, and pushed open the heavy door at the bottom of the winding stair.

After the water-chuckling, bird-whistling, leaf-rustling liveliness of the summer day outside, the stillness of the house was instant, its chill more acute as one stepped from under the sun. Elizabeth knew that five floors above Kate and Gerry were hard at work, but even if they were talking over their manuscripts, the sound of their light, rippling voices would be lost instantly in the thickness of walls, and for all the difference their presence made, Elizabeth might as well have been the only living soul in the house. Treading apprehensively on feline, private feet, she crept up the worn steps of the stairway — they were already worn, she remembered, even in Elizabeth Melville's day — passed the door of the dining-room, which stood open, and climbed on to the next landing, from which, she thought, opened the drawing-room where yesterday she had practised on the spinet.

A glance told her that she had been right in her placing of this room; it was unmistakably the same. Indeed, not only the spinet, but several other items of furniture, were standing in roughly the same positions as in the Melville house of two centuries ago. Some pieces had been added, and the curtains and carpet were different, green damask and Oriental design having been replaced by blue velvet and plain Wilton. Elizabeth was later to see the original carpet in a bedroom on the floor above, and this amused her, because it was what happened in her house at home. When new things were bought for the sitting-room, old things were relegated to the bedrooms, and the living-room at the back of the house, because, her mother said, there was plenty of wear left in them before they finally went to the jumble sale at St Luke's.

Elizabeth wandered round the drawing-room, looking at chairs and tables and cupboards with glass doors, filled with elegant pieces of china and old silver, looking with a thoughtful recognition, restraining her eager fingers from probing their solidity only because she had promised Kate that she would not touch. In any case, she knew now that touching and feeling proved nothing, for yesterday everything in this room had seemed to her as substantial as it did today, but because of her experiences she was now beginning to grope towards an idea which normally she would not have had to wrestle with until she was much older; it was that you could not say that a thing was real simply because you could see and touch it. Certainly this was how she would have explained it until very recently, but now she was beginning to doubt whether you could possibly believe the evidence of your senses yesterday, if at the same time you had to admit that perhaps yesterday never existed. And could you be sure, she now wondered, that things were still there, still real, if you stood back from them and closed your eyes? Could you be sure that this room still existed if you went out of it? Common sense said yes, but surely, if your tests of reality were your eyes and the tips of your own fingers, you really had no proof that it was so. For all you knew, like yesterday's world, it only existed because you were in it. And did that mean, Elizabeth wondered, that what was real for you need not be real for other people? That you made things real for yourself by becoming involved in them? But that was silly. A spinet was a spinet, a table was a table, in the eighteenth century or in the twentieth century. It had nothing to do with whether Elizabeth Martin was looking at it or not. Or had it?

Oh, dear, thought poor Elizabeth, questions, questions, questions, and never an answer in sight. What she did not yet understand, what she needed Kate to explain to her, was that questions are far more important than answers, that it is by asking questions that we begin to get at the truth of things. At that moment, it seemed to Elizabeth that she was failing, because no clear answers presented themselves to her, whereas actually she was succeeding; her lazy mind was growing and working as it never had before. But just because it had been idle for so long, the effort exhausted her, and she thought she was beginning to understand why Kate Jenkins had headaches.

Next she went to the window to check on the telegraph poles, and found that the view from this window was exactly the same as the one she had seen yesterday. She knew that the main road was on the other side of the wall — at least she supposed it was, since she could not see that either — with the telegraph line between Kelso and Robinsheugh running along it, but through the greeny tangle of leaves and branches neither road nor poles were visible. So the problem of whether it could be the eighteenth century inside the house and the twentieth outside was not going to be solved at this point. Elizabeth turned away, resisting the temptation to try a little stealthy tune on the spinet, and made her way back to the door. Now, she thought, forcing herself to be brave, for the nursery.

Elizabeth thought that finding the nursery again would be the easiest thing in the world, starting with the drawing-room as base. She had come down to the drawing-room yesterday, with Grizel as escort, and she had had no difficulty at all in finding her way back, when Lucy came to take her place at the spinet. She had simply gone up the next flight of twisting stairs, passed through the second door on the left when she came to the landing, walked down a long narrow passage, and the nursery door was at the end of it. No problem. So she closed the drawing-room door, climbed the stair, came to the landing, opened the door, and walked into a cupboard. It was not the sort of cupboard Elizabeth would have expected to find in Robinsheugh, although if she had considered the matter she would have realised that any house so spick and span must be much scrubbed and dusted. It was a broom cupboard, with three rough wooden shelves along a plastered wall facing the door, containing dusters and polishing cloths, tins of Vim and Brasso, handbrushes and a dustpan.

Underneath the shelves was a small sink with a tap, and on the floor, propped against the wall, an assortment of mops and brushes. There was also a large zinc bucket, which Elizabeth walked into with a surprised clatter. She had made a mistake about the door. Strange, when she had been so sure, but then, one made mistakes. So she closed the door, and tried the next one. Wrong again. She tried all the doors on the landing, although she was so sure it was the second on the left; they led to boudoirs and bedrooms and rooms with no clear function at all, but not one led into a long narrow passage. Well, she thought, it must have been on the landing above, but it was not on the landing above, and the more Elizabeth went searching, the more confused and bewildered she became; but one thing was sure, the way into the nursery was not now through any door opening off the main staircase. Nor through any other part of the house that she could recognise; it was like being in a maze, where she went round and round, crossing and re-crossing her own path, getting nowhere.

Finally, exhausted and defeated, she made her way downstairs again, meaning to go back to the cottage, but as she passed the open door of the dining-room, she decided that she would just go in for a moment, and look at Robin. Feeling very small and unimportant, she scuttled down the side of the table, avoiding the stares of the assembled Melvilles, haughty, irascible, impudent, condescending, kind, according to the character of the subject and the truthfulness of the artist. She wondered, as she came to a halt in front of the vast, cold hearth, and tipped her head back to look up at the Melville family group, how honest the painter had been about Robin, for instance, with his soft fair hair and laughing eyes, and joyous, careless pose. She could only judge by her knowledge of James and Lucy — Alexander was only a rosy blob in a frilly bonnet — but James and Lucy were very like themselves, so she supposed it would be a good likeness of Robin too. If only she knew what had happened to Elizabeth, why she had been excluded from the portrait when even the baby was there. It was almost as puzzling as the question of where the real Elizabeth was when impostor Elizabeth was taking her place; the elusiveness of Elizabeth was complete.

Elizabeth was just about to go away, back downstairs into the fresh air, when as she turned away some irregularity in the bottom right-hand corner of the painting caught here eye. Peering up at it, she saw that a piece of the original canvas, perhaps three square feet, had been cut out from the corner, and patched, not very expertly, with a piece of a coarser texture. The patch had been painted over with a continuation of the grass and broom of the original, but with the afternoon sun slanting in at the south windows, the glued outline of the patch stood out harshly, disfiguring the whole work. Elizabeth was just wondering whether she dared stand on a chair to examine it more closely, when she had reason hastily to be thankful that she had done no such thing, because a door at the far end of the room opened, and Kate came through it, carrying a great pile of books in her arms. She looked more dishevelled than ever, in an old tweed skirt and a crumpled gingham shirt which was supposed to be tucked into the skirt, but was all flopping out at one side. Her hair was tumbling wildly in her eyes, because she had no free hand to push it back; she kept tossing her head like an irritable pony, clearing her vision only to have it obscured again next moment as the unpinned golden strands fell back across her forehead. Elizabeth looked at her with a mixture of exasperation and some other feeling to which she could not give a name, but which made her ache somewhere deep down.

'Hello,' said Kate vaguely, and would have passed by, had not Elizabeth stood across her path and said, 'Hold on a minute, please — I want to ask you something.'

Kate stopped at once. Whatever else, she was a courteous answerer of questions.

'Yes, of course. What is it?'

'I wondered,' said Elizabeth, 'whether you had noticed that there is a great big patch in the corner of this painting?'

Kate smiled at her in the rather wan, tired manner she had acquired lately, a smile which lifted the corners of her mouth without touching her eyes, as if she were admitting that something was amusing without actually being amused by it.

'Well, you're a very good detective,' she said. 'I didn't notice that until I had been here — oh, a very long time.'

'It's because the sun is shining on it,' explained Elizabeth. 'I don't suppose I'd have noticed it otherwise. Why is it patched?'

'I really don't know, Elizabeth.'

'Do you know why Elizabeth Melville isn't in the picture?'

It was another point in favour, although Elizabeth was reluctant to concede it, that, unlike most grown ups, Kate never asked you why you wanted to know things. It was a kind of curiosity which did not seem to afflict her at all. Elizabeth's explanation was that she was not sufficiently interested to ask; what never occurred to her was that it might simply be a kind of politeness on Kate's part, a respect for privacy which adults tend to allow each other as a right, but rarely extend to their children. It was a respect which served Elizabeth now, for although a flicker of surprise crossed Kate's eyes, she did not ask her how she knew about Elizabeth Melville, but answered a straight question with an equally straight answer.

'It is supposed,' she said, 'that Elizabeth Melville was portrayed in the original painting on the part which is now patched. For some reason, she was later cut out. What that reason was, I cannot tell you.'

'Who told you about it, Kate?'

'Lady Melville. She doesn't know the reason either.'

'Isn't it surprising,' Elizabeth went on, 'that Giles would allow his painting to be messed up like that, and his daughter cut out? Did they quarrel about anything?'

She thought Kate looked at her rather queerly, although it might just have been that she was expecting to be looked at queerly, and fancied it.

But the matter-of-fact voice said, 'Oh, no, nothing like that. In any case, almost certainly the cutting wasn't sanctioned by Giles. If it had been, presumably he would have had it done by the same painter, who actually outlived him. But if you look closely, you'll see that that daub in the corner was done by a much less professional hand.'

And while Elizabeth was looking closely, she went abruptly, like the Cheshire Cat, leaving not a smile, but yet another mystery, hanging behind her on the air.

10

The Secret of the Glass

Tired and puzzled, Elizabeth went back across the courtyard to the cottage, where already Gerry had begun to prepare the supper. She too was looking tired and rather dispirited, which surprised Elizabeth, who had thought she only had two moods, cheerful and furious. She wondered whether perhaps Gerry was also having a trying time with the Melvilles. Or perhaps she was just having a trying time with Kate. Elizabeth did not envy Gerry her afternoons.

'Did you get a lot of work done today?' she asked, in an effort to be friendly, and start a conversation. She supposed that Gerry was still cross with her, and if she had felt like it, she could have been equally cross in return, but she found that at this moment what she wanted most in the world was a bit of friendly, commonplace chatter. The silences in this house could be so unnerving.

'Oh, yes,' said Gerry, in a despondent voice. 'We always get a lot of work done, or at least Dr Jenkins does, only there never seems to be any less to do. I'll swear that wretched trunk is bottomless. Lay the table for me, will you, Elizabeth? I have to keep stirring this sauce.'

'Yes, all right,' agreed Elizabeth. She had no objection to helping around the house. It helped to pass the time. She went to the drawer to fetch the tablecloth, and tossed it over the clear half of the table, saying, 'Do you suppose Kate will finish her work by September?'

'Oh, yes, certainly,' said Gerry. 'She'll kill herself, I dare say, but if she has decided to finish by September, she'll finish by September.'

Elizabeth laid out the forks and knives, and watched Gerry's unhappy face. She had never seen her look like this before.

'Is there something wrong?' she asked uncertainly. 'You look upset.'

Gerry was just about to say no, there was nothing wrong, but if she had one thing in common with Elizabeth it was that she too was far away from the people she knew and loved, and was living with a person she cared for, but was quite at a loss to understand.

And sometimes she felt the need to talk to somebody, anybody. She would not have chosen Elizabeth if there had been anyone else available, but there was not, so she told her.

'It has just been a horrible afternoon,' she said. 'I got everything wrong, and muddled up a whole bundle of letters which Dr Jenkins had spent the whole of yesterday putting in order.'

'Was she cross?' asked Elizabeth.

'No. She never is, which makes it worse. I was the one who lost my temper. I told her I was sick of Giles Melville and his letters, and all I wanted when I got my degree was to be a suburban housewife and teach part-time in a Comprehensive.'

'Well, what's wrong with that?' said Elizabeth. It seemed to her a perfectly reasonable ambition.

'There may be nothing wrong with it, but one doesn't say that sort of thing to Dr Jenkins.'

'Why not?'

'It's heresy, as far as she's concerned. She was very offended.'

Elizabeth stood with the salt cellar in her hand, and gazed at Gerry in perplexity. She felt that she was getting out of her depth.

'But — it doesn't really have anything to do with Kate, what you do, does it?' she asked.

Gerry took her sauce off the hob, and poured it into a jug.

'In a way, no,' she said, 'and goodness knows, she would be the last person to interfere in anybody's affairs. That isn't why I'm upset. I'm upset because I hurt her over something she feels very strongly about, and now I feel mean and nasty.'

'What does she feel strongly about?'

'People making the most of their brains. She says that it is positively wicked not to use your mind to its full capacity, because it is the greatest gift you have, and you only have one short life to use it in. All the wonder of the world, she says, and you will never have time to know more than a tiny fragment of it. Of course I know what she means, but the trouble with these scholarly women is that they just don't understand what ordinary people are like. They think that nothing matters except ideas. Dr Jenkins doesn't care about being married, or having children, or money, or security, or any of the things ordinary women want. To her, learning is the only thing in the world worth caring about — it's the gold at the foot of her rainbow, and she can't see anything else.'

Elizabeth, who knew Gerry pretty well by now, did not try to

83

console her by pointing out that Kate was a freak, because she knew that Gerry would immediately jump to her defence. She was like that. So she said, 'Do you mean she wants you to be like her?'

'Lord, no,' said Gerry. 'She knows I couldn't be. She's about a million times more brilliant than I am. But when I said so, she said that wasn't the point, the point was that I should try to be as good as it was possible for me to be. She said I was just being lazy. It was really awful.'

Elizabeth would not have known what to say to all this; she was not sure that she really understood half of it. But she sensed that she did not have to say anything. Gerry just wanted to get it off her chest to someone. So she continued laying the table, and after a pause, Gerry went on again.

'And what makes it worse,' she said dismally, 'is that she only brought me here out of kindness. There were about a dozen people who wanted the job, and most of them were far better qualified than I was. But she chose me, because I hadn't a home to go to in the holidays, and Peter is working for exams. And I've been no use to her at all.'

'You're a very good cook,' said Elizabeth, meaning to be comforting. But Gerry was not to be consoled.

'She wouldn't notice if I put corned beef and beans in front of her every night,' she said bleakly.

'Oh, yes, she would,' replied Elizabeth. 'She hates beans, and she can't abide corned beef. You think she doesn't notice what she's eating, but she'd notice soon enough if she didn't like it. Granny says she's very pernickety about her food.'

Before Gerry could make another pessimistic reply, their conversation was interrupted by the arrival of Kate, with a bag of chocolate toffees which she had bought from the travelling shop which came twice a week to the cottages at Robinsheugh. She knew that Gerry was greedily fond of them.

'Not that I should encourage you,' she said, tossing the bag into Gerry's lap. 'They're very bad for your teeth.'

This gift caused Gerry to go and sniff at the sink, and Elizabeth, suddenly exasperated by the incomprehensible behaviour of all grown ups, felt thankful that she had already made her plans for going upsairs early. Because after all, she reminded herself, with a secret surging of excitement, she had more important things to think about than Gerry's tiff with Kate. She would use the silent supper hour to stuff away as much food as she possibly could, because if her theory that night was the time for slipping away to the Melvilles should prove correct, tomorrow might well be another day of salt beef and porridge. As soon as supper was over, and she had helped Gerry to wash up, she would go upstairs, get into her nightdress, and. . . .

And she was utterly, bewilderingly, flatly mistaken. After she had eaten such a huge supper that even Kate, who usually was quite blind to such things, looked at her in mild alarm, and had helped to tidy up the Cooking End of the table, she left Kate to her scribbling and Gerry to her cookery books, and later, no doubt, her apology, and rushed upstairs to her room. Because all through supper her confidence in her idea had been growing, she was convinced that the glass performed its magic by night, that like that other journey to Babylon hers could be accomplished by candle-light, fire-light, star-light, any light but the light of day.

But she was wrong. It did not matter what she did. It was no use. She tried in her nightdress, she tried in her day clothes. She tried standing up, she tried sitting down. She tried lying in bed, and in other poses too ridiculous to describe. She said silly spells, like Hocus Pocus, and Abracadabra. Nothing happened at all. No matter what she said, or did, the only image the glass threw back to her, with mocking indifference, was that of her own face, with strained, glaring eyes and sulky, pouting mouth, so unlike, Elizabeth thought, her usual pretty face, that suddenly she didn't want to look at it any more. In a fury, she pushed the glass under her pillow, and flounced into bed, too angry and bitter to find relief even in tears.

So that was that. It was all over, before it was properly begun. The one chance she had of making this dismal life exciting, of having other children to play with, of being with a grown up who liked her, or even noticed she was there. She would certainly never see Robin now. And she had another seven and a half weeks to spend in this house, before her parents' return set her free. Seven and a half weeks of hush, and boredom, and other people's headaches. As always, when Kate came to her mind, her grievances multiplied, fighting furiously against one small voice that repeated insistently, 'Unfair, unfair.' For Elizabeth knew that Kate had never once complained about her headaches, although she was looking so ill that some days Elizabeth scarcely recognised her, and she could not help thinking that if her mother, or Granny, were to see Kate now, there would be the most dreadful fuss of anxiety and alarm. And what was it Gerry had said? 'It won't be Oxford she'll be going back to in October, it will be a nursing home.' Elizabeth turned over uneasily, and bit her thumb nail. What if there were really something the matter with Kate? But then, just when for a moment she was allowing herself to care, the old excuses began trotting themselves out again. She had loved Kate, and Kate had thrown her love away. Kate didn't care about her, so why should she care about Kate? But if, niggled that small voice, Kate were really ill. . . . Angrily, Elizabeth told it to be quiet. Of course she wasn't really ill. She was pale because she never bothered to put make-up on her face, and she had headaches because she had weak eyesight, and would insist on spending more than twelve hours a day reading ancient letters in faded, cramped handwriting. It was her own fault. And in any case, it was no concern of Elizabeth's; she had more important things to think about.

She was still tossing to and fro, getting hotter and hotter, and more entangled with the bedclothes, when she heard Kate come upstairs and go into her room. Now the rattling of that dratted typewriter would start again, and go on half the night. That was the trouble with Kate, she was so selfish, she had no consideration for anybody but herself. And she had never brought Elizabeth a bag of chocolate toffees.

But after ten minutes or so, Elizabeth realised that Kate was not going to work tonight. She listened to her moving around in her room, presumably undressing and brushing her hair. Then she heard her go into the bathroom, and run water into a glass. Presumably taking aspirin. Presently she heard her go back into her room, the light switch clicked off, and there was a faint protest from elderly bed springs as Kate got into bed and drew up the blankets. Then there was silence for a while, before — only of course it couldn't be. But if Elizabeth had not known the sheer impossibility of such a thing, she would have said that through the wall she could hear the torn, broken, stifled sound of Kate's sobbing into her pillow. Of course it was nonsense, because everyone knew that Kate never cried, but even so, Elizabeth wriggled deeper down into her sleeping-bag, and pulled the flap over her head, just in case the sound became any louder, and she was forced to believe in it.

For the next few days, Elizabeth went around with the looking-glass in her pocket, trying it out occasionally, but becoming less and less optimistic about the likelihood of its ever working its magic for her again. Gerry had apparently made things up with Kate, for she was as perky as ever, while Kate, though still with nothing to say, seemed a little more cheerful. This led Elizabeth to discard finally her suspicion that she had been crying, and to convince herself that what she had heard had been only some trick of sound. And so she dismissed the matter from her mind, and with it everything else relating to Kate and Gerry and their concerns. Because something was happening to Elizabeth, something very strange, and which she felt quite powerless to stop, even if she had wanted to. And perhaps the strangest thing about it was that she did not want to, that she made no effort at all to fight against an enchantment which weeks ago, on her return from her first visit to the Melville nursery, she had recognised as being full of danger and sinister power. Then she had wanted to fight against it, had tried to do so, till loneliness and unhappiness overcame her resolution, and she gave way to temptation. But what she had known to be dangerous then, she thought right and natural now, and did not even know that she was being changed, far less what she was being changed into.

For as the days passed, and her hand lay almost constantly on the silver glass in her pocket, it seemed that her dominion over her own mind and will and understanding loosened and fell away, and with the diminishing of Elizabeth Martin everything she looked at seemed to pale too. The pure blue of the sky faded, the bright green of the grass and the sharp hues of the wild flowers in the hedges washed out into a sickly, pastel pallor which was a travesty of their truth. The song of the birds, the sighing of the wind, the clear chattering of the river water died in her ears as if deafness were stopping them. And it was the same with people. The images of Kate and Gerry, along with the remembered aspect of her father and mother, Granny, Uncle Kenneth, Susan, her cousins in Wimbledon, people whose faces had been printed on her memory since her early childhood, now seemed to Elizabeth to be becoming oddly blurred and distorted, as if she hardly knew them, while at the same time Grizel and the Melvilles, whom she had tried in vain to contact, grew in power and clarity until they assumed for her a bright sharpness of familiarity, at the expense of people she knew and loved, and had lived with all her life. It seemed too that all the lost colour of the everyday world had drained out of it into them, and Elizabeth saw constantly before her eyes the orange flames of their nursery fire, the reds and blues of their striped woollen dresses, the wild

87

rose of their rounded cheeks, the brightness of their hair.

With the same want of effort on her part, she found knowledge of them flowing into the empty shell of her, things no one had ever told her, but which she knew suddenly as if she had always known them. She knew that their father, Sir Giles Melville, was away from home, because he was British Ambassador to the French Court of King Louis XVI at Versailles, but was expected back in time for the New Year; that their mother, Lady Melville, whose name was also Elizabeth, had recently returned from France to see her children, and make some arrangements about their education, and that she could hardly wait to get away again; so dull and boring did she find the country life at Robinsheugh; that the fifteen-year-old heir, Robin, was away at school in the south of England, but would be home for the holidays any day now, and that his coming was awaited, as Kate's had been long ago, with a joy and longing which the children certainly had not felt before the arrival of their mother. For Robin was their hero, but Lady Melville was a mother they scarcely ever saw, a haughty, stately person who never took them on her knee, for fear they would crush her silken gowns, never allowed them to finger her glittering jewels, in case they had sticky hands. She was beautiful, but she was like an exquisite, embroidered bird of paradise behind a glass, she was not to be touched. Which was sad, but not as sad as it might have been, for the children had Grizel Elliot — Elizabeth did not notice how that name too had become part of the furnishing of her mind — and Grizel was all the mother to them that they could ever want, with warm lap and strong arms, and her sweet voice singing,

> O hush a ba baby, and balililoo!
> And hee and ba birdie, my bonnie wee doo.

And Elizabeth knew all this, and more, and the knowledge burned itself deeply into her being, as if it really belonged there, until her sense of anger and desolation at being shut out from all that she loved became so intense that she felt she could bear it no longer. So on a wet, dismal Saturday afternoon, with despair in her heart, she plodded across the yard to the great house, and climbed the winding stair tō the dining-room, so that she could at least look at the painted forms of those she could not find in the flesh. And it was as she stood there, looking up at Robin and Lucy and her own dear little baby brothers, that she felt the last rushing, hurting, desperate longing before the heart breaks, and understood at last the secret of the glass. You passed into the Melville world, not because it was night, or because you wanted to get away from Kate for a while, or because you thought it might make a pleasant change. You went when your whole being ached with the desire of it, when no corner of your will was withheld, when the pain of your separation finally became unbearable. Then you took the looking-glass out of your pocket, and you looked into it, and the frame shimmered and began to melt away, and you had your heart's desire.

11

Robin

Robin Melville was sitting on the edge of the nursery table in a lordly fashion, swinging his long legs, his bold brown eyes laughing at Elizabeth who was perched on a stool by the window, sewing her sampler, an everlasting trial to fingers which seemed naturally hopeless with a needle. It was a very delicate and intricate sampler, a rectangle of cream linen on which had already been stitched, in threads of various colours, the letters of the alphabet, the numbers one to nine, and the name, ELIZABETH FRANCES MELVILLE. There was a time when this had been a source of mild annoyance to Elizabeth Katherine Martin, who had felt that she was doing all of the work, and getting none of the credit. But now she hardly ever thought of it. For the last few days she had been embroidering some red and yellow flowers along the border of the cloth, loving the beautiful names of the stitches, Algerian Eye, Rococo, Satin, Florentine, hating the needle which pricked her fingers, and the tedium of having to do again so much that Grizel insisted on unpicking. Now she was filling in the verse which was to occupy the centre of the cloth, which one day would be put in a golden frame, Grizel said, and hung in Mamma's drawing-room to be admired by everyone. She said it to encourage her, but secretly Elizabeth did not greatly care whether it was ever hung in the drawing-room or not. There was no love lost between Lady Melville and her eldest daughter.

> Have thou no other gods but me,
> Before no image bow thy knee,
> Take not the name of GOD in vain,
> Nor do the Sabbath day prophain.

She was outlining the 'o' in 'other', when the needle ran into her finger again, and she let her work fall with an anguished squawk.

'Ow!' she cried, putting her injured finger into her mouth and sucking it furiosuly. 'Why, oh, why do I have to learn to *sew*?'

'Because you are a girl, of course,' replied Robin, mocking her with his dark, mischievous eyes. 'We all know that girls have to do all sorts of silly things, like sewing and drawing, and making pretty wax flowers. That is, when they are not busy making pickles and pastry, and laundering muslin caps.'

Elizabeth uttered a dramatic groan.

'Stop it, Robin!' she implored him. 'What a future you make out! Why cannot I forget about pickles and pastry and laundering muslin, and learn Latin and Greek and Mathematics like you?'

Robin put back his fair head and crowed with laughter, swinging his legs in their blue woollen stockings until he nearly fell off the table. Elizabeth watched him with loving exasperation.

'Now what on earth would you want to do that for, you silly little creature?' he demanded, when he had recovered himself. 'What could you want with Latin and Greek? What man do you suppose wants a wife with Classics that cannot sew a shirt or make a posset?'

Elizabeth snorted contemptuously before this display of male arrogance, but she did not bridle. She had heard it all before.

'I don't want to be a wife,' she muttered, jabbing her needle viciously into the letter 'o'.

Robin's demonstrations of affection were always violent and frequently painful. They also had a way of taking one off one's guard. It was so now. Suddenly he jumped down from the table, and picked Elizabeth off her stool in a great, rough bear-hug, so that her nose was squashed against the hard brown broadcloth of his coat, and her feet, nine inches off the floor, paddled about helplessly in the air until her shoes fell off. She could feel every muscle of his strong arms, taut with young power.

'Put me down,' she spluttered through a mouthful of hairy cloth.

Robin deposited her back on her stool, and stood over her, shaking with laughter. Elizabeth looked up into his pale, clear-boned face, with its wine-brown eyes and funny, curly mouth, and she was torn as usual between adoration and fury.

'Don't want to be a wife, eh? And what, pray, do you then intend to do all your life, madam? You cannot stay here with me for ever, you know, for I shall have a wife of my own, and what is she to say when she finds I have an old spinster sister sitting in the ingle, shouting at the servants in Greek? And what will the neighbours say if it gets about that Melville of Robinsheugh cannot get Miss Melville a husband? We shall not be turning dukes and earls away from the door for ever, I promise you.'

'Now you sound like Mamma,' said Elizabeth, 'except that she thinks I shall do well to get a lawyer or a clergyman. But I shall not listen to either of you. I shall ask Papa when he comes home at the year's end, to let Mr Cockburn teach me Latin. He is allowing Lucy to learn drawing, for which she has no talent, so why should he refuse to let me learn Latin, for which I have?' She paused for a moment, then added tentatively, 'You could support my claim, Robin.'

Robin looked down at her, his face suddenly serious.

''Tis a pity you are in earnest, Elizabeth,' he said gently. 'I doubt not Papa might wish to indulge you, for he is a man who loves learning. I am willing to do what I can to press him on your behalf, but if he refuses, as he almost certainly will, remember that he does not do it to grieve you, but because he too is a man with a wife.'

And Elizabeth sighed with understanding, and pricked her finger for the twentieth time that day.

It would have been a strange conversation for Elizabeth Martin to have, but then it was not Elizabeth Martin who was having it. For Elizabeth had been with the Melvilles for several weeks now — she was not herself certain how many — and most of the time she felt that she had been with them for ever. All the pain and horror of those colourless days before her coming had faded from her mind, and although now and then she remembered that she was Elizabeth Martin, who came from London, and was spending a summer of the nineteen seventies with Kate, in a cottage behind Robinsheugh, and that she had come into this world on a visit, through the power of an enchanted looking-glass, far more often as time went by she assumed, like everyone around her, that she was Elizabeth Melville, daughter of the Laird of Robinsheugh in the seventeen seventies, who had been born in this house, and had lived in it all of her twelve years.

After the first few mornings, when she had kept expecting to find herself back in her camp bed in the cottage, she even forgot about the problem of her return, although as if by instinct she still refused to be separated from her looking-glass. For this she received many a teasing, especially from Robin, who had once sent it to her from London, when he was there on a day's outing from his school at Harrow. He was always asking her whether she was admiring her funny face in it, but Elizabeth did not tell him, or anyone else for that matter, that when she looked in the glass she saw nothing but a grey mist swirling and writhing on its face, hiding equally the past, the present and the future. When she was feeling most like Elizabeth Martin — usually in bed in the morning, before anyone else was awake — she used to wonder about this, and try to puzzle out the answer in Elizabeth Martin's fashion. She was not completely successful, but she came to accept it by pointing out to herself that she knew that it was a glass with power to show the past, but not that it had power to show the future. So, she argued, although in the twentieth century it might have power to show what happened in the eighteenth century, that did not mean that in the eighteenth century it must have the power to show events which were to happen in the twentieth. From this, she went on to say that being new in the eighteenth century, the glass probably had no past to show, but why it should veil its face in the present, she could not say. This was where her reasoning broke down again, because, after all, what was the present? What was then and what was now?

She was back to questions again, the old questions of what was real and what was not, of whether what seemed to be the present inside this house was the same as the present outside it. And that she had no way of telling, for in the weeks she had spent here, she had not been out of doors once. Sometimes the other children went out, for walks with Grizel, or occasional rides in the carriage with their Mamma, and people came; Miss Latouche, the French teacher, a ludicrous figure in flamboyant silk dresses and wooden pattens with iron hoops on the soles to keep her dainty feet out of the mud — she screeched in French and English like a distracted parrot, and wore a fantastic bonnet called a calash, which was like the hood of a baby's pram, and could be pulled up and down by means of a string attached to the brim; Mr Galt, the dancing master, who was little and thin, with pointed toes which always looked as if they were about to leap up into a wild pirouette, but seldom did; Mr Boston the music master, who was large and fat, with a pigtail wig and plump white hands which made Lucy and Elizabeth shudder as they watched them wriggling over the keyboard. . . . Certainly many people seemed to come and go, but Elizabeth was not one of them. She had been ill, she was told, and the doctor said she must stay indoors till her cough was gone; at least, that was what Grizel said, and Elizabeth Melville accepted it, although Elizabeth Martin, looking out sometimes from the nursery window into the same pale, smudged, indefinite landscape of her last days in the cottage, was inclined to wonder if there was another, darker reason for her captivity.

But such thoughts troubled her less and less; she turned from the colourless world without with relief to the vivid life within, and as the days went by, if she remembered her life in the twentieth century at all, it was as one might remember a picture once seen clearly, but now so long neglected that all but the memory of its outline had been washed away. For Elizabeth Melville became the other Elizabeth's reality, her life the truth. The process of gaining knowledge of the Melvilles, which had been begun through the power of the glass while she was still shut away from them, continued without her being aware of it. What Elizabeth Melville knew, Elizabeth Martin knew too. She no longer found it surprising that when Grizel drew her down on the rug beside her, and asked, 'What is the chief end of man?' she could at once reply, 'Man's chief end is to glorify God, and to enjoy him for ever.' It was so, and that was a relief, because it meant that the days were gone when every event was a test to be passed, and life a constant struggle to hide the fact that she was not who they thought she was. Now, in her mind at least, she was that person, but still, in her Martin moments, Elizabeth sometimes puzzled over the question of how Grizel and Robin and Lucy and the others in the house could really believe that a stranger was their Elizabeth. And where was Elizabeth Melville? Elizabeth could answer none of these questions, and for the time being, she knew that she must simply accept things as they were.

It was as if, she thought, when Elizabeth Martin's body had come to occupy Elizabeth Melville's place, Elizabeth Melville had left her mind behind to occupy Elizabeth Martin's body. And Elizabeth Martin, while she was still able to make such a comparison, realised that it was a mind as different from hers as it was possible for one mind to be from another. For whereas Elizabeth Martin, although she was clever enough to do reasonably well at school without trying, would never have dreamed of burdening herself with 'Latin and Greek and Mathematics' if she could possibly have avoided it, here was Elizabeth Melville, living among wealth at a time when no one considered it necessary for girls to know more than sewing and music and perhaps a little French, spurning a fine marriage and hungering desperately after subjects for which Elizabeth Martin could easily opt next year at her local Comprehensive School. If she were silly enough. And then Elizabeth Martin was tidy, and loved pretty clothes, while Elizabeth Melville was for ever in a pother because her stockings were falling down and her cap was all awry, and she had a smudge on her nose. She would have spent the whole day reading, had she been allowed to, the huge, leather-bound books which she carried up so carefully and lovingly to the nursery from her father's library on the ground floor, the *Plays* of Shakespeare, the *Pilgrim's Progress*, the *Poems* of Pope and Thomson, and, most wonderful of all, George Chapman's great translations of the *Iliad* and the *Odyssey*, which fed her desire to know Greek until it was like a pain inside her. But she had little enough time for reading, for it was not considered a priority by anyone in her life except herself, and Robin, who had little power to help her. Her days were filled with sewing and dancing and singing, with practising on the spinet and doing arithmetic, and learning passages by heart from the Bible, and the ever-present Catechism.

It was not that Elizabeth found any of these things, apart from the sewing, difficult, but they irked her because they seemed a pointless waste of time, and here she was, all but thirteen, and she had not even begun to learn Latin, or Greek, or any of the things that really mattered. And the future looked bleaker still, for soon now she would have to learn how to make pastries and jellies and jams, to brew beer and make wine, to launder shirts and starch muslin gowns, for in the Scotland of these days it was not considered enough that a lady should be able to supervise her servants while they did these things, she had to be able to to them herself. No lady went to her husband unable to cook, and sew, and do the household accounts, and Elizabeth was a lady, and must learn. If she preferred Latin and Greek and Mathematics, so much the worse for her. So such moments as she could snatch for reading were truly precious, and even then she was constantly interrupted by Lucy, wanting to play hopscotch, or James, wanting her to tell him a story, or Robin, who liked to tease her simply for the amusement of seeing her temper flare.

And then, there was Mamma. Elizabeth could not help wishing that her Mamma would go to Edinburgh, to London, to Paris, go anywhere so that Elizabeth did not have to listen to her constant cry, 'La, la, what in heaven's name did I do to deserve a clever daughter?' She spat the word out, making it sound as if cleverness were a deformity, like a crooked shoulder or a missing leg. 'How shall we ever find her a husband?' As the days went by, her hopes of a clergyman faded, and she was heard to ask plaintively whether anyone thought that a tradesman, or perhaps an apothecary, would be willing to overlook Miss Melville's deficiencies for the sake of an alliance with the house of Robinsheugh?

For Lady Melville was fashionably dressed, and fashionably uneducated, she was perfectly turned out from the summit of her high-piled red hair to the toes of her small silk slippers, she thought of nothing but her own pretty face, and considered that her only duty to her daughters was to get them the richest possible husbands when the time came. And it would come soon. Lady Melville had been herself marrried at sixteen; she was now thirty-two, and the mother of five children living and three dead. She did not love any of her children, although Robin amused her, and she was irritated beyond endurance by Elizabeth. Her occasional visits to the nursery to inspect her family were nightmares to her elder daughter.

'Elizabeth, have you washed your face today?'

'Yes, ma'am.'

'Then why cannot you keep it clean? Straighten your cap this instant.'

'Yes, ma'am.'

'And why cannot you keep your head up? Do you not know that a lady is recognised by her carriage?'

'Yes, ma'am.'

'Then it is time you put your knowledge to use. And cease saying, "Yes, ma'am", like a poll-parrot.'

'Yes, my lady.'

Then Lady Melville would hiss through her teeth with annoyance, and look as if she would like to box Elizabeth's ears, but feared to soil her hands. She would turn to Grizel, and say, 'Mistress Elliot, if you cannot make this wretched girl stand straight, she must be tied to the back of a chair till she learns. If it gets about the country that she is a hunchback, how shall we even get her a fishmonger as a husband?'

And Grizel curtsied, and said, 'As you wish, my lady', but when Lady Melville had swept imperiously out of the nursery, with her feathers nodding and her silken skirts swishing, she would hug Elizabeth, and give her a piece of candied ginger out of a box which she kept in the press. And Elizabeth quickly forgot about her mother, for she knew that we can only be hurt by

96

people we really love.

In fact, James was the only one of the children who really loved his mother. 'Pretty lady!' he shouted, as soon as Lady Melville appeared. 'Pretty lady!' At which Lady Melville preened herself, and simpered, and looked pleased, because flattery was the food she fed on, even the flattery of a child of three. But Elizabeth laughed secretly, and wondered whether her mother would have been quite so pleased if she had realised that James had no idea at all of who she was.

As for herself, in spite of the many annoyances and occasional heartbreaks of her life, Elizabeth was a very contented person, for she was always busy, and she had Lucy to play with, and Grizel to talk to, and the babies to look after, and she had Robin. She would have given up everything in the world for Robin, with his merry eyes and grand air, who sometimes told her stories about the Greeks and the Romans, who had made her a whistle from a rowan twig, and taught her to play 'Robin's Rant' on it, who was like a young lord, and handsomer than Prince Charlie. She was so proud of Robin, who would do all the things that she could never do, because she had been born a girl. But if Robin could do them, that was almost as good, for he would come home and tell her about them, and her admiration and enthusiasm would know no bounds. Already he was making a name for himself as a fine scholar at Harrow, where surely all the boys must admire him too; next he would go to Oxford, to New College, where his father had been before him, and then.... Then, what would he be? A great statesman, perhaps, like Mr Pitt, or a great general, like the Duke of Marlborough, or a great explorer, like Captain Cook. The magnificence of Elizabeth's ambitions for Robin was matched only by the magnificence of Robin's ambitions for himself; the world was before him, waiting for Robin Melville, and meantime, he thought, he could afford to be kind to a little girl who loved him.

One night he sat down in his room above the nursery, where the other children lay fast asleep, and wrote a letter to his father at Versailles.

12

Gold at the Foot of her Rainbow

'Grizel! Grizel!'

Elizabeth came bounding down the twisting stair from Robin's room, in great danger of breaking her neck, flew up the passage to the nursery, and threw herself into the room with such vehemence that Grizel, who was sitting on a stool by the fire, giving Alexander his bath, looked up in alarm, wondering whether the English had unexpectedly invaded.

'Elizabeth,' she said, 'what is the matter with you? You must not run about so — it will make you cough again. Now sit down, and tell me what has happened.'

Elizabeth flopped into the armchair by the fire, throwing out her arms in an ecstasy of triumph. She was far too excited to notice whether she was coughing or not; in fact she was only somewhat out of breath. 'Robin,' she gasped, 'Robin — Papa — Latin.'

Grizel watched her, torn between anxiety and amusement.

'What is it?' she asked, beginning to laugh. Alexander began to laugh too, kicking his curved legs in the bucket which served him for a bath. Elizabeth recovered her breath, and withdrew from the splashes.

'Oh, Grizel,' she sighed. 'The most wonderful thing. Robin has written to Papa, to ask if Mr Cockburn might teach me Latin, and Papa agrees — Robin showed me the letter — only he says that in the holidays Robin is to teach me himself. And Robin says he will. Is not that kind of Robin? Oh, I am so happy.'

Grizel lifted Alexander out of the bath, and wrapped a towel around his dripping little body. She looked at Elizabeth's flaming, eager face, and her lips went on smiling, but the laughter had died out of her eyes.

'And Master Robin says he will, does he?' she asked, but before Elizabeth had time to notice anything odd in her voice, Robin himself replied from the doorway.

'Master Robin,' he said, 'says that he will take his medicine like a man — since he has poured the dose himself.'

He strode purposefully into the room, carrying a pile of books, an ink pot, pens, and a sheaf of paper, which he put down firmly on the table.

'Come then, Mistress Elizabeth,' he commanded, 'to work, if you please,' and while Elizabeth dragged a chair to the table, and eagerly climbed up on it, he grimaced wryly at Grizel over her head.

'In truth, it was not what I had in mind,' he said, laughing at himself and her. 'But have no fear, Mistress Grizel, I will not see the child disappointed.'

Elizabeth was barely three years younger than he was, but she was a child to him, as he was a man to her. He pulled up a chair beside hers, and sat down.

'Now, madam,' he said, 'I hope I shall not have reason to whip you today, since I have not yet had time to provide myself with a stick.'

Elizabeth laughed dutifully, her fingers creeping out towards the books. Robin pulled a battered volume, much stained with ink, towards him from the top of the pile, and continued, 'Here is the book we shall work from first. It is called *Fell's Latin Primer*, and when you have conned everything in it, I shall reward you by allowing you to con all the other books in the pile.'

Elizabeth made a snatch at *Fell's Latin Primer*, and opened it at its first tattered page. 'Oh, stop talking, Robin, please,' she implored, 'and start teaching me.'

For the next half hour there was peace in the nursery. Lucy was down in the kitchen, helping the cook, Jeanie Rigg, to make marmalade, James and Alexander were both asleep, and Grizel was sitting by the fire with her mending, enjoying a respite from the constant bustle of her day. The only sound was the murmuring of Robin's and Elizabeth's voices, Robin's explaining, Elizabeth's questioning, his indulgent, hers bright with pleasure. Never before in her whole life had Elizabeth been so happy, and if she were never so happy again, it hardly mattered, because she had known what many people never know, even if they live to be old, a moment of perfect, unspoiled delight, in which the past and the future equally are of no account. She was sitting at the table with Robin at her side, and Robin was teaching her Latin.

'There, now,' said Robin suddenly, slapping the book shut. 'It is time to see how much you remember. The present tense of the first conjugation, amo, I love. Begin, please.'

Elizabeth shut her eyes, and puckering up her face into such a terrible expression of concentration that Robin almost suffocated with mirth, she began to repeat, slowly and softly, as if it were a spell, 'Amo, amas, amat, amamus, amatis, amant. I love, thou lovest, he or she loveth, we love, ye love, they love.' She opened her eyes, and smiled at Robin, the intimate, private smile of one enthusiast to another. 'Was that right, Robin?'

Robin grinned at her, rocking himself perilously on the back legs of his chair. It was impossible for him to be serious for long. 'Amo, amas,' he sang, 'Amo, amas, I love a lass,

As a cedar tall and slender,
Sweet cowslip's grace
Is her nominative case,
And she's of the feminine − '

'*Robin!*'

'Forgive me, madam, if I am carried away on wings of song. Yes, it was well said. But now we come to the difficult part. I shall say the English, and you are to tell me the Latin. I love.'

'Amo.'

'We love.'

'Amamus.'

'They love.'

'Amant.'

'He loveth.'

'Amas. No, I should say Amat.'

'You should. Have a care, or I shall have to bring that stick tomorrow. Thou lovest.'

'Amas.'

'I love.'

'Amo,' cried Elizabeth, jumping down from her chair and throwing her arms round Robin's neck. 'Amo you, Robin, for being so kind and good as to teach me, and amo Papa, for saying that I might, and − oh, Robin, I am so happy!'

Robin put his head on one side, and gave her an impudent, beady stare, very like the look of the bird he was called after, then he shook his head so that his queue, tied with brown velvet ribbon, danced from side to side.

'Well, 'tis a strange whim,' he said, 'but I wished to indulge you.' He laughed ruefully, and added, 'I do not say I should have been so eager to plead your case if I had guessed I would be bidden to teach you myself.'

'But you will, Robin?'

'Did I not say so, silly one? But now I must be off − I have business of my own to attend to. Do not forget what I have taught you, or I shall be obliged to whip you.'

Elizabeth could see that this was to be a new joke between them.

'When will you teach me more?' she asked hopefully.

'Tomorrow, at the same time. And now, good day to you, Mistress Elizabeth.'

He made her a sweeping bow.

'Good day to you, Master Robin,' laughed Elizabeth, honouring him with a curtsy to match his bow. Elizabeth's curtsys were always magnificent, except when she was curtsying to her Mamma.

With caressing hands, she began to gather up the books, and Robin went, almost colliding with Mr Cockburn, who was coming in at the door as he went out.

The Reverend Adam Cockburn, was the parish minister at Robinsheugh; he was also chaplain to the Melville family, which meant that he baptised the children, tutored the sons, catechised the daughters, reproved the servants, conducted Sunday morning services and gave a great deal of free and very wise advice to everyone in the house, all in return for very little money. In his earlier days, he had been tutor to Sir Giles Melville, looking after him while he was at school, and later when he went to Oxford, and then made a Grand Tour of Europe to finish his education, as was customary among the sons of the nobility in those days. Mr Cockburn had been quick to point out that it was a mistake ever to speak of finishing one's education, because death alone could do that, and he was himself a good example of what he meant, for he was a very distinguished scholar, despite his humble way of life. For twenty years he had lived in the cold, bleak little manse which adjoined the windswept church on the hill above the village, and because he had a roof above his head, and a cabbage patch, and three shelves of books which were his own, he thought himself the most blessed and happy of men.

He looked older than his fifty-three years, with shoulders rounded by much stooping over books, and legs stiffening with rheumatism brought on by the creeping damp which rose through every stone of his sparsely-heated dwelling, but his face, surrounded by streamers of wispy grey hair, was a good face, a face to be trusted. Perhaps there was only one person in the world who really disliked him, and that was Lady Melville. Because he was a clergyman, and the close friend of her husband, she was obliged to be civil when he called, but although she relieved her feelings by sneering privately at his homespun blue coat and heavy, cracked shoes, she found him an uneasy companion, perhaps because the truth of him forced her to see something of the truth of herself. Her children, on the other hand, loved him openly, and his visits to their nursery, although usually made for the purpose of testing Elizabeth and Lucy in their Psalms and Catechism, were never feared, except in the sense that they feared to disappoint him.

So now, after he and Robin had laughed, and passed the time of day, and squeezed past each other in the narrow doorway, Elizabeth ran to him, and took his roughened hand in hers, and drew him kindly to the fire, telling him how pleased she was to see him. Grizel too had got to her feet, smiling with pleasure, and, dropping a curtsy, invited him to sit down and warm himself.

'Will you be staying to dinner, Mr Cockburn?' she asked, and Elizabeth, leaning against the arm of his chair, eagerly joined her voice in the invitation.

'Oh, yes, please do stay, Mr Cockburn.'

But the minister shook his head.

'Nay, I thank you both kindly, but I had just looked in to speak to Her Ladyship on a matter of business, and thought I would look in on you too, before I go. I have to visit an old body up at Bieldhall, that is not long for this world, and I must start soon if I am to get back before nightfall.' Then, seeing Elizabeth's disappointed face, he added. 'But next time I come, I promise to dine with you.'

Elizabeth brightened, and Grizel was pleased too, because she knew from his thinness that the old man — fifty-three was old in these days — often did not have enough to eat, less because he was sunk in poverty than because he thought it was more blessed to give than to receive.

'Try to let us know you are coming,' she said, 'and we will have a clootie dumpling, and collops with our kale.'

'It will be a feast indeed,' said Mr Cockburn, his eyes twinkling as he drew Elizabeth round from the side of the chair, and placed her squarely before him.

'Well, now, Mistress Elizabeth,' he said, 'you are looking very pleased about something this fine morning. Am I allowed to know what it is?'

And Elizabeth, who was longing to tell someone about her good fortune, let it all come tumbling out, the story of Robin's letter to Papa, and Papa's letter to Robin, and how Robin had promised to teach her Latin.

'And I know some already,' she said with pride. 'And tomorrow I shall be learning more. Is it not kind of Robin to teach me?'

And she waited for the praise of her hero which was so sweet to her ears. But to her surprise, Mr Cockburn did not rush into agreement. He looked at her very closely, and said, 'You say your father has asked Robin to teach you, Elizabeth?'

'Yes,' said Elizabeth, a little taken aback by the gravity of his tone. Could it be that Mr Cockburn thought that he — but no, she dismissed that idea at once. Mr Cockburn could never think that he alone should teach. 'There is no reason why I should not learn Latin, is there?' she asked, uncertainly.

'Why, no, no, my child,' said the minister hastily, looking at Grizel over her shoulder. 'I see no harm in it, provided that it does not interfere with your womanly duties. I did not know you were minded to be a scholar, Elizabeth.'

'Oh, I am,' whispered Elizabeth, looking at him with shining eyes. 'I want to read all the books in the world, and know everything there is to know. I want to know the truth about everything.'

He smiled at her then, and nodded his head sympathetically.

'Ay, that ambition I understand,' he said softly. 'All the knowledge and wonder of the world, Elizabeth, and such a little time to know it. It is like the pot of gold at the foot of the rainbow, you spend the whole of your life seeking it, and know you will never find it, but it matters little. It is the seeking that counts, in that we are truly blessed.'

'Gold at the foot of the rainbow,' said Elizabeth, and the phrase was an echo in her mind of something heard long, long ago, so long ago that no sooner had she thought it than it faded away again, and was gone.

'I hope you have other ambitions too, Elizabeth,' said Mr Cockburn, who was a man of his time, after all. 'I hope you are minded to be also a good wife and mother when the time comes, for that is a woman's true vocation.'

And Elizabeth, who knew that a woman's vocation was not necessarily a woman's choice, and knew too the impossibility of making anyone understand that she would prefer to remain a spinster and read books, than to become a wife and mother and make pickles, merely said politely, 'I shall do my best to be what is required of me.' She wondered how many books she could read, how much Latin she could learn, before these requirements were demanded, and her real life came to an end.

'You are a good girl,' said Mr Cockburn, 'and I trust Master Robin will keep his promise. But now, I must away.'

While Grizel went to the door with him to see him out, Elizabeth took her sampler out of the press, and drew her creepie to the window, before she was told to do so. She was always happy to see Mr Cockburn, and he had been kind about her Latin, but somehow the sunshine had gone out of her day. There was something in the air, something she could not understand, something Grizel and Mr Cockburn knew, and were not telling, something which sighed with a grey breath over her happiness.

'Grizel,' she said, as she threaded her needle with brown silk, and began to outline the letter 'w', 'what does he mean, he trusts Robin will keep his promise? Does he think that Robin might not?'

'Oh, 'tis but a way of speaking,' said Grizel soothingly, as she drew a stool close to Elizabeth's. Then, changing the subject firmly, 'Now come, we have much to do. We must see if we can finish today all we had to unpick yesterday.'

13

Hide and Seek

So the days followed each other like stitches in the formal pattern of the children's samplers, each on its own simple and unremarkable, but, woven one into another, making a design of varied colour and rich texture as the small life of the nursery, and the great life of the house, continued in their accustomed rounds. Of course things were not going to go on like this indefinitely, and Elizabeth Martin, at least, had never supposed that they would. Although after the first few mornings she had stopped feeling with her toes for the spars of the camp bed as soon as she awoke, she had continued to suppose, when she did think of it, that that was how she would eventually make the passage back to her former life. But when it happened, it was not like that at all.

It was late in the afternoon, and Elizabeth, snatching a short rest between sewing and Catechism, was sitting on her creepie by the fire, reading *Robinson Crusoe*. Robin had lent it to her the week before, and she thought it was the most marvellous book she had ever read in her life. For once, she was alone, and for Elizabeth Melville, surrounded as she was by other human beings at every minute of the day and night, to be alone was a luxury and a relief. Usually, if such a treat came her way, she spent her time of solitude learning her Latin, but today she had all her preparation for Robin up to date, and felt free to indulge herself in a little reading for fun.

Lady Melville was entertaining friends to tea in the green drawing-room on the ground floor, and Robin, in his best velvet coat and silk stockings, had been summoned to help amuse them. Alexander and James had also been taken down to be admired; Grizel had gone with them, and would wait to bring them back when their Ladyships tired of them. Which might be soon enough, thought Elizabeth, trying to read faster, because Alexander was cutting teeth, and had been red-faced and howling all day, while James, however angelic and adorable he might look in his pink satin frock and green velvet sash, was quite capable of emptying the cream jug over the head of any formidable and feathered old dowager to whom he did not take a fancy. Lucy and Elizabeth, being too old to be admired, and too young to be amusing, were not required in the drawing-room, a state of affairs which pleased them both, since it left them free to pursue other occupations more to their taste. So when their sewing was done, Elizabeth took her book, and Lucy went off to help the maids, Jessie and Alison Hume, who were folding sheets and pillow cases in the linen cupboard at the end of the passage. Lucy liked this kind of work; she was a born housekeeper, and with her pretty face and unadventurous mind was sure to do credit to her mother when the time came for getting a husband. But there must have been few sheets to fold today, because long before Elizabeth expected her, or the downstairs party was even properly underway, she was back, hovering restlessly at her sister's shoulder, with her usual cry, 'I have nothing to do now. Come and play with me.'

Elizabeth sighed, realising that so soon her precious peace was at an end, but she put up a little resistance, just the same.

'Go away, Lucy. I want to read.'

'You're always reading.'

'I wish I were.'

'You never play with me.'

'I do, often.'

'Then come and play with me now.'

So sadly Elizabeth closed her book, and laid it on the stool. She did not have much in common with Lucy, with her airs and graces and her undeniable bad temper, but because Elizabeth was good-natured, they got on fairly well together.

'What do you want to play?' asked Elizabeth patiently, stooping to pull up her stockings.

'Hide and Seek,' said Lucy promptly, with the perversity which will always choose the wrong game for the wrong occasion. Elizabeth looked anxious.

'Oh, Lucy, I do not think we should, not when there is company in the house. It is too dangerous. I do not want a whipping, even if you do.'

'Pooh,' scoffed Lucy, 'there is no danger. They are in the green drawing-room, for mercy's sake. However could they hear us from there?'

'I do not know. But they might.'

Lucy pouted, and raised her foot to stamp it, and poor Elizabeth thought hopelessly that there would be trouble whatever she did. So she said, 'Very well, then. But remember, no lower than the Great Hall.'

It was still called the Great Hall in Elizabeth Melville's day, although the walls had been panelled, and such portraits as then existed hung. It was used as a ballroom, not a dining-room.

And so the game began. At first they hid in easy places, close to the nursery, the linen press, the box bed, the peat closet. But after a while, easy places became difficult to find, and they ventured on to the floor below, Lucy leading, Elizabeth reluctantly following, and began to hide behind curtains and in fireplaces and under beds. As usual, while Lucy continued to look as fresh as a daisy, Elizabeth got dirtier and more dishevelled by the minute, until she was in such a state that she expected trouble even from Grizel. And the sound of Lucy's high, childish screams ringing out piercingly all over the house made her tremble, because she was sure that Lady Melville and her guests must hear, as they sat at their tea and conversation far below. And if they did. . . .

'Lucy,' she said anxiously, 'I think we should stop now. Mamma, you know.'

Lucy looked at her, and burst into a peal of high-pitched laughter.

'La, la, if you could but see yourself,' she said, imitating her mother. 'You have peat-dust on your nose, and feathers in your hair, and your cap is all askew. You do look a fright.'

'Yes, I expect I do. So please, let us stop now.'

But Lucy never knew the right time to stop, either.

'Just one more time,' she insisted. 'You hide, and I shall seek for you.'

She threw her apron over here head, turned to face the wall, and began to count. She was past twenty before Elizabeth had gathered her wits at all, thirty before she realised that they had already exhausted all the hiding places on this landing. Almost without thinking, she snatched up her skirts, and leaping away down the spiral staircase, her stiff leather shoes snapping on the stone steps, gained the lower landing and ran into the Great Hall. She was halfway down the room before she realised that she was running along the side of a table, and glancing down at her feet, saw two brown sandals and a pair of white nylon socks. And as her appearance changed, so in an instant did her mind; like a kernel bursting from its shell, Elizabeth Melville's mind broke free, and Elizabeth Martin knew herself again. But as she skidded to a halt in front of the cold, empty fireplace, she was not prepared for the voice which uttered in sudden fullness close by, was not prepared either for the voice, or for what it had to say.

'Weel, noo, Elizabeth, ye maun fair like that picture. Ye've been staunin' there keekin' up at it thae twenty meenits. I was beginnin' tae think ye maun be awa' wi' the fairies.'

Elizabeth jumped, and swung round on her heel to find herself face to face with Mrs Lindsay, the gamekeeper's wife, a large, comfortable woman, in large, comfortable overalls, who was their neighbour in the yard, and a part-time caretaker in the Great House. She was standing by the table, with a can of spray-polish in one hand, and a large duster in the other, and looking at Elizabeth with a broad smile on her pleasant, reddish face. She was fond of children, and she was always waylaying Kate in the yard to point out to her what a pity it was that Elizabeth had no one of her own age to play with. With this Kate agreed, in her usual vague fashion.

'I dinna work on a Saturday efternoon as a rule,' she went on, unaware of the miracle which had just occurred under her nose. She sprayed some polish on to one end of the table, and laid into it with the strongest arms Elizabeth had ever seen wield a duster, continuing placidly, 'But I didna get this feenished this mornin'. It's braw furniture in this hoose, but it taks an awfu' lot o' polishin' tae keep it shiny.'

'Yes,' said Elizabeth. 'Yes, I'm sure it does.' She glanced down and saw the looking-glass in her hands — it had been in the pocket of the other Elizabeth's dust-gown — and pushed it away into the pocket of her waterproof. 'I didn't hear you come in, Mrs Lindsay,' she added, thinking as she said it that it was a silly thing to say. I didn't hear you come in, three months ago.

'I ken ye didna. I've polished the sideboard, and the wee press, and a' thae chairs doon this side o' the table, and ye've no' moved. I doot ye wis dreamin'.'

'Yes, something like that,' agreed Elizabeth, thinking rather sadly how one could never even begin to tell anyone. And with the weight of a three months' dream, that she knew was not a dream, because it was more like living than anything she had ever experienced, lying across her heart, she said goodbye to Mrs Lindsay, and made her way down the stair, stepping out silently into the lowering, grey-roofed afternoon. Gerry had already lit the lamps, and there were rags of light hanging in the cottage windows among the geranium leaves. The door was open, and as Elizabeth walked across the yard towards it, Gerry's voice floated out to her, singing a pop song, then the rich brown smell of Irish stew.

Elizabeth went up to bed early that night, not because she was tired, not because she wanted to look in her glass again, but because she wanted to be alone, to think things over. It was unlike her actually to seek solitude, but her weeks in the Melville household had taught her to put a new value on peace and quiet, and as for thinking, although she was well aware by now that it was not going to explain anything in a way that she could fully understand, it was a habit she had fallen into. Indeed, without noticing the change, she had in her own right become a much more pensive, contemplative person than she had ever been before, probably because for the first time in her life she was living with people who did not talk all the time. It so happened, however, that they were talking now; at least Kate was. In an unusually conversational mood, she was explaining to Gerry the economic policies of the Whigs under Queen Anne, warming to her subject with an enthusiasm which she freely admitted she never felt for anything dated after 1820. Gerry, who did not altogether approve of lessons at the supper table, after a long day's work, was sitting on the edge of her chair with a look of intelligent politeness on her face, and a glazed look in her eye, which Elizabeth would probably have found funny had she not had other things on her mind. So she got into bed, put her looking-glass under her pillow, and curled up under the blankets to think.

Despite her happiness in the Melville nursery, and the brutal abruptness of her departure, Elizabeth did not at once experience the anguished, unbearable longing to return to it. She knew that that would come; the low murmur of sadness and loss, which even now she heard, would grow even louder and more insistent until it culminated in a final crescendo of yearning desperation. Then she would go, because she had to. But until that happened, she could not; nothing would hasten her going back. It was beyond her power. And meanwhile, it was as if after weeks of early rising, poor feeding, and very hard work, she was glad of a respite, a little while when she could sleep well, eat heartily, and rest from the laborious task of being Elizabeth Melville.

What surprised her most was that from the moment she had run into the Great Hall, believing herself to be Elizabeth Melville, she had known that she was Elizabeth Martin. It was surprising because she had for so long believed herself to be Elizabeth Melville, had thought her thoughts, worn her clothes, learned her lessons, known her joys and sorrows, with only a rare, floating remembrance of Elizabeth Martin to disturb the serenity of her mind. Then in an instant, the being of Elizabeth Melville had fallen from her, like a garment one drops to the floor and steps out of, and she had had her own identity restored to her. Her knowledge of the Melvilles, her closeness to them, seemed as intense as ever, but she did not think she was one of them. Her certainty of her own identity was a relief, but it also gave her a sense of security which events might yet prove to be false.

When she considered it, Elizabeth was not so greatly surprised by the manner of her return, although it was not what she had expected. Obviously the way the charm — she used the word because she could not think of a better one — worked was to bring her back to the spot she had started out from. If she started out by looking in the glass in bed, she was returned to her bed. If she looked in the glass in the Great Hall, she was returned to the Great Hall. That had a tidiness which Elizabeth liked. There was however one point which puzzled her. Mrs Lindsay said that Elizabeth was in the room, looking at the portrait, when she came in. She had polished for twenty minutes, during which time Elizabeth had continued to stare at the portrait, without moving. Mrs Lindsay had made no mention of the looking-glass at all. But during that twenty minutes, Elizabeth knew, she had been playing hide and seek upstairs with Lucy. How was it possible, she wondered, to be in two places at the same time, even in two centuries at the same time? For that, one would need two bodies, one for the eighteenth century and one for the twentieth, and the thought of this was one which Elizabeth simply could not countenance, because although there might be two centuries, there was only one Elizabeth — one bodily Elizabeth, at least. When she went into the glass it was in her own body; she had no feeling of leaving it behind her, like an empty shell waiting for her return. She found this idea so offensive that repeatedly she tried to push it away from her — and yet. . . . She tried to remember how she had found the Melvilles when she had looked in the looking-glass in the Great Hall all these weeks ago — only of course it was this afternoon — and thought she could remember walking through the nursery door, and finding Grizel helping Lucy with her sampler, while James played on his hobby-horse.

. . . Yes, that was it. It had been afternoon. And here was yet another puzzle, in some way tied up with the puzzle she had just been thinking about. On her previous visit, she had gone to bed in the nursery, and had wakened in her cottage bed in the morning. Even supposing it had been the same day, and she was not at all sure that it had been, or what she had been, how was it that Grizel had not noticed her absence between getting up time and afternoon, had not asked where she had been, or what she had been doing? Exhausted by unanswerable questions, Elizabeth put out the light, and fell asleep.

As the days went by, however, she realised that the return to her own identity was not quite as simple and complete as she had at first imagined. For one thing, although she no longer thought she was one of them, the Melvilles still occupied her whole mind, she thought about them constantly, and their vividness continued to make everything else around her unimportant and indistinct. At first, she spent hours wandering about in the house of Robinsheugh, trying to find her way into the nursery, but the room and the way into it seemed to have vanished completely, and none of the Melvilles' furniture and belongings, standing spick and span under Mrs Lindsay's polish, had the power to whisper in her ear what she wanted to know. Finally, she gave up the search; the empty house still oppressed her, perhaps because in the silence she was always listening for Robin's laughter, the silken swish of Lady Melville's skirts, the sharp patter of Grizel's shoes over the stone floor. So instead she wandered the fields, never noticing the lark rising sweetly from the yellow corn, or the redness of heather beginning to flush the hillside, because her eyes were always on the Robin of her imagination, Robin who seemed to be everywhere, running ahead of her in his brown coat and old breeches, jumping streams and leaping through the bracken, turning to wave to her, beckoning her on.

And even while she was quite sure that she was Elizabeth Martin, somehow shreds of Elizabeth Melville's personality clung to hers, so that sometimes Elizabeth thought a thought with Elizabeth Melville's mind, or did something which Elizabeth Melville would have done, and only afterwards realised that she had acted out of character. She supposed that in a way this was to be expected; you could not be someone else for three months and more, think her thoughts, dream her dreams, desire her desires, and not be left with something of her rubbed off inside you, influencing you to think thoughts which, if you were not careful, had a habit of turning themselves into words before you had remembered to clap your teeth over them. This happened most embarrassingly one evening, when Elizabeth was drying the dishes for Gerry, and Kate was sitting at the Study End of the table, copying something in her spiky, crabbed handwriting from a reference book into a large notebook. Suddenly into the silence, Elizabeth heard herself say, 'Kate, do you suppose I could go to Oxford?'

Unfortunately it was not one of those occasions when Kate was so deeply absorbed that a thousand silly questions would not have roused her. She lifted her head slowly, and looked at Elizabeth over her spectacles with a most insulting expression on her face, one of complete astonishment. Elizabeth felt herself shrivelling.

'You?' said Kate, an octave above her usual low-pitched note.

'I only wondered,' muttered Elizabeth, slinking away and getting very busy at the cutlery drawer.

Kate laid down her pen.

'Well, really,' she said, in a voice which startled Gerry by its unaccustomed bitterness, 'you do surprise me. Why, only at Christmas you were telling me — very loudly — what a waste of time and money higher education is for a woman, and pointing out how mine had been a distinct disadvantage, since because of it I had failed completely to get myself a husband. You gave me other reasons for my failure, I remember, but that was the main one. Perhaps you have forgotten, although that I can't believe. You were positively offensive about it.'

So it had hurt, thought Elizabeth, caught between a stab of guilt and a little thrill of triumph. Behind the cold, impassive eyes that had studied her across the dining-room table on Christmas Day, the arrow had gone home, and the wound still stung. And she felt pleased that for once she had goaded Kate into making a sharp retort, had forced a crack in that terrible patience. The strange thing was that it had happened when she was not even trying to be provoking. But afterwards, when Kate, looking miserable, had returned to her writing, and she was forced to leave the kitchen to escape the reproach in Gerry's fieldmouse eyes, a most unaccustomed remorse swept over Elizabeth, and she wished she had not been so unkind to Kate. Normally, if this had happened, she would at once have called up a whole string of grievances to prove that she was not to blame, and make herself feel better, but this time she did not think of one. Of course it was Elizabeth Melville's sorrow she felt, and in a way she was aware

112

of this, but it did not prevent her opening her door when she heard Kate coming upstairs, and going out to meet her in the passage.

'Kate.'

'Yes.'

'I'm very sorry I was rude to you at Christmas.'

For a moment Kate looked slightly confused, as if an apology from Elizabeth was something of a shock, but then she smiled at her, and said, 'It doesn't matter, Elizabeth. It was a long time ago, and it was wrong of me to bring it up again. I'm sorry too.'

She hesitated, but there seemed nothing more to say, and touching Elizabeth's cheek rather uncertainly with the back of her hand, she turned to go into her room. Then she stopped in the doorway, and turned back, adding, 'I didn't answer your question downstairs, did I? Of course I have no idea whether you could go up to Oxford or not. I've never seen any of your work, and in any case it's probably a bit early to say. But if you are really serious, we must discuss the matter properly at a later date. Good night, Elizabeth.'

Elizabeth went back into her room again, and shut the door with a sigh. Of course it was all Elizabeth Melville's fault, with her Latin and Greek and Mathematics. Now, when the matter was raised again, as it surely would be, she would have to tell Kate that it was all a mistake, she didn't want to go to Oxford, she wanted to be hairdresser when she left school. Then Kate would be offended, and things would be worse than ever, if that were possible. Which was just too bad, she added firmly. Yet as she took the looking-glass out of her pocket, and put it away under her pillow, she could not help having a sad and guilty feeling that she was breaking faith not only with Elizabeth Melville, for whom the University would have been a dream so golden and wonderful that she never even thought to dream it, but with Kate, whose hand she still seemed to feel against her face in the first fondling of three long years. It was such a painful, difficult thing to share your mind with someone else. That it was also a very dangerous thing was something she had previously known, but had forgotten.

However, as Elizabeth Melville had learned from her Bible, a soft answer turneth away wrath, and it appeared throughout the next couple of days that Kate, having accepted Elizabeth's apology, was now making an effort to let her see that no hard feelings remained. She lent Elizabeth a guide-book to the

Scottish Borders, with a section in it about Robinsheugh, and gave her a letter from Uncle Kenneth to read. (It began, 'Dear Mrs Skinny,' and was so full of brotherly teasing and affectionate rudeness that Elizabeth felt thankful she had not made a fool of herself by writing to him, as she had intended earlier.) Then on the second day, when she came over to supper in the evening, Kate brought with her a minute cotton and lace mitten, smaller than an egg cosy, which she had found pressed among some papers in the trunk, and called Elizabeth down to look at it. Elizabeth took the frail scrap of glove on the palm of her hand, and examined its yellowed stitchery with delight.

'Isn't it tiny?' she said. 'It must have been Alexander's.'

Kate seemed surprised by this.

'Why Alexander's?' she asked with interest.

'Well, he was the baby, wasn't he?'

'Oh, yes, I see — you're thinking about the portrait. Yes, I suppose it would be his, but don't you think it might have belonged to all the children in turn? I expect they passed things down in their family, just as we used to do in ours. I'm sure I never had a new stitch to my back — it's why I make such a point of dressing beautifully nowadays. Elizabeth, did I tell you what the Melville children were called?'

Coming right on top of the straight-faced joke, this question sounded casual enough, but when she said, 'No, Gerry did,' Elizabeth was sure she did not imagine the flash of relief in her aunt's grey eyes.

'Well, put it in a envelope, Elizabeth,' said Kate. 'There are sure to be some deep down in the Study End, if you delve. I don't want to put it back in the chest, so if you write 'mitten' on the envelope, and put it in the dresser drawer, I can give it to Sir Gilbert when I see him. Don't let me forget where it is.'

With which she went off upstairs to wash, leaving Elizabeth feeling quite light-hearted as she began to search for an envelope and a biro among the litter of Kate's belongings.

But of course it was too good to last. It was only a truce, brought about by Elizabeth Melville's intervention, and sooner or later Elizabeth Martin was bound to break it. What was really sad was that things were spoiled again by a misunderstanding, not because Elizabeth was angry, but because she was frightened. She could never understand why it was that being frightened made you sound angry, but it did. She had noticed it before, and that was how it happened now, later that same evening, when she was coming out of the bathroom after her bath, and met Kate coming along the passage with her arms full of papers and books. For Kate had a far-away look in her eyes, and she was singing to herself in a low, murmuring voice, a song which made Elizabeth's ears sting with alarmed recognition.

O can ye sew cushions, and can ye sew sheets?
And can ye sing balaloo when the bairn greets?

For a second, she could not believe it, and then she panicked. It was panic that made her strident, that made her shout as if she was furious, 'Why are you singing that song? Where did you hear it? Tell me where you heard it!'

She saw Kate wince as the harsh words seared her head. She seemed completely bewildered, then, very mildly, 'Oh, dear,' she said, 'I don't know. I really don't know. It's quite a well-known song, isn't it? I'm sorry if you don't like it, Elizabeth.'

Then she went into her room, and shut the door. And Elizabeth wished she had slapped her, shouted at her, shaken her, done anything except answer her with that horrible, deadly politeness. For it also said in Elizabeth Melville's Bible that grievous words stir up anger, and that was something Elizabeth would have understood. Grievous words should stir up anger, so that people could quarrel, and get things off their chests, and make up. But how could she ever understand anyone who met grievous words with a composure so unnatural that she wanted all the more to smash it, just for the normality of seeing her roused? And as always happened, when sorrow and mis-understanding widened the terrible gulf that now stretched between her and Kate, Elizabeth began to feel first the lonely fear of a situation which she could not handle, then the familiar ache of longing for the warm bundle of Alexander in her arms, for Robin's teasing laughter, for Grizel's comforting knee. . . .

14

The Birthday

When Elizabeth walked into the nursery it was morning, and she was wearing her best green silk dress, which meant that it was Sunday morning. If she had needed more proof, this was provided by Alison Hume, who was standing by the table, her dirty weekday apron tied over her brown Sunday dress, her large red hands busy dropping generous spoonfuls of treacle over the stiff porridge which she had already ladled into the children's little wooden porringers.

'Fine porridge for ye the day, Miss Elizabeth,' she said, giving Elizabeth a frightful smile which laid bare her irregular, blackened teeth.

'Yes,' said Elizabeth, trying not to shudder, either at Alison's teeth or at the treacly porridge, which she loathed, and only ate so as not to hurt Grizel's feelings. For the treacle was supposed to be a treat, kindly supplied by Grizel because she knew that for the little Melvilles Sunday was the most terrible day of the week, just as Monday was the happiest, because it was farthest away from the next Sunday. Elizabeth had time to notice that Lucy, also dressed in green silk (both dresses had been made out of an old one belonging to their Mamma, who did not believe in wasting money on finery for daughters still in the nursery) was already seated on her creepie, learning her Catechism and looking as sullen as she could without spoiling her complexion with a frown; James, who had already learned that he was not allowed to raise his voice or play rowdy games on the Sabbath, was sitting disconsolately on the hearthrug in his silk gown, chewing the end of his green velvet sash until it resembled a strand of very slimy and disgusting seaweed. Grizel was washing a howling Alexander — Alexander always behaved badly on Sunday, which Lucy said was a sign that he was very clever. She said he knew what it was going to be like later, and was taking the opportunity to be bad while there was no danger of a whipping for it. Lucy always spoke as if whippings were daily events at Robinsheugh; in fact there were far more threats of whippings than were ever actually carried out. Grizel was wearing a large apron over her Sunday finery of blue wool, and she was looking rather harassed, as she often did on Sunday mornings, when there seemed twice as much to be done as on any other morning, and she could not count on co-operation from anyone.

All this Elizabeth Martin saw, and Elizabeth Melville understood it, because she had seen it every Sunday morning of her life. And Elizabeth Martin realised that although she had been out of this room for fifteen days, no one had missed her, even although — and this was the really odd thing — however different their time was from hers, a gap must still exist between her going and her coming, because she had played hide and seek with Lucy on a Saturday afternoon, and now it was Sunday morning. One night at least, fifteen at most, and no one had noticed she was gone. Then another peculiar thing happened.

'Did you find it, dearie?' Grizel asked, and she heard herself saying, 'Yes. I must have left it on the japan table when I went down to say my Psalms to Mr Cockburn yesterday. Here it is, Grizel.' And glancing down she saw that she was carrying, as well as her looking-glass, her Bible, which apparently she had just been down to the drawing-room to fetch. She took out her Catechism from the back of the Bible, and went to sit down by Lucy, and she knew that they were to learn the answer to Question forty-one, 'Where is the moral law summarily comprehended?' She also found that she already knew the answer, because she had learned it yesterday to save time.

It was all very puzzling to Elizabeth Martin, but before she had time even to begin to think about it, she slipped back, gently and easily into the being of Elizabeth Melville, and was troubled no more.

Robin did not eat breakfast in the nursery, because that would have been beneath his dignity. Instead, he took coffee in his own rooms on the floor above. Shortly after they had finished, however, he strolled in, looking very fine in a blue silk coat and breeches, with buckles on his shoes, and offered to escort the ladies down to the Great Hall for morning service.

'That would be very kind of you, Master Robin, if the ladies were ready,' said Grizel, with the closest approach to tartness which her gentle nature allowed, 'but Mistress Lucy is missing a shoe, I see, and if Mistress Elizabeth does not pull up her stockings and rub that black spot off her nose, I fear Her Ladyship will be fretting about husbands again.' Grizel only ever called Elizabeth and Lucy 'Miss', or 'Mistress', in the presence of their parents, or when she was feeling cross; it was a warning sign, and they scuttled to put the finishing touches to their toilettes.

Robin grinned at Elizabeth, who was trying to pull up her stockings and adjust the ridiculous train which trailed out behind her gown, while holding her Bible under her chin, and her Psalter between her teeth. She grinned back, and the Bible fell, then the Psalter. Robin came striding over to her, taking a large handkerchief, bordered with lace, from the pocket of his breeches.

'Spit,' he ordered, and Elizabeth spat, whereupon he rubbed away at her nose with the damp spot until she was sure she had no nose left. Then he stood back, surveyed her critically, with his lower lip pushed out, and said, 'Have no fear. Already the Dukes are at the door.'

But Elizabeth was not listening. She had bent down to pick up her Bible and Psalter, and was now straightening up with an expression of comical dismay on her face.

'Oh, dear,' she said. 'Grizel, I am very sorry, but my garter seems to have broken.'

Eventually another garter was found, and substituted for the broken one, eventually everyone was brushed, combed and ready, and they all descended to the Great Hall with the kind of expression on their faces which people wear when they are going to a funeral. Hating Sunday was a tradition among the Melville children, and certainly it was not a cheerful day, being given over entirely to Divine Service, Sermon Reading and learning passages from the Bible, with some extra Catechising thrown in for good measure. 'Six days shalt thou labour and do all thy work, but the seventh day is the Sabbath of the Lord thy God; in it thou shalt not do any work. . . .' However rebellious, a Melville would as soon have jumped out of the nursery window as have learned a Latin declension or sewn a sampler on the Sabbath Day. It was not, as Lucy said, that one particularly wanted to sew one's sampler on any day, but if it were a choice between that and learning the Catechism, Lucy knew which she preferred. As for Elizabeth, she had always hated the gloom of Sunday, but now it seemed a thousand times worse, because to know that *Caesar's Gallic Wars* was in the press, along with *Robinson Crusoe* and *Gulliver's Travels*, and to be forbidden to touch them, was a kind of torture she sometimes felt she could not bear.

The family never went to the little Parish Kirk on the hill above the village; instead, Mr Cockburn came at half past nine to conduct a long service in the Great Hall, which everyone in the house, from Lady Melville down to Effie Gray the scullery maid, was obliged to attend unless actually at Death's Door. They were a considerable company, family in silk and lace on one side of the hearth, servants on the other in their Sunday clothes of hodden grey and striped wool; Tam Rigg the steward, Jeanie Rigg the cook, the Hume sisters, Alison and Jessie, their brother Jack, who was Robin's manservant, and a throng of under-servants, footmen, scullery maids, waiting boys, chambermaids, all as familiar to Elizabeth Melville as her own brothers and sister. Many a boring Sunday morning she had whiled away studying their faces, amusing herself by making up stories about their lives and loves, inventing for them escapades which would have shocked and outraged their douce minds, had they had but an inkling of them; for Elizabeth had long ago learned that though her body might be disciplined and imprisoned, her spirit and her imagination were free. . . . Under Grizel's watchful eye, she filed into the row of chairs set out for the family, and settled herself between Robin and Lucy to await the arrival of the minister. As always, her nearness to Robin made her happy. She put out a furtive finger and touched the embroidered silk of his sleeve. He grinned, and flicked her finger off the cloth, as if it had been a fly. 'Forbidden on the Sabbath,' he muttered out of the side of his mouth, and Elizabeth, who was much too well brought up to laugh out loud on Sunday, laughed silently inside. Lady Melville arrived last, whisking into the room in a flurry of mute indignation, subsiding on to her tapestry cushion with a sigh and a rustle which reminded Elizabeth of the wind breathing through the sedges by the Wishwater — although even as she thought it, it seemed to her like a sound she had once heard in a dream, so long it was since she had been out of the house to hear it.

Then Mr Cockburn came in, a bent, shrunken figure in his black Geneva gown and white bands, and the service began.

'Let us worship God. Let us sing to His praise and glory in Psalm one hundred. . . .'

There was no organ, no spinet, because these were frivolous instruments which the Church did not permit to be associated with sacred music. Mr Cockburn had a tuning fork in the pocket of his gown, and when he had given them the note, they all stood, and dolefully raised their voices.

> All people that on earth do dwell,
> Sing to the Lord with cheerful voice,
> Him serve with mirth, his praise forth tell,
> Come ye before him and rejoice.

Anything less like rejoicing would have been difficult to imagine. Only Robin, Lady Melville and Grizel could even keep the tune, and as for the rest — Elizabeth was afraid to look at her mother, whose expression of pained, protesting distaste on these occasions always made her want to smile — and smiling was yet another of the things one did not do on the Sabbath.

She did not look at Robin either, although she was aware of him as she was of nobody else; it was always like this now, as if there were only two people in the world, Elizabeth and Robin. And what she would do, she thought, as she bowed her head for the prayer, when he left her to go back to school, she did not know. But then, as the rolling voice of the minister prayed above her bent head, she remembered something that she ought not to have forgotten; the strangeness of her having forgotten made her anxious for a moment, before that little anxiety was swallowed up in a far greater one. For the whole house was astir with the news. Master Robin was not going back to school. It had gone round the house in a long whisper, passing from mouth to mouth, accompanied by nods of the head and pursing of the lips and muttered remarks which cut themselves off abruptly if one of the children should happen to appear. Elizabeth had heard from Robin himself. He had told her last week, when he came to give her her Latin lesson, and she had asked him what would happen about her lessons when he went back to Harrow. The recollection swept over her as she sat there, bringing mixed feelings of relief and anxiety, pleasure and pain.

'Oh, did I not tell you? I am not going back there, ever.'

'Not going back? Robin, why not?'

'Because I hate it, Elly. The boys are so unkind to me. They are so rough, and they hate anyone who loves learning as I do. So I wrote to Papa, and asked him to take me away, and let me come home, and study here at Robinsheugh, with Mr Cockburn.'

'And Papa agreed — to that?'

'Yes. Oh, I had hard work to persuade him, but he did agree in the end. I am to stay here for the next two years and study with Mr Cockburn, and learn the management of the estate, until it is time for me to go to Oxford — '

He said the word 'Oxford' the way Kate Jenkins said it, with a kind of chime in the voice, as if it were Eldorado or the Rainbow's End. A thin memory of Kate Jenkins slipped fleetingly through Elizabeth's mind, and was gone.

She should, she thought, have been delighted that Robin was going to be at home with her for two whole years, which seemed a time so long that she could scarcely imagine its ever coming to an end. And she was, of course, she reminded herself quickly, delighted. Yet there was something clouding her happiness, some restless worm of anxiety wriggling in her mind, and not only because when he was telling his story, Robin had not once looked her in the eyes. It was the story itself; something in the story did not ring true, and that frightened Elizabeth, who expected truth from Robin as she expected warmth from the sun. Elizabeth knew how great a store her Papa set by a good education for his sons, she knew that Harrow was an excellent school, better even than the High School in Edinburgh, which Papa had himself attended, and surely he would not have allowed Robin to leave, simply on the strength of a letter, without going to Harrow himself, to find out what was happening, and to ask the masters to see to it that Robin was not ill-treated. She glanced sidelong at Robin's handsome profile, at the silky fall of his fair hair, and to be on the safe side, she began to pray for him. Her education, if it had not taught her much else, had taught her how to talk to God, and she began now silently, using a grand style of language with all the ease of one talking confidentially to an old friend. 'Almighty and eternal God, look down in mercy upon Thy servant, Robin Melville, and grant him Thy grace, that he may walk before Thee in the paths of righteousness, forsaking evil, all the days of his life. . . .' What the evil was that Robin should be forsaking, she had no idea, but however much she tried to push the idea away from her, back it came. Somewhere, there was something not right.

So Mr Cockburn preached, and Elizabeth prayed, and Lady Melville yawned behind her fan, but what Robin was thinking, as he contemplated the silver buckles on his satin shoes, only Robin knew.

On the sixteenth of November, 1779, Elizabeth Melville was thirteen years old, and when she awoke that morning, a floating wisp of Elizabeth Martin's mind registered the thought that time must indeed be topsy-turvy, since in her other world, it was still only the middle of August. Also, she had reached the age of thirteen ahead of time, since her own birthday was not till December. But then she forgot again, as the clock chimed seven, and she had to get up in the shivery darkness, by the glimmering light of the cruisie-lamp, to begin another day of much work and little play. Birthdays were not celebrated in the eighteenth century as they are now, and Elizabeth had no birthday cake with candles, and no birthday cards, but she did receive two presents, one of which she would have got anyway, but which just happened to be ready on that day. It was a new frock, made from a length of material which Sir Giles, perhaps pitying their second-hand finery, had sent from Paris to be made into dresses for his daughters. Lucy had hers already, laid away carefully in an oak chest, to be kept good for high days and holidays, but Elizabeth's had only that morning arrived from the dressmaker. Lady Melville sent it up to the nursery after breakfast, with instructions that Elizabeth was to put it on, and come down to the blue room, so that she could see if it needed alteration before the dressmaker was paid. Elizabeth's heart sank.

'Grizel, I do not want to go,' she whispered.

'Tush, now,' said Grizel, shaking out the folds of the dress, and holding it up to the light, 'we'll not be having any of that nonsense, please. If Mamma sends for you, she must be obeyed, and if you remember to keep your head up, and speak out when you are spoken to, what have you to fear! Just you wait till she sees you in this bonnie frock!'

So Elizabeth sighed, and said no more, but stood before the fire, and took off the striped woollen gown she was wearing. Woodenly she held up her thin arms, and Grizel slipped the new dress over them, and began to fasten it down the back. It was a pretty thing, intended for the celebration of the New Year, which the Scots kept as a holiday instead of Christmas, and although she was not as interested in clothes as Lucy was, Elizabeth looked down at it rather admiringly, smoothing it down over her hips, and enjoying the whispering ripple of the silk under her fingers. The material was in small, uneven checks of green and blue, like a plaid, with fashionable tight sleeves to the elbow, below which deep flounces of white lace fell almost to the wrists.

'Do you think my Papa will like it?' asked Elizabeth hopefully.

'Like it? He'll think you're the bonniest wee girl in Scotland, or in France either,' said Grizel delightedly, as she stood back to view the effect. She was safe to say so, since Lucy was downstairs practising at the spinet. 'Now just you wait till I get a blue ribbon to tie up your hair, then off you go to your Mamma. I'll swear she can find nothing wrong with you today.'

But Elizabeth knew better than that, and it was with her usual feeling of sick terror that she descended the chilly stair to the blue room, a small, stuffy apartment on the floor below, where Lady Melville took her breakfast, and dallied half the morning in her pink damask gown and huge lawn cap, sighing for France and making her maid's life a misery with her demands and complaints, shrieking in her affected, Frenchified voice that the poor girl was an idiot who could do nothing right in the world. Elizabeth often thought she would rather be a tinker than her mother's maid. Still, she rather hoped that Betty would be there now, arranging her mother's hair, and being abused because she could not do it properly, for abuse shared is abuse halved, and at least Lady Melville could not be shouting at both of them at the same time. But when she knocked at the door, and the shrill little voice ordered her to enter, she found to her surprise and confusion that the only other occupant of the room, besides her mother, was Robin. Resplendent in a yellow silk nightgown — what Elizabeth Martin would have called a dressing-gown — he was lolling in a chair by the fire, with his slippered feet on a stool, and there was something so relaxed and confident in his manner that Elizabeth knew at once that this was not the first morning he had spent idling in this room. And a finger of anxiety poked her, for she knew too that at this hour he should be dressed, and at his books. He screwed up his nose and winked at her, as she was rising from her curtsy to her mother, but before she had time to respond, a trill of derisive laughter rang out from the other side of the hearthrug.

'La, la, 'tis a mercy *you* are not required to curtsy before the Queen of France. The whole Court would die of the shock. Have you the rheumatics in your knees, that you bend like a wooden doll? And why cannot you keep your head up, and your poky chin in? And why are you here?'

Tears sprang to Elizabeth's eyes, but she would not let them fall. It was bad enough to be humiliated, to be humiliated in front of Robin was intolerable. She could not bear to look at him, because she knew that if she saw sympathy she would weep, in spite of herself, if she saw amusement she would die. So she kept her eyes fixed on her mother, and replied tightly, 'You sent word I was to come, my lady, so that you could see if the gown was to your liking.'

'Did I so?' enquired Lady Melville provokingly. She passed a languid, indifferent eye over her daughter, and added, 'It will pass, I dare say. See you keep it clean, and try not to look more like something out of a tinker's pack than you can avoid. What do you say, Robin? Are you proud of your sister?'

Her tone prompted the kind of answer she required; Robin was to laugh, and shrug his shoulders, and make some disparaging remark to add to Elizabeth's misery. But however much Elizabeth might squirm to order under her mother's tongue, Lady Melville had never succeeded in subduing her eldest son.

'I am proud of her,' he replied firmly. 'I say she looks very beautiful, and I doubt not the King of France would agree with me, and any other king with two eyes in his head.'

Then Elizabeth knew she was really going to cry.

'Psht!' hissed Lady Melville, in a pique. 'And a pretty couple you make! Well, get out of here, girl. You have your brother's opinion, and you are well acquainted with mine. Get out of my sight.'

Elizabeth fled, tumbling upstairs with tears running down her cheeks. Robin caught up with her half-way up, where she had stopped to dry her eyes on the fine lace of her sleeve. He threw his arm round her, and gave her one of his rough embraces. Elizabeth sniffed, and leaned against his arm.

'Oh, Robin,' she whispered, 'why is Mamma so cruel?'

Robin sat down on the step, and drew her down beside him.

'She is bored,' he said, 'she is stupid, she is disappointed. She is married to a man who cares a thousand times more for his work than he does for her, and she has not the brains to find out interests for herself. And of course she is jealous, because you are young and pretty, and have all your life ahead of you. But fear not — she returns to France after the New Year, and so she will not plague us much longer. Then la, la,' he mimicked, 'we shall all be very jolly with Master Robin to find you husbands. Do you care for my nightgown?'

Elizabeth laughed shakily.

''Tis very fine,' she said, 'but you should not be wearing it in the middle of the day, Master Robin. You should be at your books.'

Robin gave her hair a friendly tweak, and they climbed to the landing.

'Yes, madam, I should be at my books. But you will mind your business. You are not mistress of the house yet.'

'Shall I be, when Mamma is gone?'

'Most certainly. I shall be master, and you will be mistress. But now — wait. I have something for you.'

'For me? What is it?'

'A gift,' said Robin, 'for your thirteenth birthday. I wonder where I can have put it?'

He searched the pockets of his nightgown slowly, laughing at her wide-eyed impatience, and just when she thought she was going to burst with suspense, brought out a small gold ring, which he dropped lightly into the palm of her outstretched hand.

'I bought it for you the last time I was in Edinburgh, in a little old jeweller's shop in the Canongate, but I kept it so that you might have it today. I thought it might please you.'

'Oh, it does, Robin. You are so good to me.'

Elizabeth took the ring between her finger and thumb, and held it up to the light to examine the engraving.

'Why, look,' she exclaimed. 'There's writing on it. Did you notice that, Robin?'

'No, as I say, it was a little shop, and dark. What does it say?'

' "QUHAIR THIS I GIVE, I WISS TO LIVE",' read Elizabeth slowly.

'A friendly ring, I see,' said Robin lightly. 'Shall I put it on for you?'

'Yes.'

Elizabeth handed the ring back to him, and stretched out her hand. He took the little gold band and held it up, spinning it cleverly in the air. Then with a flourishing bow, he put it on her finger. It fitted perfectly.

It seemed to Elizabeth that she could not be happier, but then, 'Since it is a special day,' Robin said, 'I shall grant you one wish. You may ask anything it is in my power to give. What will it be?'

Elizabeth shivered with delight.

'Anything?'

'Anything.'

She did not even have to think.

'Robin, when Mr Galt comes this afternoon to teach us dancing, will you come too, and dance with me? Not with Lucy, just with me?'

His merry eyes laughed down into hers.

''Tis a little wish, but granted,' he said. 'And for you, I shall

125

even wear my best velvet coat.'

'And your white silk stockings,' pleaded Elizabeth, 'and your shoes with the diamond buckles.'

Robin said that that too would be arranged.

Late in the afternoon, when the sun's rays were slanting in through the south-facing windows of the house, Kate Jenkins left her work room and walked down the stair, preoccupied with her own thoughts as usual. It was as she passed the open door of the drawing-room that her attention was drawn by a moving flash of colour, and for a minute she paused, her austere face touched by a rare tenderness of delight at the sight of a little girl dancing alone in the middle of the floor, giving her hand to an unseen partner, smiling and nodding with all the intensity and seriousness of a child playing grown up. A moment passed before the strangeness of the sight obtruded on her enjoyment, another before she grasped in what that strangeness consisted. For Elizabeth, in what appeared to Kate's short-sighted eyes to be a long tartan nightdress, was dancing a stately measure, in perfect time to silent music which suddenly began to throb inside Kate's head, and she was familiar with every step and turn of a dance which Kate was sure she could never have seen before in her life. Her pleasure faded, and with a dark puzzlement she watched the dance end, saw Elizabeth's sweeping curtsy to her imaginary partner, saw her walk away with him hand in hand down the room.

And Kate was going to go after her, to ask her where she had learned the dance, and who it was she thought she was dancing with, when Reason stopped her, and because all her life she had listened to Reason, she did so now. And Reason told her severely that of course lonely children played such games, and of course Elizabeth must have learned the dance at school, and of course she was letting this house and its past get on top of her in a way that was neither wholesome nor rational. And that as a scholar she should be ashamed of herself. But there were tears in her eyes as she laid her forehead against the cool wood of the doorpost, and tried to remember where she was going, and what she was going to do, when she was diverted by the sight of a tartan frock dancing in the sun.

15

All in French Garlands

'I should be starting school today,' said Elizabeth one morning in late August, and as she said it, she had a sudden homesickness for green blazers against black asphalt, bare legs running to and fro, and excited voices shouting greetings in the cloakroom, as everyone joined in the good-natured pandemonium of the first morning of a new school year.

Kate looked up from a letter she was reading. 'Oh, dear,' she said, with her unfailing instinct for saying the wrong thing to Elizabeth, 'should you really? I think Margaret mentioned in one of her letters to me that I might help you with some lessons when term time began, but quite honestly I can't afford the time. I suppose you had better try to work a bit on your own, and if you get really stuck, tell me, and I'll try to find ten minutes.'

She got up abruptly, and began to gather her belongings together, while Elizabeth stared at her dumbly, trying to tell herself she didn't care. But if she didn't care, why was it that when the last thing she wanted was to sit at the kitchen table, writhing and stuttering over French verbs and the dates of the Wars of the Roses, while Kate sat seething with ill-concealed exasperation at her side, it should hurt so much to know that it was the last thing Kate wanted either? And what did it matter, when there were so many other, important things to think about? But it did matter, and Gerry at least noticed that it did, because after Kate had disappeared across the yard, and they were left together in the kitchen, she patted Elizabeth sympathetically on the shoulder and said kindly, 'I wouldn't take it to heart if I were you. She doesn't mean it, you know. It's just that she has a lot on her mind, and she really isn't very well.'

'Yes, I expect that's it,' said Elizabeth. She was grateful to Gerry, but she could not help noticing that her way of comforting her was to make excuses for Kate. Miserably she trailed upstairs, and shut herself in her room. There was no escape from unhappiness now, it seemed, either here or in her other world. Everywhere trouble was closing in upon her.

Looking back, Elizabeth remembered that day when she had danced with Robin in the drawing-room, while Miss Latouche played the spinet, and Lucy sulkily partnered the dancing master, as the last occasion in either of her existences when she had been really happy. It was like the last day of summer, before the clouds begin to gather, and the sharp wind to blow, a day remembered because then for the last time one felt the warmth of the sun. After that, while life in Kate's cottage continued in its customary, boring routine of silence and neglect, broken only by the occasional unpleasant incident like this morning's, life at Robinsheugh, which used to provide her with an escape into happiness, also began to spoil.

Shortly after Elizabeth's birthday, Lady Melville had left Robinsheugh to stay with friends in Edinburgh, saying that she could not bear the boredom of country life for another hour, and would not return till her husband came home. No one was sorry to see her go; they were sorry for Betty, who had to go with her. Elizabeth was perhaps even more relieved than anyone else. An end to complaints and criticism and peevishness and everlasting talk about husbands — it seemed too good to be true. But all her pleasure in her mother's departure had been wiped out by her anxiety over Robin, anxiety which had begun during a Sunday morning service as no more than a vague shadow in the corner of her mind, but which had since then grown and blackened till she could think of nothing else. For although he was as jolly and joky and kind to her as ever, and had never once neglected to come for her Latin lesson, Elizabeth knew that all was not well with Robin.

It was not just that his outward appearance had changed, although perhaps that was the beginning of it. She never saw him now in his old schoolboy clothes, rough woollen breeches and worn brown coat, his long wrists dangling from the cuffs because he outgrew everything in months. Instead, he was for ever riding off to Edinburgh to visit the tailor, and when he was at home, he sat about the house in silks and laces, perfumed like a London dandy, playing cards and drinking with the farmers' sons who came to visit him, and cheat him of his money. They were all much older then he, and Elizabeth knew they were not the kind of young men Papa would have chosen as companions for Robin. He neglected his studies, too. There was a suspicion of a sneer in his voice when he mentioned Mr Cockburn and his Greek accidence, and he never spoke to her of Oxford now, the city he used to tell her was all shining spires and rivers and bells beating on the sky. And because she loved him more than all the other people in the world put together, because he was the sun that warmed her and gave her life, Elizabeth Melville was deeply unhappy.

Elizabeth Martin was unhappy too, and often in her own world she longed to turn her back on Elizabeth Melville and her troubles, and know her no more. But this, she now realised with a hopeless certainty, was no longer possible. In earlier days Elizabeth had gone through her looking-glass into the Melville world because she had desired it, because it was the place she most wanted to be, because there she was with Robin. She had told herself that it was safe, because always sooner or later she was restored to her own life, her own personality. She still was, more or less, but now things were different, because Elizabeth Melville was no longer happy, and sometimes the burden of her distress, placed on top of her own, seemed more than Elizabeth Martin could bear. So the answer, she knew, was to stay in her world, and leave the Melvilles alone.

The problem was that she was unable to take her own advice. For in spite of all the pain he was causing her, Elizabeth Martin loved Robin as much as Elizabeth Melville did, and she went to him now because she could not help it. There was no use telling herself that Robin had changed, that he was not as he used to be, that he had let her down. There was no use trying to be reasonable at all. It had nothing to do with reason. The old need for the warmth and comfort of the nursery, the companionship of the other children, so understandable when compared with the loving security of life in that room with the lonely austerity of life in the cottage, had somehow shrunk till it became no more than a ceaseless, single-minded craving for Robin; for good or ill, she had to be with Robin. It was a feeling Elizabeth could not even begin to control, and although she was not yet as frightened as she should have been, she was becoming uneasy.

For the result of her desire was that every time she returned from Elizabeth Melville's life into her own, a shorter interval seemed to elapse before the need to look again, to return to Robin, overcame her. At first more than a week might pass between her visits, but then the spaces narrowed to five days, two days, one day, a few hours, and Elizabeth was far too intelligent not to see what the outcome of this could be. But while one part of her understood the danger, and warned her that she should be trying to fight against it, the other, stronger part was for ever urging her to forget and discard her old life and loves, and cast her lot with the past that seemed so vividly like a future. It was easier to think this way because by now her old life seemed so far away and unimportant; only now and then scenes from it, like this morning's vision of school, flashed poignantly on her mind's eye, reminding her, calling her to return.

Sometimes Elizabeth wondered how much of what was happening was caused by the ring. There was something very odd about the ring, that was obvious. Since Elizabeth Melville's birthday, when Robin had given it to her, the little gold ring with its strange inscription had never left her finger. This was for the simple reason that she could not get it off. No matter how much she pulled and twisted, licked her knuckle, rubbed it with soap from Gerry's soap box, Elizabeth Martin could not remove the ring. Elizabeth Melville of course did not try. And — this was the queerest thing of all — Elizabeth discovered one day that the ring was not visible to anyone in the cottage except herself. She had been standing by the kitchen window, wetting her finger and pulling at the ring, when Gerry came up behind her suddenly, and said, 'What's the matter? Have you hurt your finger?'

Elizabeth was beginning to say 'No', when Gerry took her hand, and looked closely at the knuckle, which she had scraped and bitten and worried almost to the point of bleeding.

'Elizabeth! What have you been doing?' she demanded in horror.

Elizabeth thought it was obvious enough to make this a silly question.

'Trying to get my ring off,' she said, impatiently.

'Well,' said Gerry, 'and I should think so too. It's a good thing you did get it off, before we had to take you to the jeweller to have it cut off, and your finger too, most likely. It must have been far too small. Just wait there, please, till I get a piece of plaster. It looks horribly sore.'

With which she went to the dresser, found a tin of Elastoplast, and came back with a dressing, which she stripped off and applied to Elizabeth's finger, on top of the ring.

Of course it was uncanny, and at one time it would have upset Elizabeth, but now she was so accustomed to the extraordinary that when she found out, in the evening, that Kate could not see the ring either, she was not even surprised.

'How does your finger feel now?' Gerry asked her at supper.

'It's all right,' said Elizabeth.

Kate paused with her hand on the coffee pot.

'What's wrong with your finger?' she asked.

'Nothing,' said Elizabeth.

'She has been wearing a ring that's too small for her,' Gerry explained. 'She's got it off now, but it has left her knuckle in a nasty mess.'

'Let me see it, Elizabeth,' ordered Kate.

'It's all right, Kate, Don't fuss.'

'Take the plaster off, Elizabeth. I want to see it.'

Elizabeth sighed. It was just like Kate, who never noticed anything, to notice the one thing you would rather she had not noticed. At the same time, on the odd occasion when Kate did give you an order, there was something about her which made you obey. So she pulled the strip of Elastoplast away, revealing the golden gleam of the ring below.

Kate put on her spectacles, lifted Elizabeth's hand and drew it up close to her eyes.

'Hm,' she said, not unkindly. 'That could have been very nasty. It's a good thing you got the ring off. You had better keep it covered for a day or two until the swelling goes down, and if it doesn't get any better, tell us.'

And Gerry covered the ring with a fresh plaster, which equally inexplicably seemed to have disappeared half an hour later, when she was back in the nursery, learning her Adjectives of the Third Declension, because Robin was setting her an examination on the morrow, and if she failed he was going to put her on bread and water for a month. The sore finger had gone too, but Elizabeth Melville did not notice that either. She had forgotten all about Elizabeth Martin, as she concentrated on her precious Latin. So much to learn, and so little time, before the pickles and the wine and the laundry claimed her.

'Elizabeth,' said Grizel, from her chair by the fire, 'it is time for your sampler. Bring it from the press, please.'

Reluctantly Elizabeth raised her head, and looked imploringly into Grizel's face. Grizel laughed.

'And you need not woo me with your black eyes,' she said. 'Even great scholars must learn to sew in this house. Now close your books, and bring me the thread box when you come.'

Elizabeth got down from the table, with a sigh.

'I wish I had been a boy,' she said, 'then I would not have to sew.' But she went obediently to the cupboard to fetch her work.

'If you were a boy, you would find other tasks to distract you, I dare say,' said Grizel gently. 'There is always something to keep us from the things we want to do in this poor old world.'

131

'What do you want to do, Grizel?' asked Elizabeth, as she drew her creepie close to Grizel's knee.

'Oh, I want to sew cushions,' said Grizel, 'and beautiful hangings, that will still give people pleasure long after I am dead. And sometimes I think I want to work in a garden, like my father. But I do not want these things as you want your learning, little one. I am not going to break my heart for the want of them. I suppose I am one of life's fortunates — I love best what I have now.'

Elizabeth unfolded her sampler, and smoothed it out on her knee. She pondered for a moment in silence, as she threaded her needle, then she said, 'I thought — if I could not have the things I wanted, at least Robin could have them, and I was glad for him. But now — ' she dropped her voice to conceal its tremor ' — now I think Robin no longer wants the things I want for him. He is so very changed, Grizel.'

Her disloyalty to Robin was like a knife in her own heart, but she was so desperate that she had to ask someone, someone who loved Robin too, whether the change was really in Robin, or in herself. And Grizel loved Robin. He had been her first baby, when she came to Robinsheugh as a nursery maid at the age of twelve — younger than Elizabeth was now — and she had always loved him best. Elizabeth knew this, and she felt no jealousy. It seemed to her only right and fitting that Robin should come first with everyone else, as he did with her.

Grizel put a reassuring arm round Elizabeth's narrow shoulders.

'Now you listen to me,' she said, 'and stop worrying over him like an old mother hen. Surely you can see how it is — the Laird is away, and our Robin is thinking he is the Laird himself. So off he goes and buys himself some fine new clothes, instead of these old brown tatters, and struts about like a peacock, enjoying himself. There is no great harm in it, Elizabeth.' She laughed suddenly, the clear, fluting sound which was one of the things Elizabeth liked best in the world to hear, and added, 'And no doubt he knows that the time is short for strutting, for the Laird will soon be home, and then Master Robin will have his wings clipped, I'll be bound.'

This was very comforting, and Elizabeth wanted to believe it, but — 'He neglects his books,' she said sadly.

'Well, he does not neglect yours, I am happy to see. I wondered — but never mind. He has kept his promise to you, and

I have no doubt he will settle to his studies again when his father comes home.'

'Yes,' said Elizabeth, thinking of the father she loved, and hardly knew, 'I expect you are right, Grizel. Everything will be well when Papa comes home.'

'That is my good girl. Now look — see how little we have to do. Three lines of French Running here, three bonnie gowans in Satin there, and only the last two words, and the date.'

' "Day", and "prophain",' said Elizabeth. 'But I think I shall make my gowans first.' She poked in the thread box for a skein of white silk. 'White for the petals, and yellow for the little sun in the middle. Do you suppose gowans are daisies for giants, Grizel?'

'If it pleases you,' said Grizel, indulgent to such childishness. Sometimes she thought that despite her cleverness, Elizabeth was very young for her age. But then, she had long enough to be grown up, and Grizel sometimes thought sadly that being grown up would bring few pleasures to her Elizabeth. She rumpled her hair affectionately, and said, 'Now stop your blethering, and get to work.'

Elizabeth, who could laugh at herself, did so, and stitched away in silence for a few minutes. Then, 'Shall I finish this before my Papa comes home, Grizel?' she asked. 'I should like to surprise him with it. Last time he was here, he said I should have a golden guinea to myself if I finished it to his liking.'

'Now what would you do with a guinea?' asked Grizel teasingly.

'I would buy you all a present, of course,' said Elizabeth. 'But shall I finish it, Grizel?'

'In four weeks? You could finish it and make another one,' laughed Grizel, enjoying the expression of horror on Elizabeth's face.

Some days later, in another time and place, Elizabeth was bouncing her red ball against the cottage wall, and as she played, she was singing to herself.

> We are three brethren come from Spain
> All in French garlands,
> We come to court your daughter Jean,
> And adieu to you, my darlings.

My daughter Jean she is too young
All in French garlands,
She cannot bide your flattering tongue,
And adieu to you, my darlings.

'What I would like to know,' remarked Gerry, pausing in the middle of beating up a batter pudding to peer out through the geranium leaves at Elizabeth, 'is where that child picks up these songs. It isn't as if there are any other children around here for her to play with.'

Kate, who was sitting at her own end of the table, supporting her forehead on her spread fingertips, looked up from her book with a reluctant, guarded expression on her thin face.

'Then one must assume,' she said in a flat voice which conveyed neither concern nor alarm, 'that she heard them before she came.' She hesitated for a moment, then she added, 'That's how it is with these childhood songs, isn't it? You hear them once, and they go on singing themselves in your mind. . . .'

Her voice faltered, and Gerry looked at her with troubled eyes. It was a sign, she thought, of how terribly tired and overworked Dr Jenkins was that these days she so often failed to grasp a point that one was trying to make. It was as if she were never really concentrating on what one was saying, and that was frightening, because Gerry had been taught by her for two years, and she knew her well enough to realise that underneath her vague, untidy exterior, was one of the most brilliant, incisive minds she was ever likely to encounter in her life.

'But, Dr Jenkins, that's a Scottish song,' she said hesitantly. 'They're all Scottish songs. I've never heard them before. Has Elizabeth been to Scotland before this summer?'

'No.'

'Well, then.'

Kate tutted, and made a fluttering, irritable gesture with her hands.

'Well, then, I don't know. Perhaps she learned them in school — they teach the most unlikely things in schools nowadays. It's called Projects. It's why they come up to the University unable to spell. Or maybe she heard them at the Lindsays'. She goes over to see them quite a lot, doesn't she?'

She turned over a page, and dropped her head deliberately over her book again, which was always how she dismissed a conversation she was tired of, and Gerry, who had been opening her mouth to remark that Mrs Lindsay did not seem to her the kind of woman who would sing songs about French garlands, changed her mind and shut it again. For after all, she thought, there was no reason why she should get herself into a disagreement with Dr Jenkins over Elizabeth. Quite often she felt sorry for Elizabeth, and felt that Dr Jenkins might pay her a little more attention, but on the other hand there was no denying that Elizabeth was awkward, and could sometimes be abominably rude and unhelpful, so that just as often she felt sorry for Dr Jenkins, who seemed unable to please Elizabeth whatever she did. The trouble with children, Gerry mused, was that they were always wanting to be treated as grown up, then when someone took them at their word, they didn't like it. Of course what Dr Jenkins thought about her niece, Gerry had no idea, because she was far too loyal to discuss Elizabeth with anyone, and somehow she was not the sort of woman who could ever be lured into that kind of discussion against her will. But just the same, said Gerry to herself, as she attacked her bowl of batter again with a wooden spoon, there was something very strange about Elizabeth these days. She had always been querulous and discontented, but at least at the beginning her unpleasantness had been straightforward. She had not been — well, furtive was the word which came to Gerry's mind. She was certainly furtive now, and there was something about her eyes. . . .

Gerry looked down at Kate's untidy fair head, bent over *Scottish Border Fortifications 1300—1700*, and for a moment she wondered what was going on inside it, whether she too noticed a change in Elizabeth, or whether, because she was tired and in pain, she shied away from the consequences of noticing, and pretended there was nothing to notice. Even very clever people, Gerry had observed, were good at practising this kind of self-deception. But then, such being Gerry's own capacity for self-deception, as soon as she had got herself to a point where she not only acknowledged a problem, but even had begun to admit that it might be a very unusual kind of problem indeed, her great ally, Common Sense, came to her aid. And of course, Common Sense said to Gerry, she was being absurd, and letting herself imagine things. Living in this out-of-the-way place for so long with an Oxford scholar, who, however nice, was certainly more in touch with the seventeen seventies than she was with the nineteen seventies, was beginning to get on her nerves. Of course there was nothing wrong with Elizabeth, really — how could there be?

Adolescence, said Gerry, that was what was wrong with her; adolescence, of course being the convenient way of explaining anything that was wrong with a girl of Elizabeth's age. And in any case — Gerry now addressed herself very firmly, falling back on the unfailing excuse of everyone who knows that another person needs help, but for various reasons does not want to be the one who gives it — it was none of her business. Her business was to look after Dr Jenkins, who, poor woman, was quite unable to look after herself, and see that she got enough to eat, and persuade her that midnight was a more reasonable bedtime than half past three in the morning. It was not for her to worry about Elizabeth, who would be perfectly all right when she got back to London, among her own family and friends. And so, having come for the first, and perhaps the only time of her life, to within a hair's breadth of believing the unbelievable, Gerry put her pudding into the oven and dismissed the matter from her mind.

Meanwhile Kate, intent on *Scottish Border Fortifications 1300—1700*, turned a page, reached for her fountain pen, and opened her notebook. She too had shelved the problem of Elizabeth, not because she was unaware of it, but because it was one of the things which would have to be dealt with later, when she did not have so much work to do. What she did not understand was the extent of the seriousness of the problem, or that the time when it would still be possible to deal with it was rapidly running out.

16

The Winter Rose

September came. The summer flowers that Elizabeth once had loved faded from the hedgerows, the rose petals fell, and the rose-hips ripened. The fresh leaves of July, which in August had darkened to a duller, dustier green, now began to show the first crackle of rust around their edges, spreading inwards as the month passed on in a blaze of gold. Red berries hung in clusters in the hedges, and on the rowans by the Wishwater, the bracken was a dapple of yellow and russet and bronze along the hill's foot, while above it the first mauve faintness of the opening heather deepened quickly into a purple-red which was like a wild fire in the evening sun. And Elizabeth Martin would have loved it, would have looked at it all with eyes wide open to the brave, flaunting beauty that clothed the last days of the year that would never come again. But Elizabeth Martin no longer walked in the lanes and woods, and for the strange, hybrid being of whom she now formed a rapidly diminishing part, colour outside the flame-lit, abnormal world of Robinsheugh was something which had long ago ceased to have any meaning.

Everything beyond that world of garish light seemed by contrast flat and monochromatic, and Elizabeth, who would often now have turned her tired eyes for relief to the greyness without, found that she could not do so. It was like being in a darkened room with a coloured television in the corner; remorselessly her eyes were drawn towards the light. For what had begun for her as an exciting, extraordinary, astounding but in no way frightening experience, was turning rapidly into an appalling nightmare, the worst part of which was the terrible certainty that she would never wake from it again. It was not only that as Elizabeth Martin she was losing her identity, was in fact in the process of becoming another person. The really horrifying thing was that as she changed, what was left of her own consciousness was aware that she was changing. It was like knowing that she was dying, yet different, because it was not annihilation that Elizabeth faced, nor even the continuation of her own life in another, spiritual world. When the moment of her death came, it would be because she had become somebody else.

For a long time after she had begun to move from one existence to the other, in each she had at least known who she was. One aspect of her personality had always been stronger, its only disturbance the odd, floating thought or memory which came to it from the other, weaker part, lingering on when the rest of the mind had taken flight. It had been a strange, but perfectly tolerable situation, one which Elizabeth Martin had been sure she had firmly under control. Over and over again she had assured herself that since she looked into the glass because she wanted to, she could equally well stop looking when she wanted to. But this was where her reasoning was at fault; she did not know the difference between looking because she wanted to, and looking because she had to, because the symptoms of these two feelings were so alike — perilously so, as it turned out, because by the time the remnant of Elizabeth Martin's mind realised what was happening, it was too late to do anything about it. She looked because she must, and she could not stop. She had thought she controlled the glass, and all the time the glass, or the power behind it, had really been controlling her.

The fact of the matter was that at some time during the past strange weeks, or perhaps gradually during them, life with Kate and Gerry in the cottage had assumed all the sensations of dream-living which Elizabeth had found so markedly absent in her first contact with the Melvilles. At that time, each world, each life, had seemed equally real. At the same time, she had been perfectly clear in her own mind about who she was and what was happening to her. She had been Elizabeth Katherine Martin, of 17 Cranbury Avenue, London N.6., and because she had found a magic looking-glass, she was able sometimes to pass into a world which she recognised as that of the eighteenth century, where at first she had pretended to be Elizabeth Melville, then later had believed she was Elizabeth Melville — while she was there. It had been strange, exciting and adventurous, and Elizabeth had been lulled out of her first qualms into the belief that it was not dangerous by the fact that when she returned to her twentieth-century life, she had never been in any doubt as to which was the real she.

Now all that was changed, and the opposite had come to pass. It seemed to her that in the first instance she was Elizabeth Frances Melville, of Robinsheugh House in the county of Roxburghshire, who sometimes dreamed herself into another, alien existence which only the last lingerings of Elizabeth Martin

138

helped her to understand at all. Because the positions in which the two girls found themselves were different in one very important respect. When Elizabeth Martin went into the past, there were signposts to guide her; memories of a project she had once done at school on the Georgians, Kate's conversations with Gerry about her work, the belongings the Melvilles had left behind them, their letters in the chest in the tower room, their cradle in the lumber room, their portraits in the dining-room, the house itself. All these told their story. For however little we may know or understand of history, we are never totally ignorant of the past; it is familiar in one degree to the Elizabeths, in another to the Kates, of the present day. But when Elizabeth Melville found herself, as she now seemed to do, in the twentieth-century world of what in her lifetime had been a blacksmith's cottage thatched with peats, she had taken a step into the future, into the totally unknown. There was no background knowledge she could rely upon to help her understand where she was, or what was happening to her. Elizabeth Martin was not a person she could possibly recognise; she was the future which is always a question, rather than the past which can be caught, put in order, and tidily laid away. And yet she was completely dependent on Elizabeth Martin, for without the help she received from the fading remains of Elizabeth Martin's mind, she could never have coped with the blind, stumbling uncertainty of being a child out of her own time.

She was bitterly unhappy and afraid, and Elizabeth Martin, stifled, trapped, but still alive within her, was bewildered and absolutely terrified. She wandered around the cottage like a little ghost, sat at table with Kate and Gerry, eating food which had no taste, looking into a greyness in which for some reason the only colour she could still distinguish was the gold of Kate Jenkins's hair. And this was odd, because very often when she looked at Kate she had great difficulty remembering who she was. Sometimes, in a burst of concentration which nearly tore her apart, she threw off Elizabeth Melville and knew herself for who she was, and it was then she wanted to run to Kate, and hold on to her, and cry, and tell her everything. But if she did — for she did Kate the justice of knowing that she would take her story very seriously indeed, even if for the wrong reasons — Kate would take her away, and then she would never see Robin again. And that was what she could not bear. Not to see Robin again was the very worst thing that could possibly happen, and Elizabeth felt that she could never wilfully take the step that would separate them, because the agony of her loss would kill her.

> What's this dull town to me?
> Robin's not near,
> He whom I wished to see,
> Wished for to hear.
> Where's all the joy and mirth
> Made life a heaven on earth?
> O they're all fled with thee,
> Robin Adair.

She could not remember who it was she had heard singing it, whether it was Grizel, or Kate, or Lady Melville, or Miss Peel who taught singing at her school in London, only that it was true. No joy, no mirth without Robin.

At such times, when there seemed to be enough of her old self present to think properly about such things, she sometimes wondered whether Kate was suspicious. It never occurred to her to worry about Gerry, but now and then she thought she saw Kate looking at her with an odd expression in her eyes, especially after the incident of the carpet. It happened on an evening when Elizabeth, by dint of great effort, was just managing to keep Elizabeth Martin uppermost in her ravaged, conflict-torn mind. Not sufficiently, however. Kate had been to Edinburgh, to the University Library; she arrived back sooner than expected, when Gerry, who had been taking things easy, was only half-way through making the supper.

'Well, don't worry,' said Kate, who was not one to fuss about that sort of thing. 'It doesn't matter. I'm not hungry anyway. We'll eat when you have it ready.'

With which she sat down by the fire, fished her spectacles out of her pocket, and was soon engrossed in one of the tomes she had brought back with her. Apparently.

'Elizabeth,' begged Gerry, 'be kind, and lay the table for me. I'm going to get in an awful muddle in a minute.'

'All right,' agreed Elizabeth, and getting up from the table, where she had been pretending to do a crossword, she went to the dresser drawer to fetch the tablecloth. It was not there.

'Gerry,' she said, 'the carpet isn't in the drawer. Shall I bring a clean one from upstairs?'

'Eh?' said Gerry. She glanced in perplexity at the stone floor, then at the scrubbed wooden table, then at Elizabeth, who was still standing by the open drawer, unaware of having said anything amiss. They stared at each other with blank eyes, then turned, both conscious at the same second of a sudden quickening in Kate. Her vague eyes were instantly alert, although when she spoke, her voice was carefully casual.

'I wonder,' she said, 'how you come to know that in the eighteenth century the Scots called a tablecloth a carpet?'

Elizabeth stiffened.

'I — I don't know,' she stammered. 'I — that is, I must have heard someone say so. You, probably.'

Kate contemplated her with the kind of shrewdness which can make normally abstracted people frightening.

'Certainly you did not. It's a piece of information I only acquired myself this morning.'

'Gerry, then.'

'Gerry, did you know that a tablecloth was called a carpet in Scotland in the eighteenth century?'

'Was it?' said Gerry, looking uncertainly from one serious grey-eyed face to the other. 'How very strange.'

'Then I read it somewhere,' shouted Elizabeth, losing her temper. 'Why do you keep asking me questions?'

'Why do you never answer my questions?' replied Kate, who in truth was never known to ask anybody anything. She returned to her book then, but when Elizabeth looked at her, she knew by the way she stared fixedly at one spot on the page that she was not reading, and that in itself was strange enough to be unnerving. She must be very careful, thought Elizabeth Martin, not to let Elizabeth Melville betray her again.

All through supper, she went on struggling hard to remember that she was Elizabeth Martin. At the end of the first course, Kate excused herself, saying that she felt unwell, and went upstairs to her room. Gerry looked gloomily at Elizabeth over the pudding.

'This can't go on,' she said in a worried voice. 'I feel so responsible, but I just don't know what to do. She won't rest, and she doesn't eat, and she won't see a doctor, and I don't see how she can possibly survive another three weeks like this. But she won't listen to a word I say.'

Elizabeth's two minds, which at that moment were almost evenly balanced, floated in and out of each other, making all this familiar, yet impossible to understand.

'What do you think is wrong with her?' she asked, not because she cared, but because she supposed it was a correct reply yo such remarks.

'Overwork, obviously,' said Gerry, 'and worry, although what she has to worry about, I've no idea. It's awkward, because she is who she is, and I am who I am, and although she's so very nice to me, I don't feel inclined to take liberties. If I did, I'd write to her mother.'

'I expect that would make her very angry, wouldn't it?' asked Elizabeth.

'I know.' Gerry paused, then added, rather as a last, forlorn hope, 'I was wondering if you might talk to her. She might tell you.'

'No,' said Elizabeth. 'No, I couldn't possibly do that. You see, I don't really know her.'

It was perhaps fortunate that Gerry could not understand the truth of this statement.

'Ah, well,' she said, shaking her head, 'we must just hope for the best, I suppose. I wonder if she would like a cup of coffee? Will you take one up to her?'

And this time Elizabeth said she would; it did not matter to her whether she did or not.

She took the cup and saucer carefully in her hands, and carried them slowly upstairs, making sure that the coffee did not slop over into the saucer. She met Kate coming out of the bathroom, and it only needed one glance at her flushed, unhappy face to see that she had been crying. She put her hand over her face, and without looking at Elizabeth took the cup in her other hand, thanked her abruptly, and brushed past into her room, closing the door firmly behind her. Elizabeth stood staring at the door, too upset to move. It was not just that the sight of a grown-up crying put her into a panic, as it does most children, the fact that the grown-up was Kate made it more disturbing than ever. For Elizabeth Martin remembered that Kate never cried; it was a well known fact that she did not. That was why she had been so sure, that night weeks before, that her ears were deceiving her. Kate never cried. Even when her father had died, and Granny and Mother had wept for days, Kate had gone about with a white, stony face, her misery walled up in silence behind hard, bright eyes, and everyone had said how terrible it was that she could not cry too, and have relief. But Elizabeth was sure she never had, and yet she was crying now. And for a moment she wanted to knock on the door, and go in, and ask Kate what grief worse than

142

death had come to her, and comfort her. And she might have done it, had not at that instant Elizabeth Martin lost her grip, and Elizabeth Melville's mind flooded their shared consciousness. For although Elizabeth Melville was compassionate, more compassionate certainly than Elizabeth Martin, she did not know Kate, and as Elizabeth was to discover later on in her life, it is very difficult to care very deeply for someone to whom we cannot put a face. So she turned away, groping in her pocket for her looking-glass.

It was a relief, in a way, to turn her back on Elizabeth Martin's troubles, on the fear and confusion of being so terribly divided, on that endless, silent mental battle to keep herself from disappearing, and become again Elizabeth Melville of Robinsheugh, who was now rarely disturbed by the least, wispy memory of Elizabeth Martin. But there was no other relief.

In the nursery, life went on as usual; Alexander was learning to crawl, James was even wickeder now he was four than he had been when he was three, while Lucy, thought Elizabeth, was getting more like her mother every day with her 'La, la's' and her constant interest in her appearance. But none of this seemed important any more, which was sad, really, because Elizabeth loved the two little boys dearly, and Lucy, in spite of their differences, was the only friend of her own age she had ever had. Now the younger children wearied her, with their demands for stories and games, for the fun they always had with her.

'Go away,' she said. 'Not now. Perhaps tomorrow.'

Their puzzled eyes hurt her, and when they turned away from her in disappointment, she wanted to call them back, to make them happy. But she was too tired to bother. James was probably the one most bewildered by her neglect, because he adored Elizabeth, and he could not understand why she no longer wanted to read to him, or have him climb into her bed, and huddle up beside her in the early morning. He watched her reproachfully from a distance, and Elizabeth hated herself, but suffering made her selfish, and she made no effort to console him. Listlessly she moped by the fire, aware of Grizel's anxious eyes on her, not caring any more.

For the dreaded moment had come and passed. Robin had stopped coming to teach her Latin, and he had blown out the candle he had lighted in her life, leaving her in the dark. It had not happened all at once; she had seen it coming. For weeks, she knew, he had come so as not to disappoint her, but that he had lost interest was obvious. She could see from the way he lounged at the table, fidgeting and polishing his finger-nails on the embroidered cuff of his coat, thet he was bored, and all the joy she used to have in sharing an enthusiasm with him was gone. Then he began to come late, then to miss days, then he stopped coming at all. For a while she had tried to keep him.

'Robin, I learned my nouns of the fourth declension, and I can construe my passage. Will you not hear it?'

He flicked an imaginary speck of dust from his satin sleeve, but he would not look her in the eyes.

'Ah, of course — tomorrow, Elizabeth, be sure I shall hear it tomorrow. Today I have promised to dine with the Scotts, and they, being simple creatures, still take their dinner at three. 'Tis a long road, and longer with that old fool Cockburn riding his nag at my heels.'

Elizabeth's horror at this reference to the minister almost swamped her misery over Robin's neglect, but when he had gone, she said to Grizel, 'He will hear my Latin tomorrow, but tomorrow never comes.'

And all Grizel would say, with an unaccustomed frown between her dark brows, was, 'It is high time the Laird was home,' as she lifted Alexander out of the cradle, and began to untie the ribbons on his little bonnet. Elizabeth crept to her side, and sat down on the floor, burying her face in Grizel's skirt. 'My head aches,' she said.

Grizel's remedy for an ache in the head was a dose from a black bottle which she kept in the press; it was evil-tasting, and it made Elizabeth feel ill. It did not cure her headache, and for her real sickness there was no cure. She did not ask Robin to teach her again; it was pointless, and his excuses were as painful as his neglect. She went on living as bravely as she could, but he had taken all her joy away.

Then one morning, when she had not seen him for a week, and her desire for a sight of him was like teeth gnawing ceaselessly in her mind, Robin came to the nursery to see her. She was alone in the room; Lucy and Grizel were downstairs at the spinet with Mr Boston, while James and Alexander were out in the garden with Alison. Elizabeth was huddled up on her creepie by the fire, sewing her sampler. It was all but finished now; two flowers, the last six letters of the word 'prophain', and the date, were all that remained to be done. She looked up at Robin, and in spite of everything that had happened, the sun came out for her, and she smiled up at him with a surge of happiness. He smiled back, standing before her like a young prince, she thought, in his velvet coat, and she saw that in his hands he was carrying three pink roses. He bent down and laid them in her lap.

'They were growing down in the corner by the front gate,' he said, 'where they are sheltered from the wind. Roses in December, Elly — are they not lovelier than roses in June?'

Elizabeth looked down at them, thin, delicate things, more like our wild roses than the plump, overbred cushions we grow in our gardens now, and she breathed in the sharp, sweet scent that seemed to her like the very odour of happiness.

'They are so beautiful, Robin,' she said.

Robin squatted down in front of her, and took her face gently between his hands.

'How thin you have grown,' he said, suddenly worried. 'What ails you, little sister?'

Elizabeth shook her head.

'Nothing,' she said.

'Then listen,' said Robin. 'Tonight I ride to Edinburgh to see Mamma, and attend to some business I have there. I shall be back on Thursday afternoon. Then we must see about starting your Latin lessons again, eh? I have been neglecting you, I know, but I have had much to do. Have ready your work on Thursday, and I promise it shall be my first concern when I come.'

Elizabeth wanted to shout and sing and dance and laugh and cry all at once. She did none of these things. She said goodbye to Robin, thanked him for the roses, and told him pertly to have a care he did not fall in the ditch. Then after he had gone, she went to the press, and found a pewter cup for her roses. She filled it with water from the ewer which Grizel kept in the corner by the box bed, and carried it carefully to the window-sill. She floated the short-stemmed flowers on the water, admiring the shape of their deep pink petals, which faded out to a pearly paleness at their softly puckered edges. It was then, as she was thinking of nothing in particular, that Elizabeth Martin came fleetingly, and noticed that these flowers were the last colour she could distinguish before the greyness began on the other side of the glass. Beyond their tender pink began the shimmer of uncertainty, the landscape which she could never establish definitely as belonging to her own time, or to the other. The fact of the greyness told her nothing; what she saw from Kate's cottage was as grey and thin as this, but if there were some clue, something by

145

which she could answer the question of whether Kate and Gerry and her father and mother were alive outside, or would not be born for two hundred years, she would know whether hers was an enchantment limited to this house, or a more unspeakable enchantment by far. Elizabeth looked out of the window now, her eyes straining sorely into the mirk of dun hillside and ashen leaves. Then she noticed. Leaves. Leaves on trees, in December? And the roses, had Robin picked the roses in December, as he said, or was he too under the spell of time gone all awry? It was so great a problem that her concentration gave way under it, and Elizabeth Melville remembered that it was time now to sew her sampler. She sat down on her stool, and looked for a skein of yellow silk in the box.

And so she turned her mind to other things, which was a pity, in a way, because that night Elizabeth Melville had an experience which would have helped Elizabeth Martin to solve the riddle of her outdoor world. She was playing a game of hide and seek with James and Lucy — she was so happy that she had been playing games with the delighted children all day, and Grizel, relieved beyond words, had let her — and while she was hiding in the wine closet at the back of the house, waiting for Lucy to come and find her, she happened to glance out of the tiny window into the courtyard far below. And there she saw Kate, thin and mistily familiar in her old brown waterproof, with her bag of books under her arm, making her way slowly back across the cobble-stones to the cottage. Familiar — yet as Elizabeth watched her go, fading and melting silently into the gathering night, she could not remember who she was, or where she had seen her before.

'I see you!' cried Lucy, bursting in, and a moment later Elizabeth was leaping upstairs, with her skirts kilted up around her, shrieking with merriment as James leaped out on her from the shadow of the nursery door. They all fell into the room in a laughing heap, and it was not till she had disentangled herself from the other two, and staggered to the fireplace to collapse on her stool, that Elizabeth noticed that Grizel was not sharing their amusement. She was sitting in her chair with the baby on her knee, and she was watching the children with disturbed, brooding eyes. Elizabeth went to her side.

'What is it, Grizel?' she asked, her laughter fading. 'What is it? Has something happened?'

Grizel put an arm round her, and shook her head.

'But there is something? You look — afraid? Tell me, Grizel.'

The other children had drawn near now, and they were looking at Grizel too, their eyes grave.

'Oh, it is likely nothing,' said Grizel. ''Tis foolish to worry over such things, I know. But Matthew Grimble rode as far as Gilmerton with Master Robin this afternoon, and he is just this minute back. He says there is smallpox in Edinburgh.'

17

At the Letter 'O'

'Damn,' said Kate explosively into a letter that had come by the morning post. 'Damn and blast and damn again.'

Gerry looked up in great alarm from her own letter from Peter, and even Elizabeth, who as usual was having to fight very hard to remember where she was, and who these people were, stared at her aunt in some surprise. Kate was not at all a cursing type of woman.

'What's the matter?' asked Gerry, trying to think of the worst thing that could possibly have happened. 'They haven't sent back your Income Tax returns *again*, have they?'

'No,' said Kate with a groan. 'It's much worse than that. It's too awful for words.'

Gerry's mouse-eyes dilated with fright as she wondered which College or Library had been burned to the ground. Elizabeth, for a moment really intrigued, found it easier to concentrate on being Elizabeth Martin; she looked at Kate in something approaching amusement.

'Well, tell us,' urged Gerry, 'if it's so awful. Don't keep us on tenterhooks.'

'I'll read it to you,' said Kate, in a doom-laden voice. 'It's from Sir Gilbert Melville.'

She lifted the sheet of writing paper, looking at it with an expression which suggested that she really thought her eyes must be deceiving her, and began, ' "Dear Dr Jenkins, as you perhaps know, it is our custom to open the house of Robinsheugh to the public on five Sundays in the year, in aid of charities in which my wife and I are interested. The next occasion is Sunday, 17th September. Advertisement of the opening has been arranged with the local press, and through the publicity of the 'Scotland's Gardens' scheme. I understand from my factor, Mr Grimble, that arrangements are well in hand, and that those members of the Robinsheugh community who usually help us are willing to do so again. However, we have a problem. Usually my wife, my eldest daughter, Elizabeth, and I try to be at home on open days to act as guides to parties of visitors, but unfortunately we find that this time we all have engagements which will keep us in London, and will therefore be unable to come north. I wonder if we might ask you and Miss Temple — " Miss Temple? Oh, that's you, Gerry, isn't it? I'd forgotten " — you and Miss Temple to undertake the task of acting as guides on our behalf? You know more about the history of Robinheugh than we do — " So we do, Gerry, that's for sure " — and it would be a load off our minds if we knew that parties were going round under adequate supervision, although of course security will be in the capable hands of the local Police Force — " I hope it brings its truncheon.'

She tossed the letter down in front of Gerry, and said, 'There, you can read the rest yourself if you like.'

'No, thanks,' replied Gerry. 'That's enough. Do we have to?'

Kate sighed impatiently.

'Yes,' she said. 'At least I do. It's a small request from a man who has been very good to me, and I can't possibly refuse. Of course I can't make you do it, but I'd take it as a great favour if you would.'

'Well, of course I will,' said Gerry, adding half-teasingly, 'It's a small request from a woman who has been very good to me, and I can't possibly refuse.'

'Rubbish,' said Kate automatically, her mind already on something else. She finished her coffee, kicked back her chair, and stood up, pushing at her hair with distracted fingers. She began to gather her books together, pocketed her spectacles, and was just about to leave when Gerry said, 'Dr Jenkins, I was thinking — Elizabeth could act as a guide too. She knows almost as much about Robinsheugh as anyone.'

This might have startled Elizabeth Martin, but she was already slipping back to Elizabeth Melville.

'Yes, she does, doesn't she?' said Kate, looking at her niece with a mixture of pride and anxiety which Elizabeth was past noticing, but which was not lost upon Gerry, who was beginning to have her own ideas about what was worrying Dr Jenkins. 'Would you like to be a guide, Elizabeth?'

Elizabeth shook her head blankly.

'That's all right, then. I expect they'll be chasing you up to help with something else.' She turned away, and went over the the door, muttering to herself, 'Lollipops. Ices. Poodles. Screaming infants. Oh, *Lord*.' She shuddered, and disappeared.

Elizabeth did not give another thought to the Robinsheugh Open Day. For Elizabeth Melville, it was an event with no meaning at all, and it was with Elizabeth Melville's affairs that she was now exclusively concerned, passing to and fro by means of the looking-glass sometimes as often as eight times in one day. Robin had not come back from Edinburgh on the Thursday when he was expected. He did however send a note to Elizabeth — it made her feel very proud and important that the note was addressed to her — to say that Mamma wished him to stay with her for a few days, and that he would be back by Monday at the latest. Elizabeth quite understood that if Mamma wanted Robin to stay, Robin was honour-bound to obey her, and she spent the next few days happily enough. It was pleasant waiting for Robin, preparing her Latin, knowing that Robin had promised that her next lesson would be his 'first concern' when he came home. To begin with, she had worried a bit about Robin's being in Edinburgh when there was smallpox about, but after a while she sensibly put that worry behind her. The smallpox in Elizabeth Melville's day was rather like road accidents in our own, an accepted hazard of life, and something which was a thousand times more likely to happen to other people than to oneself or one's family. So she forgot about it, because she had her Latin to revise, so that it would be perfect for Robin's return, and her sampler to finish for her father's return, and there were all the usual lessons and chores to be got through as well. And despite the fact that her mind had been set at rest by Robin's kindness, Elizabeth still was not feeling as bright as usual; she was tired all the time, and her head ached badly. But she bore it patiently, and did not tell Grizel, for fear of another dose of physic from the black bottle in the press. Most of the time she sat by the fire with her work, reading and stitching and waiting for Robin. She was waiting for her father too; he was expected in less than two weeks, and then Lady Melville would also return, so that the family would all be at home to celebrate the New Year together.

Already the house was agog with preparations; beds were being aired, rooms were being swept and dusted, while in the kitchen the preparation of meats and cakes and plum puddings and every kind of confection went on from morning till night. Lucy spent every spare moment in the kitchen, putting her finger into every bowl and pot when Jeanie Rigg was not looking, and she was for ever running upstairs with excited reports of the brewing and baking, roasting and stewing, which were going on below. There was nothing, she boasted, of which she had not already had a taste. But Elizabeth, who had no appetite, sat by the fire, and felt secretly glad that nothing was expected of her.

'I shall just be in time to put the year 1779 on this sampler,' she remarked to Grizel. 'At least I shall not have a sampler to sew in 1780. But I expect there will be something else to try me. See Grizel — one petal of this gowan, and "ophain" to write. Then my date. December 1779. 'Tis a pity "December" is such a long word. I wish I had finished in May.'

They looked at each other and laughed cosily. In spite of her sore head, Elizabeth Melville had not found life in the nursery so pleasant for a long time.

She came out of the Melville world, as she had on that occasion gone into it, in a split second of the morning of the Robinsheugh Open Day, to find herself caught up in preparations for an event which she was totally unable now to understand. She came into the kitchen from the downstairs passage, where she had been standing when she last felt compelled to look in her glass, and found Gerry rushing around trying to tidy up the room, which Kate had left in an uproar after ransacking it in search of her glasses, which she lost on average three times a day.

'I don't know why she doesn't padlock them round her neck,' said Gerry crossly. 'Oh, by the way, Mrs Lindsay was here a minute ago. She wants to know if you'll go over and help her to lay tables in the barn. I said you would when you'd had your breakfast. Help yourself to sausages — I must rush up and make the beds.'

While she was eating her sausages, Elizabeth Martin made a great effort of concentration, and with a last thought of her own, remembered what Mrs Lindsay looked like. After that, Elizabeth Melville took over completely. She knew where the barn was, and she thought she would know how to lay tables, although it was not really a task for Miss Melville of Robinsheugh, whose table was always laid by Alison Hume. However, when she had finished her breakfast, she went out in the rain across the courtyard to the barn, and spent her morning running to and fro with piles of saucers and plates, laying out teaspoons, filling sugar basins and cream jugs, at the beck and call of Mrs Lindsay and several other women from the estate who had come to help with the teas.

'You're richt quiet the day, Elizabeth,' said Mrs Lindsay, when they were all sitting down having a tea-break in the middle of the morning. 'Is there onything wrang, dearie?'

'No,' said Elizabeth. 'No, thank you, I am quite well.'

'I'm glad tae hear that,' replied Mrs Lindsay, sounding relieved. 'We dinna want twa o' ye no' weel. Gerry was tellin' me your Aunt Kate's no' been richt a' summer. I was sayin' I doot she works far owre hard.'

Elizabeth had not the least notion what she was talking about. She nodded in agreement, but in fact she could not think who her Aunt Kate was. Her only aunts were her mother's sisters, Mrs Fraser and Mrs Austin, and their names were Charlotte and Mary. Perhaps Aunt Kate was one of Papa's aunts, who lived away in the glens beyond Dundee, and never came to Robinheugh because the roads were far too rough for a carriage, and they were too old to ride. . . .

The afternoon came at last. Elizabeth saw that a signpost with five pointing fingers had been erected in the middle of the courtyard. 'TEAS AND ICES; SOUVENIRS; PONY RIDES; GUIDED TOURS; EXHIBITION', announced the fingers drippily, as the rain washed into the felt pen writing, and black streaks ran down the wood. Long before two o'clock, when the house was supposed to be open, cars and buses were droving steadily down the drive in the downpour, much to the chagrin of Kate, who had been saying hopefully all morning that of course no one was going to be silly enough to come out on such a dreadful day. They turned in at the white gate marked CAR PARK, churning up great spurts of grass and clover and chocolate-coloured mud as their wheels remorselessly destroyed the turf of the Great Meadow by the Wishwater. Crowds of men, women and children, in waterproofs and golfing caps and polythene rain hats, leaned valiantly into the wind as they ploughed cheerfully across the ruined grass to the courtyard, where they paused to decide which delight they wanted to sample first.

Elizabeth watched them sullenly from the window of her cottage bedroom, where she had gone for refuge. Mrs Lindsay had wanted her to stay and help with the teas, and someone else had asked her to sell tickets for an exhibition of historical costume which had been got together hastily in the stable. She had refused, aware of their puzzlement, and had hurried away to the empty cottage, meaning to hide there, to lie on the camp bed until it was all over. But the sight of these outlandishly dressed strangers fascinated her; she had no idea who they were or what they were doing here at Robinsheugh, and now that the last of Elizabeth Martin, who would have known, was gone, there were no answers to her questions. As she watched them scuttling here and there in the rain, laughing and calling to one another, eating ices and hot dogs and dropping their papers, as often as not, on the clean cobbles, her interest turned to resentment; how dare these common people come here, when Papa was away, with their children and their dogs, and walk about the place as if they had every right to be there? Where were Tam Rigg and Matthew Grimble, and why were they allowing this to happen? But it was not until she looked across the courtyard, and saw that the strangers were actually going into the house that she acted; she wanted to know what they were doing, these dim, faceless people who were stamping so rudely over her home, so she put on Elizabeth Martin's waterproof, put her looking-glass in the pocket, and ran downstairs, out of the cottage, across the courtyard and up the stair. Jostling and pushing, she forced her way up to the drawing-room floor, paying no attention to the angry looks and mutterings of the paying visitors, who thought she was only one of themselves. In the drawing-room doorway she catapulted into Kate Jenkins, who was emerging with her first party of sightseers in tow.

'Steady on,' said Kate, and put her hands on Elizabeth's shoulders. Elizabeth did not know who this woman was; she never remembered having seen her before in her life, but for some reason her touch calmed her. She looked up into her clear eyes, and said, in her stilted, eighteenth-century voice, 'I beg your pardon. I did not mean to hurt you.'

'You didn't hurt me,' said Kate. She looked at Elizabeth as if she knew her, and said, 'Why don't you come round with me, if you've nothing else to do?'

Elizabeth did not know why she should, but she had nothing else to do, so she fell in at the stranger's heels, and followed her as one would follow a tiny lantern on a pitch dark road. They went downstairs, and into the dining-room.

If she had been herself, Elizabeth might have got a lot of amusement out of Kate's guided tour. It was not that there was anything about it which an outsider would have found funny — on the contrary, it was, as one would have expected, extremely competent. But to someone who lived with the untidy, unbuttoned everyday Kate, much would have been entertaining in a private sort of way. For Kate had lost her customary air of being put together more by accident than design, and looked instead as if she had been put together by Gerry, which was the truth. Her grey flannel dress was pressed and properly buttoned. There were no holes in her stockings. Her hair was secured with purposeful hairpins, and with her gold-rimmed spectacles set firmly on her long nose, she looked like a rather snooty headmistress in charge of a party of badly behaved schoolchildren with whom she was only associating under protest. Not that the party was really badly behaved. Obviously it was far too much in awe of Kate to do anything out of order; ice creams, dogs, lollipops and umbrellas had all been discarded without a murmur, and when Kate was speaking they stood around her in respectful silence. It was not so with Gerry, who lacked the power to intimidate, and later reported having had a terrible time with a child who had put an ice cream down another child's Wellington boot, and two eager American ladies who kept referring loudly to 'this dear little English castle', much to the indignation of the many Scots in the party. She had thought, she said, that a fight might break out any minute. It was not like that in Kate's group; recognising authority, her sightseers behaved in a subdued but exemplary fashion. Elizabeth Martin might have noticed too, for she had noticed it before, a certain reluctance in Kate's manner of speaking, something beyond the natural shyness and dislike of crowds which were making this task agony for her. She gave her explanations and descriptions fluently, but in a remote, cold voice which suggested that discussion or questioning would be unwelcome. But of course Elizabeth Melville did not notice any of these things. She followed Kate in frightened bewilderment, wondering whatever had happened to the house, for the people thronging it were only one of the puzzles that beset her.

'This,' the strange woman was saying, 'was originally the Great Hall of the castle, which was built as a fortified tower around the year 1560. At that period it had stone walls, a vaulted roof, and presumably arrow-slits rather than the present windows which were cut in the last quarter of the seventeenth century. The walls were panelled in 1760, and the present ceiling dates from 1800. The room has been in continuous use since the sixteenth century, first as an assembly and living-room, then as a ballroom, and since the middle of the last century as a dining-room. The furniture is mainly Victorian. . . .' Elizabeth gazed about her in astonishment. She was in the Great Hall. There was the fireplace, the door into the pantry, the firescreen with its fleur-de-lys and the Melville coat of arms which Grandmamma had embroidered. There was the portrait of great grandfather Melville, and there was Papa. But where had all these other portraits come from? And what had happened to the ceiling? Her puzzled eye travelled round the walls, and came to rest on the picture above the fireplace, the one painted last summer when Robin had been home from Harrow, and Papa had been home from Versailles, and they had all been so happy. She veered towards it, drawn by its familiarity, by the happy associations it held for her. She and Lucy had had new dresses for the portrait. She and Lucy . . . Elizabeth stared up at the portrait in terror, her ears buzzing, her knees turning to water where she stood. For she saw that she had disappeared; where she had sat among the sweet grass by the Wishwater, with a posy of gowans in her hands, only the broom and the grass grew now. They had rubbed her out, as if she had no right to be there. Too grief-stricken to cry aloud, she turned away with a silent sob, and stumbled after the woman who had said, 'Come round with me.'

They went downstairs again, down the long cold passage which ran from the back to the front of the house, and into the Library, a room Elizabeth Melville knew well, because she was always stealing down to borrow books from its well-stocked shelves. Elizabeth Martin would not have known it at all; it was kept locked, and although Kate had a key, she had never taken Elizabeth into it. Elizabeth looked around her in some relief. Everything here was as it should be, surely. She tried to listen to what the strange woman was saying, although the extreme Englishness of her accent was so unfamiliar that she found it difficult to follow every word.

'The Library contains many books of great historical and antiquarian importance, as well as some of the best furniture in the house. I would draw your attention to these chairs by Hepplewhite. The escritoires are by Sheraton, and if you would care to look at these Meissen figurines on the chimney-piece. . . .'

The intruders moved towards the fireplace with polite murmurs of appreciation, but Elizabeth, who had seen the Meissen figurines a hundred times, and did not care for them anyway, since one of them was the image of her Mamma, moved towards the shelves at the other side of the room, and began to run her eye lovingly along the familiar, gilded, calf-bound spines. While the others pried impertinently, the strange woman came up beside her.

'You haven't been in here before, have you?' she asked

casually. 'They keep it locked, because most of this stuff is priceless. But if you'd like to have a proper look, I'll bring you over before we leave.'

Elizabeth had no idea at all how she should reply to this extraordinary offer, and perhaps fortunately she did not have to, because just at that moment a stout young woman in a pink anorak and a tartan hat approached them.

'Excuse me, Miss — ?'

'Jenkins,' said the stranger.

'Miss Jenkins. I've been looking at two rather beautiful pieces of embroidery on the wall by the window. I was wondering if you could tell me anything about them?'

The stranger left Elizabeth, and with slow, hesitant steps crossed the room to the window. Elizabeth followed, because she could not help it. Hanging on the wall, behind glass and surrounded by narrow gilt frames, were two samplers. A glance confirmed that they were hers and Lucy's. Only of course they could not be. Lucy's was finished, and laid away in the press, waiting to be stretched and framed after the New Year, but hers. . . . Hers was lying on her creepie beside the nursery fire, the needle still threaded, stuck through the cloth, at the letter 'o' of the word 'prophain'. The word was still unfinished. She looked at the samplers, and knew she was going mad. But what was the woman called Miss Jenkins saying?

'These were the samplers of the two little daughters of Sir Giles Melville, who was Laird of Robinsheugh from 1755 till 1797. They are rather remarkable work for children of twelve and eleven, I think. You can see that the top one is dated 1779 — ' That was Lucy's ' — and the other, although undated, is in fact known to date from the same year.'

Elizabeth watched the young woman who had asked the question put her nose close to the sampler, and heard her say, 'No, it isn't dated, is it? Why, it isn't finished either. Look, the needle is still sticking into the material. Why was that?'

She turned her inquisitive, thrusting face towards Miss Jenkins, but Miss Jenkins was not looking at her. She was looking at the sampler, and Elizabeth, who was looking at her with a scream of terror frozen just inside her lips, saw that her face was for a second contorted as if by intense pain. Then she turned on her questioner, and in a tight, reluctant voice which cursed her for an intrusion on a private and terrible grief, she said, 'It is unfinished, because the child Elizabeth died before she had time

156

to complete it.'

Then Elizabeth did scream. It was the last sound she heard, high and piercing, as the walls fell, the floor came up to meet her, and she reeled into Kate's arms in a dead faint.

18

Darkness at the Shut of Day

When Elizabeth came round, she was lying on her own camp bed in her little square room in the cottage, and Kate, her face haggard with anxiety, was sitting on the edge of the bed, rubbing Elizabeth's hands ineffectually between her own. Elizabeth knew at once that it was Kate, she knew that she was lying on her camp bed, she knew, then and every day for the rest of her life, that she was Elizabeth Martin and nobody else. She also knew that she had just had some terrible experience, but she could not for the life of her remember what it was. She tried to sit up, felt dizzy, and was glad when Kate gently pushed her down again.

'What happened?' she asked weakly.

'You fainted,' said Kate. 'It's all right. Lie still.'

'Where was I?'

'In the Library. Don't you remember? It was stuffy — maybe.'

Kate knew it had not been stuffy. It had been cold, all afternoon it had been so cold she thought she would never be warm again.

Elizabeth withdrew her hands from Kate's awkward clasp, and closed her eyes over Kate's perplexed, unhappy face. She wished she would go away and leave her alone.

'I'm all right now,' she said.

'Yes.'

Kate got up, and went over to the window. Elizabeth watched her under the flickering lashes of her right eye. She looked at something outside for a moment, then she turned back hesitantly.

'Elizabeth, I'll really have to go,' she said. 'That queue will be at Berwick-on-Tweed if I don't. Mrs Lindsay is going to bring you over a cup of tea, and Gerry and I will be back as soon as we can. You should try to sleep for a while — you're probably overtired.'

After wanting her to go, Elizabeth felt aggrieved when she did. It was just like her to abandon a person who had just had a nasty fainting fit, and was still feeling very groggy. And what was this queue she was talking about? And what was all this nonsense about a Library? She had not been in any library. Where she had been was much more difficult to say with certainty. In fact there seemed to be a lot of gaps in her memory which at present she felt too tired and woolly to fill. She drank the tea which Mrs Lindsay brought, along with much sympathy and good advice, none of which Elizabeth wanted, but when Mrs Lindsay had eventually lumbered away with the empty cup, she found that she was glad enough to lie down again, because of the airy, uncomfortable feeling in her head. She tried to think why there was so much unaccustomed noise outside her window, people talking, and the sound of many feet. She ought to know, but just at that moment she couldn't quite recall. . . . She would lie quietly for a while, she decided, and perhaps she would even do as Kate and Mrs Lindsay suggested, and have a little sleep. . . .

So Elizabeth closed her eyes, and through that light, uneasy afternoon sleep that is almost a kind of waking, she remembered the looking-glass, and the nursery, and Grizel Elliot, and Robin, and she remembered that she had been Elizabeth Melville. But it was a selective remembering, and the most important thing she could not remember at all. And through a mist that swirled thickly before her leaden eyes, Robin Melville came to her, and stood in his blue coat with silver buttons, and his white silk shirt open at the throat, and he was smiling, and holding out his hand. For a moment, Elizabeth Martin could not think what it was he wanted. She stared blankly, but he went on smiling, and holding out his hand, until she realised — he wanted her. He wanted her, and as she looked into his pleasant boyish face, with its merry brown eyes, she knew that she wanted him too. Nothing had changed. All the old aching longing for his company that she had shared with Elizabeth Melville came back to her alone, and she would have put out her hand to him then, and gone with him wherever he would have taken her . . . but something was holding her back. There was some reason why she should not go, could not go, if only she could recall what it was. But as she lingered, trying to remember, Robin laughed, and shook his head at her; the mist curled up around him, and gently he was blown away, still smiling, out of her sight. Elizabeth woke with a start, and felt under her pillow for the looking-glass.

But even as she did so, she knew it was not there. It was in the pocket of her waterproof, and she could see her waterproof hanging on the back of the door. And although she was so sure that that was where it was, there were fingers of panic clawing at her throat as she got out of bed, and went to fetch it, because if by any chance that glass should be lost, or stolen, or broken, how could she ever get back to Robin? But it was there, and she could breathe again. She took the glass back to her bed, and scrambled in, pushing it under her pillow. She might be Elizabeth Martin, but she had Robin's glass and she had his ring.

She raised her hand in front of her face, expecting to see the ring gleaming there as usual, below a knuckle that had returned to its normal size since she had stopped trying to pull the ring off. For a moment, she thought she had lost it, but then she noticed a very peculiar thing. Although she could still feel the ring on her finger, could twist it round and round, and run her nail along the engraved words which ran round it, she could not see it at all. Just as before it had been invisible to Gerry and Kate, now it was invisible to her too. It was strange, in an unpleasant way, and disturbed Elizabeth extremely. But as she thought about it, it occurred to her that perhaps it was not so strange as it at first appeared. Robin had not given the ring to Elizabeth Martin, he had given it to Elizabeth Melville. While she had been Elizabeth Melville, she had been able to see the ring. Now that she was wholly herself again, she could not. That was logical enough, if you could say that anything was logical in such a peculiar business. But why then, if she were not Elizabeth Melville any more, should she still be able to feel the ring on her finger? Surely the touch of it should be gone too. And what was it the engraving said? QUHAIR THIS I GIVE, I WISS TO LIVE. And what did it mean? Elizabeth had never given much thought to its meaning, but now, as she lay on her back and stared up at the whitewashed ceiling, it began to come to her what it might mean, and she did not like what it might mean at all. So she put the idea away from her, telling herself it was nonsense. How could anyone live in someone else? It was impossible. But of course it was not impossible. Elizabeth Melville had lived in her. Or had she lived in Elizabeth Melville? But anyway, she hastened to add, it was different with Robin. Robin had never in any way shared her identity, he had never, as his sister had, been inside Elizabeth's skin. Nonetheless, she began to realise that the casting off of Elizabeth Melville had not really simplified things for her as much as she had at first thought. One of the things which made her uneasy was that she could not remember what it was that had sundered them, only that it had been something sudden, something so violent that she had thrown off Elizabeth Melville for ever in the time it takes to scream. But she had not thrown off Robin.

After a while, the noises in the yard died away. Somewhere in the distance engines were revving up, car doors banging. Then the old, familiar silence, broken only by the musical running of the Wishwater and the rustling and dripping of wet autumn leaves. Presently Kate and Gerry came running across the cobbles in the rain. Through her open window, Elizabeth could hear Gerry's high giggle as she regaled Kate with one of her stories; it was cut off abruptly as they entered the house and closed the kitchen door. One of them came straight upstairs, but Elizabeth did not know which, because she pretended to be asleep. She heard her door being opened, and softly closed again, footsteps retreated downstairs, and no more was heard for a long time. Elizabeth lay very still in the gathering twilight, and wondered what it was she could not remember, and how long it would be before Robin pulled her, willing or unwilling through the glass. And what would happen then. She had not thought of it in this way before; she had always thought that she went because she wanted Robin. It was a new and serious thought that she might have to go because Robin wanted her, because it was his part to command, and hers to obey. But one way or another, it made no difference, because for good or ill, the only thing she had left in common with Elizabeth Melville was that she could not live without Robin. Deep down, fear stirred in Elizabeth.

Gerry brought her supper on a tray.

'Well, well,' she said, switching on the light and dumping the tray across Elizabeth's knees, 'I hear you added your own spice of drama to the afternoon's proceedings. How do you feel now?'

'Better,' said Elizabeth.

'Good. Sing out if you want anything else,' replied Gerry briefly, and departed.

Elizabeth ate her ham salad and yoghurt and thought about Robin. When she was almost finished, Kate arrived, and sat down on the stool beside her. They looked at each other with reserve.

'How are you feeling now?' Kate asked.

'All right,' said Elizabeth.

'I'm glad,' said Kate. She ran her fingers through her hair, which was now reverting to its usual state of chaos, took a breath which Elizabeth could hear, and said, 'Elizabeth — I don't want to pry into your private affairs, but, what happened this afternoon — well, it was strange, to say the least of it. If there is something worrying you, as I feel sure now there is — obviously the last thing I'd do is to try to force your confidence, but if you should want to talk about it — I would try to understand.'

Elizabeth listened to this apologetic, hesitant speech, and looked at Kate's embarrassed face with mounting exasperation. It was exactly what she would have expected.

'Of course, if you'd rather not, that's up to you. But if it's anything you can tell — '

She caught Elizabeth's eye, and broke off in mid-sentence.

What Elizabeth most needed at this moment was someone like her mother, robust, sensible and unimaginative, who would bully her into telling her story, say she had never heard such a pack of nonsense in her life, and make her put the looking-glass in the dust-bin. Instead she had Kate, delicate, thoughtful and withdrawn, who believed in things like minding one's own business, and respecting other people's right to privacy. Which might be all very well in a general kind of way, but was no use at all to Elizabeth now. It was like knowing that you were drowning, while the only person on the beach stood by the water's edge with her clothes on, diffidently enquiring whether you would like her to go and look for a lifebelt or not. Elizabeth stared at Kate's troubled, unhelpful face, and once again, panic made her cruel.

'I can't tell you,' she said, 'and I wouldn't if I could. You'd never understand. You couldn't. And if you really want to know what I want, I want you to go away and leave me alone.'

A slight flush ran up Kate's thin cheek, and Elizabeth saw her hands tremble. But when she spoke, it was very gently.

'All right, Elizabeth,' she said, getting up, 'if that's what you want. I'm sorry I asked you. Nonetheless — ' her voice took a firmer tone ' — I am not quite as stupid as you appear to think, and I may as well tell you now that I have decided to take you away from here as soon as it can be arranged. Obviously there is something in the air that doesn't suit you. It will take me a few days to get my work in order, and my books crated, but you must be packed up and ready to leave first thing on Thursday morning. You will have to stay with me in Oxford till your parents come home.' She looked Elizabeth straight in the eyes, and added, 'Until then, I think you had better stay in the cottage, and not go over to Robinsheugh again. I don't want you to have any more nightmares if it can be avoided. I hope you understand me, Elizabeth.'

With which she picked up Elizabeth's tray and went away, leaving her, as she had requested, alone.

Everything happened very quickly after that, as it always did after a dispute with Kate. It was as if there was only one way of forgetting each new betrayal, of shutting out the hurt look in those eyes that were like a reflection of her own. She would go to Robin, whose brown eyes were always laughing, who never burdened her with solemn, unhappy things. Since she had stopped thinking with Elizabeth Melville's mind, this was all she could remember about him, but it was enough. She wanted him, and whatever it was that she had forgotten, but which since afternoon had been calling out a warning, no longer seemed of any account. She got up, got out of her crumpled clothes and into her nightdress, and went to clean her teeth. Then she got back into bed, and raising the silver looking-glass in front of her eyes, she went with hope to find her one desire.

Grizel was sitting by the fire as usual, when Elizabeth walked into the nursery in her nightgown, mending Lucy's petticoat by the light of the cruisie lamp. It was dark outside. Lucy and James were playing with James's building bricks on the floor by the table, and Alexander was whimpering sleepily in the depths of his cradle. It was all as it had always been, but there was a difference. Elizabeth was no longer Elizabeth Melville. She had no idea how long she had been away, and it was so long since she had been in the nursery without the aid of Elizabeth Melville's mind and memory that for a moment she felt afraid, and would have gone back if she could. As it was, she looked at Grizel and the other children with uncertainty, thinking that surely they were bound to notice the difference in her. But James and Lucy went on building their castle, and Grizel, looking up at her with even more than her usual fondness, beckoned her to come over to the fire.

'You must not run around on bare feet when you are not well,' she said. 'Come here, now, and sit by me.'

Elizabeth crossed the floor and sat down at Grizel's feet, leaning her back against her knee. Without looking at her, Grizel put down a cool hand, and laid it against Elizabeth's forehead, saying, 'Does your head still ache, my love?'

Elizabeth remembered vaguely that Elizabeth Melville, like Kate Jenkins, suffered from headaches. She was just opening her mouth to say, 'No', when she realised that she did seem to have a headache. This was puzzling, because now that she was fully Elizabeth Martin again, why should she have Elizabeth

Melville's headache? And why should Robin's ring once more be clearly visible on her finger? She heard Grizel repeat her question.

'I don't know,' she said.

'You are fevered, still,' said Grizel, with an edge of anxiety to her voice. 'You must go back to bed.'

'Not yet,' said Elizabeth. She was thinking about Robin, who might come at any moment. 'I like to sit here beside you.'

'Not for long, then.'

'No.'

It was true that she felt uncomfortably hot.

Elizabeth gazed into the rose-red heart of the fire, and wondered where Robin was, and whether she dared to ask. Elizabeth Melville would have known of course, but without Elizabeth Melville she had become again a stranger child, groping lonely through a hidden land. She looked at little James, with his wide brown eyes and curling golden hair, and she felt a pang of sorrow that after all he was not her little brother; she had no little brother, or sister of her own. But she had Robin, surely, although he was not her brother either, she had Robin as her friend. She tried to recall when Elizabeth Melville had seen Robin last, but that did not work at all. She had some hazy idea that he had gone off somewhere, perhaps to Edinburgh, but she could not remember why or when. Of course he might still be there, might not return for days. On the other hand, he might just as well have returned in her absence, and be in the house now. At any moment, the door might open. . . . She would simply have to wait, and trust him to come, as she always did in the end to Elizabeth Melville. But where was Elizabeth Melville? She leaned her head against Grizel's knee, and tried to wrestle again with that old problem; she was occupying Elizabeth Melville's place, so where was Elizabeth Melville? But she was too tired to work out any more answers to such difficult questions. The heat of the fire was feeding the heat that burned inside her, her mouth was dry, her throat parched.

'Water,' she muttered.

She felt Grizel's hands lifting her gently aside, propping her against the front of the chair. Through half-shut eyes, she watched her take a cup from the table, and go over to the ewer for water. Carefully she carried it back, and kneeling down on the floor beside her, prepared to hold it to her lips. Then, 'Christ Jesus, have pity!' she whispered, starting up in horror, so that the water spilled, and Elizabeth, startled into wakefulness by the anguish in her voice, gazed up at her in fear. The beautiful colour was gone from Grizel's cheeks, leaving them ashen, and her soft brown eyes were wide open, full of dread and a terrible compassion which Elizabeth knew was for her.

'Elizabeth! Oh, Elizabeth!'

James and Lucy had dropped their bricks, and were staring at their sister in frightened silence.

'What is it, Grizel?' whispered Elizabeth.

Grizel did not answer, but she went on staring at Elizabeth's face until Elizabeth could bear it no longer. With trembling hands, knowing that at last she was about to see the truth, slowly she lifted her looking-glass from her lap, and looked at the clear, unmistakable reflection which at last it chose to reveal. A small, pale, pointed face looked back at her, a face with a turned-up nose, a wide, curly mouth like Robin's, and brown Melville eyes. It was a plain face, a clever face, Elizabeth Melville's face, and as Elizabeth Martin stared at it for the first and last time, in one awesome, haunted moment everything hidden was made plain. This was why no one in the Melville house ever thought to question her identity. This was why the question of where Elizabeth Melville went while Elizabeth Martin occupied her place was one that needed no answer, the reason why she was never missed out of her place by Grizel and the other children. This was why, although she knew perfectly well that she was really Elizabeth Martin, she felt the fever and the headache that afflicted Elizabeth Melville's body. She was a prisoner in somebody else's body, her mind was trapped behind a stranger's unfamiliar face, a face with six red spots across its forehead. And she remembered the fate of the stranger. She knew what it was she had forgotten, the reason why she should not have come back. Two samplers hung on the Library wall, and one was unfinished. Elizabeth Melville had died before she had finished her sampler. Elizabeth Melville. . . .

'No,' she said thickly to Elizabeth Melville's face. 'No. I won't die.'

Her words seemed to jolt Grizel into action.

'Of course you will not die,' she said. 'Who talks of dying?'

Reaching behind her, she snatched up a blanket, wrapped Elizabeth up in it, and lifting her as if she were quite weightless, carried her to her bed.

'Lie you there, now, and keep warm.'

Then she turned to Lucy.

'Lucy, go up to Master Robin's room, and tell him to get down here this minute. Then you are to take James, and go down to Jeanie Rigg, and tell her that Tam must ride to Edinburgh, to her Ladyship, this very night.'

'Mamma will not come,' said Lucy coldly. 'She fears the pox as she fears death itself. Grizel, will I — ?'

'Do as I say, will you?' cried Grizel, shouting at Lucy for the first time in her life. 'Take James, and do as you are told!'

Lucy turned tail and fled, and Elizabeth never saw her again. She lay on her back, her eyes closed, and struggled with terror and pain beyond bearing.

She never knew how long she lay there, tormented by a fire that seared her whole body, but centred most cruelly in her head, but perhaps days passed, because sometimes it seemed light, at other times she could see the cruisie lamps hanging their feeble lights against the shadow that was the wall, and the flickering of the firelight on the roof. At first she could not lie still; her fear was like a great bird imprisoned in her chest, beating frantic wings, trying to break free. She tossed and thrashed about piteously, trying to climb out of bed so that she could escape, but firm hands held her down, and she could hear someone moaning for a long time before she realised that it was herself. Later she was too weak to move at all. Water poured ceaselessly through her skin, soaking her nightgown and her tangled hair, running like acid into her open mouth. Breathing heavily, she huddled wearily on the pillow, floating in and out of consciousness as the seconds of someone else's life remorselessly trickled away.

Faces swam above her, Grizel's, Robin's, Mr Cockburn's, an unknown face that must be the doctor's, faces with smiling mouths and frantic eyes, coming like reflections in still pools that disintegrate suddenly at the dropping of a stone. She knew that Robin never left her. In his shirt and breeches, with tousled hair, he sat by the bed, his young face haggard with grief and fear; it was he who lifted her up so that Grizel could pour water down her dry, aching throat, it was he who constantly wiped her brow with a cool wet cloth, and promised her, over and over, in a voice saying a prayer, that she would be better soon.

She tried to tell him, in her cracked, whispering voice —
'Robin, it's all a mistake. I'm not Elizabeth Melville — I'm not who you think. Please, Robin — I want my mother.'

Hopelessly, she watched his blank, uncomprehending eyes.

'Want your *mother*, Elizabeth?'

'Yes, yes.'

Then she heard Grizel's voice, whispering, 'Pay no heed, Master Robin. Of course she does not want her mother. 'Tis the delirium — the child does not know what she says.'

'I do, I do,' whimpered Elizabeth, but after a while she knew it was no use, and not long after that she found that she could not speak at all. And there was mercy in the end. For with her power to speak went her power to think; whoever she was, she was too ill to know, to care what would become of her. She woke, and she slept, a little life, a little death.

Another night came. Elizabeth, who had been asleep, surfaced to a dim awareness, her first for a long time. She knew that there was a stir in the room, more shadows looming on the wall, voices murmuring by the door. Grizel's face floated into the wavering pool of her vision, and mistily she recognised it as the face of someone she loved. Very far away, she heard her voice, 'Elizabeth, my dearie, your Papa is come.'

The largest of the shadows moved; a man whom Elizabeth had never seen in her life before, but whose face she had looked at so often that it was as familiar to her as her own father's, crossed the floor on tiptoe, and sat down on the side of her bed. He smiled down at her, touching her cheek and her hair. Then she was lifted into his arms, her hot face pressed to the coolness of his linen shirt, she took one long, deep, final breeath, and darkness came down upon her.

19

The Glass Breaks

Never in all her life again would the moment of waking come as sweetly to Elizabeth as it did on the morning after that last, fearful night in the Melville nursery. For fully five minutes she lay in her sleeping-bag, with her eyes closed, listening to the delicious, happy sounds of river and trees, birds calling, dogs barking, doors banging, the milkman whistling, the sound of her own normal, healthy breathing, and thinking of nothing at all. She was alive, she had escaped. Elizabeth Martin had not died, trapped like a hunted animal in a body not her own, her soul had broken free, and returned to its proper habitation. Or had it? The face of Elizabeth Melville rose before her, and at that memory, a sudden terror chilled her; her happiness faded.

Her first thought was to pull out the looking-glass from under her pillow, to check — but in time a voice in her head cried a warning, and she dropped the cursed thing on the blanket as if it had been red-hot. Whatever happened, she was never going to look into that terrible glass again. Never. Yet she had to know. Shaking and swaying, like someone who is getting out of bed for the first time after a long illness, Elizabeth struggled from her room into the bathroom next door, where there was a mirror above the wash basin. For a long moment she stood, holding on to the edge of the basin, not knowing whether she was going to faint, or be sick. But slowly her head cleared, and doing perhaps the bravest thing she ever did in her life, she raised her face, and looked into the glass. Her own reflection, grey-eyed, pink-cheeked, straight-nosed, stared back at her, different in every way from the sallow, sickly, dark-eyed little face of Elizabeth Melville. Perhaps it was not as pink-cheeked as usual, and suddenly Elizabeth knew why; nausea returned like a wave breaking over her, and she was sick as she had never been in her life before, so much so that while it lasted she could think of nothing but the horror of it, and the disgust. It was not until she had staggered back to her room, and dropped trembling into her rickety armchair, that she even began to feel the first trickle of the relief which presently surged over her, relief, thankfulness, joy. I am safe, I am free, I have survived, I am myself. . . . She clasped her hands, the tip of her thumb brushed against the fourth finger of her right hand, her nail scraped something hard, and her joy was snuffed out. She was still wearing Elizabeth Melville's ring. She closed her eyes, and in darkness she heard Robin Melville's voice, as she had heard it before the last darkness closed upon her, 'I shall never let her die. She belongs to me.' And the words on the unseen ring, QUHAIR THIS I GIVE, I WISS TO LIVE. Like a black cloak, desolation came down and covered Elizabeth. Nothing had changed. She had not died. She was Elizabeth Martin. But she belonged to Robin Melville. When he wanted her, he would call her again.

The next three days were well-nigh unbearable. Kate and Gerry also seemed to be under a strain, although presumably not the same kind as Elizabeth's. To her, they paid almost no attention at all. It was as if each person in the house was living shut up in a private cell, where all communication with the others had been broken off. Kate was up at five o'clock every morning, working on her papers in the tower room till four in the afternoon; after that she worked in the kitchen, sorting papers and crating her precious books, reducing the apparent chaos of the Study End to a prim row of cardboard files. She was as meticulous over her work as she was careless over everything else; her papers were put in order with infinite patience and care, and packed in plastic folders, each clearly labelled with a description of its contents. The same loving attention was given to the books; each was individually wrapped and sellotaped into a protective sheath of cardboard before being put into the crate. She had all the appearance of a woman who was rapidly coming to the end of her tether, but Gerry, who watched her with serious, helpless eyes, knew quite well that this was how the work would have been done even if they had had advance warning that the world was to end the next day. She was very fond of Dr Jenkins, and she would have done anything she could to help her out of the private hell she was so obviously inhabiting, but she could not help thinking with longing of Peter, and her other friends at Oxford, and how nice it would be to return to a life where people were not strung up like guitar strings ready to snap at any moment. And she was glad that she was not going to become a scholar.

Meantime, she made work for herself to do. Dr Jenkins had dispensed with her help, no doubt feeling that help from Gerry was the last thing she could bear, so for want of anything else to keep her occupied, Gerry had undertaken to clean the whole cottage from top to bottom. Kate said that it was quite unnecessary, but Gerry said she preferred to have something to do, so Kate said she could please herself.

Elizabeth stumbled between them, supposedly helping, but in fact getting constantly in the way. She did not mean to be truculent and unco-operative, but that was how it seemed; everywhere she looked, she seemed to see Robin Melville, laughing at her, at the table, in the pantry, on the stair, in the yard. He was everywhere, and he was waiting. Stupefied by fear, she could not help being irritable when Gerry asked her to sweep the stair, and Kate told her to mend the covers of a pile of paperbacks. For what did it matter whether the stair was swept, or the books mended, when Robin Melville was waiting, and there was no escape? For Elizabeth was sure now that whether Kate took her away on Thursday morning or not could make no difference, for Robin had power to call her to his will from the ends of the world.

The atmosphere became electric, and perhaps all three of them knew that a storm of some sort was on the way. It was narrowly averted a number of times, usually by another of Kate's displays of superhuman patience. There was the time when Gerry, determined to be helpful when she had been asked not to be helpful, roped up three crates which had not been filled, tying knots which proved almost impossible to undo. There was the time when Elizabeth, glancing up at Robin, who was looking in at the window, sent a bottle of furniture polish which Gerry had been using spurting thickly over the pages of one of Kate's most valuable reference books. In a panic, she tried to rub it off, but only succeeded in spreading it over the cover as well. She thought that Kate was bound to be furious this time, because she cared more for books than she did for people, but Kate merely took the book out of her hands, went with it to the sink, wiped the pages, dried them at the fire, and wrapped up the ruined remains with the same care she lavished on all the rest. No one spoke much after that.

Wednesday came. Elizabeth spent most of the day in her room, packing her trunk and suitcase. The suitcase was to go with her in the car; the trunk, along with the crates of books and papers, was to be left for the carrier, who would come on Friday. Elizabeth put her clothes and other belongings into the trunk with less care than Kate gave to her books. For what did it matter, when Robin Melville was waiting, and in all probability she would never see her home or her family again? It was then that for the first time she cried, tears of loneliness and fear, and she wondered if even now she should go down and tell Kate all about it. But it was too late. Kate would never believe her, and she knew herself that as she told it it would sound a story beyond belief. And in any case, it would make no difference; no one could save her, least of all a poor creature like Kate. So she cried, and despair tore at her heart. She did not go downstairs until Gerry called her to supper at half past six. Kate had said they were all to have an early night, because she wanted to be on the way at seven o'clock tomorrow morning. Gerry had been to Kelso that afternoon to have the car checked and filled up with petrol, and except for a few last-minute bits of packing, nothing remained to be done. Kate was not in the kitchen when Elizabeth went down; Gerry said she had gone to pay the milk bill at the Fergus's cottage, and say goodbye to the Lindsays.

'It's a wonder she remembered to pay the milk bill,' remarked Elizabeth offensively, as she slid into her place at the table. Gerry, who was standing by the fire ladling soup, dropped her ladle, and turned round, her dark face suddenly angry.

'Listen, you little beast,' she said. 'We have one more night here, one night for her to keep her temper and not give you the beating you deserve. So just try to hold your tongue, if that's possible, and stop trying to provoke her. She has the most atrocious headache, and she must have a breaking point somewhere, for pity's sake. I know what I'd do to you if you were my niece.'

If Elizabeth had not been so furious, she would have laughed. She was supposed to feel sorry for Kate Jenkins because she had a headache. She was just opening her mouth to give Gerry a piece of her mind when the door opened, and Kate came in, with an expression on her face which made Elizabeth shut it again in a hurry. Kate lifted her book, put on her glasses, and sat down; Gerry and Elizabeth ate in silence, looking at their plates. The only sounds in the room were the ticking of the kitchen clock and the discreet clatter of knives and forks. Gerry removed Kate's soup, and substituted a plate of meat and vegetables, which Kate did not eat either. She sat with her book open in front of her, pushing her food slowly round her plate with her fork, saying nothing. Elizabeth sneezed, and Gerry jumped, as if a shot had been fired. Then silence again.

The kettle boiled over. Grateful for the opportunity to act, Gerry leapt up and made a dive towards it, lifting the coffee pot in passing.

'Elizabeth,' she said, 'gather up these plates for me, will you, and bring the coffee cups from the dresser — oh, and the cream jug is probably empty.'

It was said pleasantly, but Elizabeth was still furious with Gerry, who had said she was a little beast, and she was afraid to move from the table, because Robin Melville was standing by the dresser, watching her. . . . Yet even so, what she replied was so terrible that as it came out of her mouth, she could hardly believe that she was saying it.

'Do it yourself,' she said. 'It's what you're paid for, isn't it?'

The words dropped one by one into silence, but like all words, once they were out they could never be taken back again. Gerry went scarlet, but Elizabeth was not looking at Gerry. In frightened fascination she was staring at Kate, and in her mind a small, detached voice said three words, 'Here it comes.' For Kate had dropped her book, and now she was rising from her chair, and she was shaking with rage. Elizabeth watched her burning eyes, and the dark stain of colour running up her face, and the triumph she would once have felt at this moment was quenched in a ripple of terror. She was going to get the beating she deserved. But she need not have been afraid. Even now, Kate controlled herself. She put her trembling hands flat on the table, and a terrible stillness followed her wrath.

'I think,' she said, in a tight, expressionless voice, 'that we have had just as much of your rudeness and unpleasantness as we are going to take. You make me ashamed. There is a limit, Elizabeth, and this is it. You will apologise to Gerry at once. At once, do you hear?'

'Please, Dr Jenkins,' muttered poor Gerry, in an agony of embarrassment. 'It doesn't matter.'

'It matters to me. I am waiting, Elizabeth.'

Then Elizabeth lost her head completely.

'I won't apologise,' she shouted. 'I'm not sorry, and I won't. It's you who are unpleasant and rude to me, so why should I be the one to say I'm sorry? Gerry was horrid to me when I came down to supper, and as for you — ' she turned wildly on Kate, her eyes flaming with an anger that was mostly desperation, 'I know you don't love me any more, but please, why is it you can never look at me as if you know who I am?'

It was a terrible moment. Kate shrank back in her chair as if Elizabeth had struck her. The colour drained out of her face, leaving it paler then ever. But when she spoke, it was obvious that her anger, like her strength, was spent.

'All right, Elizabeth,' she said. 'You had better go up to bed now. You can apologise to Gerry in the morning. I'm sure when you have had time to think about it, you'll see that whatever your opinion of me may be, none of this is any fault of hers.'

It was said firmly, and finally, and there was nothing more to say. Elizabeth left the kitchen, and went upstairs to her room. Before she closed the door behind her, she knew what was going to happen. Already she could hear Robin calling, and it was a call she had no power to disobey.

Elizabeth felt oddly calm. It was as if, after all she had been through in the last few days, it was almost a relief that things were now moving to an inevitable end. And Elizabeth was certain that the end was inevitable. Once she had loved Robin Melville, and she had gone to him because to be with him was the loveliest thing she knew. Now she was afraid of him, afraid of his power over her, and yet, as she sat on her bed with her silver looking-glass in her hands, she realised that it is not impossible to love and fear at the same time. Robin was calling her, and underneath all her fear and sadness at the certainty that she was leaving behind her for ever the life that she had always known, she could recognise shreds of the old longing for the merry, affectionate boy, which had first pulled her through the glass to find an adventure beyond all mortal comprehension. Had it not been for the stirring of that old love, perhaps even yet she might have resisted the call, have sent Robin back to the shadowy land which had seemed to her more bright than the light of day. Too late for that, she knew.

She did not know how long she sat there, listening to the wind talking among the dry autumn leaves, and the river running that she would never hear again. Gerry came upstairs, and went into her room, and much later Kate came up too. She thought that Kate hesitated for a moment outside her door, as if she were wondering whether she should come in. But if she did, she decided not to, but went into her own room, and closed the door. At last, in a thrall so deep that she scarcely thought of what she was doing, Elizabeth looked down into the glass. Time passed before she realised that although her face gazed back at her entranced, nothing else had happened at all. This time, she did not even wonder if she had been reprieved. She waited, and presently her mind started to function again. At least, she would have called it her mind, but there was something about her thoughts which corresponded to the glazed, abnormal look of the eyes that stared up from the glass. The voice she had heard before, that was not quite her own, gave the explanation inside her head.

'This is Elizabeth Melville's glass. Elizabeth Melville is dead. You cannot go again to be Elizabeth Melville, only to be yourself. So if this way is closed, you must find another.' And without being told, she knew what that way was.

So Elizabeth put the glass in her pocket, as she always did, took off her shoes, and slipped like a ghost through the darkened cottage. She shut the kitchen door quietly behind her, and sat down on the doorstep to put on her shoes again. Then stepping out into the moon-whitened courtyard, she set out for Robinsheugh.

Slowly and bitterly, as if a great weight were pushing her down into a desired oblivion, Kate Jenkins awoke to the sound of the kitchen clock striking twelve. She counted the strokes reluctantly, automatically, knowing as she struggled to open her weighted eyelids that something was wrong. It took the whole striking minute for her mind to register what it was; it was midnight, yet her room was full of light. The light had wakened her. No moon ever shone so brightly, Kate knew, and with her heart vaulting into her throat, she got out of bed, and moved quickly over to the window. Across the yard, the house of Robinsheugh stood in a blaze of light. From every window it shone out, white and clear and still, like sunshine on smooth water, and it was this quality in it which wiped away Kate's first despairing conviction that the place was on fire, and left her with another, no less despairing in its way, that she was looking on something totally uncanny. She stared at it through a long moment of paralysis, then she heard her own voice say 'Elizabeth.' Feeling ran through her limbs again, and she moved.

First, she went through to Elizabeth's room. The light was on but the room was vacant. She went back to her own room, put on a skirt and jersey, and pushed her feet into her shoes. She felt fear, not so much for herself as for the child she knew she had neglected, but she too experienced something of Elizabeth's relief that things were moving towards an inevitable end. For

174

herself, it mattered less now what the end was, than that it should come. She went along to Gerry's room, switching on the light as she went in. Gerry came up out of a cosy nest in the middle of her enormous bed, looking more like a mouse than ever with her shiny eyes blinking in the unexpected light.

'I'm going over to the house,' said Kate. 'I think Elizabeth is there.' If I'm not back in fifteen minutes, you are to go for Mr Lindsay — you are on no account to come alone. Promise me you'll do this, Gerry.'

'Yes,' said Gerry, 'but — '

Kate had no time for buts. Following in Elizabeth's footsteps, she too went downstairs, through the darkened kitchen, and let herself out into the night. In the empty courtyard it was as clear as day, though with a light sharper and more intense than that of the brightest northern noon, and high overhead was the black roof of the sky. Calmly, Kate walked across the cobble-stones towards the house. A silver line down one side of the door at the bottom of the stair told her that it was open, and as she drew nearer she could see, at a window two floors above it, the silhouette of a man's body outlined against the brightness within.

Elizabeth had thought she would never get up the stairs. She felt as if her body was ten times heavier than usual, as if her feet were made of lead. She who had skipped up and down these steps as light as blown thistledown, now stumbled and tripped and fell against the wall; but Robin was waiting, and she must go on.

He was waiting for her on the landing outside the drawing-room, and for a split second, as she emerged through the archway at the head of the stair, she mistook him for his father. She had left a boy of sixteen, and found a man of — Elizabeth was too young to gauge ages accurately, but she was sure he was well past twenty. Very tall, and inclining to stoutness, he stood hunched in the doorway of the drawing-room, not in the least like his father, when one looked at him closely. There was a coarseness about his features, a dirty carelessness overlying the sumptuousness of his dress that repelled Elizabeth; there were stains on his yellow silk waistcoat, and an odd, sour smell came from his embroidered coat. He stood there, laughing at her, his lips curled in a sneer, and it was only then, when she was almost upon him, that it came to Elizabeth that of course this was what had always been wrong with Robin; Elizabeth Melville had known it too, without ever putting it into words. He was always laughing. Nothing solemn,

175

nothing sacred, but that irreverent mirth debased and diminished it. And how was it that she had never noticed before the shallow coldness in those eyes she had thought so merry? Then she knew — she should never have listened, she should never have come. . . .

In a terror of revulsion, she turned to flee, her only thought to get away from him, but as she did so, he put out his foot, and as she veered to the left to avoid contact with it, interposed himself between her and the top of the stair. Never a word was spoken, but Elizabeth knew she was in a trap. Automatically, she backed towards the window, and he came after her, his odour wafting ahead of him, sickening her. She knew she would rather leap from the window to her death than let him touch her, but the window was closed, and she would never have the time and the strength to open it. She opened her mouth to call for help, but she did not know who she would call for. She wanted to call for her father, but he was far away, everyone was far away. And so it was with a sense of surprise that suddenly she heard her own voice, shrill and piping and urgent on the air, 'Kate! Kate!'

Down in the courtyard, Kate heard it too. Half-way over, she began to run; in a dozen strides her long legs cleared the remainder of the cobbles, with flying feet she kicked open the door, and came up the stair like the wind. Elizabeth caught sight of her face as she came, and knew at last why it was that Kate never wasted her temper on little things. She was keeping it for something big. Ducking under Robin's arm, Elizabeth staggered towards her.

'Kate, help me!'

She felt Kate's hands on her shoulders, she was firmly set aside in the shelter of the drawing-room door, and Kate turned to face her persecutor across the floor.

Neither Kate nor Elizabeth could ever say clearly what happened after that. To Elizabeth, huddled shrinking in the doorway, afraid to look yet afraid not to look, it seemed that some terrible battle was raging, and it was none the less a battle because no word was spoken, nor because neither of the combatants touched the other. They were fighting with their eyes and their minds, each trying to wrest the victory by making the mind of the other surrender. They were fighting for Elizabeth, yet in some way she could not understand, Elizabeth knew they were fighting for themselves too. It was a battle of a kind Kate Jenkins was well equipped to fight with anyone, and i they had started equal, there would have been no doubt as to the victor. But Kate was handicapped; she was tired, worn out mentally and physically by the worst four months she had ever had to endure in her life, and Robin Melville was experienced as she was not in gaining power over human souls. Slowly, she began to retreat, knowing like Elizabeth that to touch him was the unthinkable thing, but it was Elizabeth who saw first what was happening. Robin was bearing down on her, pushing her backwards across the landing towards the top of the stair. While he held her mind with the power of his own, he was edging her body, step by faltering step, towards its destruction. And Elizabeth knew what she had to do.

Gripping the handle of the silver looking-glass tightly in her hand, she ran out from the shelter of the doorway. Just as Kate got to the top of the stair, she raised the glass in her fist like an axe, and brought it down with all the strength she could muster on the back of Robin's neck. There was some resistance, she thought, some substance between spirit and flesh stopped the blow; the sharp edge of the glass cut, but it did not cut through. A pain like electricity ran up her arm, her fingers splayed involuntarily, and the glass fell to the ground where, instead of breaking, it writhed and bubbled for a moment, as if it were subjected to some intense heat, before it ran itself away, like fugitive mercury, along the margin of the floor. At least that was how it seemed, but again Elizabeth was never sure, because in the same moment that Kate lost her footing, and fell backwards into the darkness, Robin too departed, and Elizabeth thought, in that last moment of nightmare, that the one who had been her love and her fear in two worlds looked at her once with the eyes of a boy of sixteen; then a rushing wind swept through the house, and in her last moment of consciousness she saw him lifted up and drawn away into the darkness, fading and folding and dispersing in a sigh, until he was no more. Then all the lights went out.

When Elizabeth came round, she was sitting in a shaft of moonlight, which was falling through the landing window, awkwardly propped against the wall. Kate was kneeling on the floor beside her, the colour of her face not entirely explained by the bleaching effect of the moon. She was trying to hold a cup of water to Elizabeth's lips, and for a moment Elizabeth could not understand why she was doing it so clumsily that most of the water seemed to be running down her chin.

'You're getting to make a habit of this,' remarked Kate, but despite the attempt at a jest, her voice seemed to Elizabeth as pallid as her face.

She struggled to sit up properly, and it was then that she saw the reason for Kate's clumsiness: she was using only her left hand. Her right arm dangled helplessly at her side, the hand sticking out from it at an angle all distorted and abnormal.

'Your arm, for heaven's sake,' cried Elizabeth.

'I suppose it's broken,' said Kate calmly. 'Don't worry — I don't seem to feel anything at all.'

But Elizabeth was already scrambling to her feet. She took the cup out of Kate's hand and laid it on the floor.

'Come on,' she said, 'I'm all right now. I've got to get you home.'

'Just what I was thinking about you,' said Kate.

Supporting each other, they made their way slowly down the narrow stair, and out into the clean, clear, frosty air of the autumn night, making their way with careful, shaky steps towards the rectangle of light that was the cottage door. There were voices, because more than fifteen minutes were past; Mr and Mrs Lindsay were both there, and Gerry, and Mrs Fergus, who had heard the commotion, and had come in her dressing-gown and curlers, and without her teeth, to see whatever was the matter. The arrival of Kate and Elizabeth was greeted with cries of consternation and alarm, but Elizabeth did not remember much more after that — only that it was Kate herself who, firmly setting aside all offers of help and relief, escorted her upstairs, supervised her undressing and getting into bed, brought her hot milk and an aspirin, and sat beside her until she fell asleep. She thought afterwards that it was very good of Kate, under the circumstances, but at the time, as she curled up under the blankets and felt Kate's hand against her hair, it seemed to her a perfectly natural thing for Kate to do.

20

Kate and Elizabeth

When Elizabeth awoke next morning, she could not at first understand why it was that her bedroom was flooded with sunlight, for the south-facing rooms of the cottage never received this amount of sun till the middle of the day. That it could be the middle of the day did not occur to her, and she seemed to have forgotten everything that had happened the night before. For a suspended, blank moment she could think of nothing, then a wild explosion of memory shattered her head.

'Kate,' she said.

But it was Gerry whose black head came round the door, followed by the rest of her, wearing a ridiculous frilly apron over her shabby denim trousers, and carrying a breakfast tray. She looked so blessedly common-place that Elizabeth thought her plain brown face the most beautiful sight she had ever seen.

'Breakfast, lunch,' said Gerry cheerfully. 'Call it what you will.'

Elizabeth sat up, battling with the covers to release herself.

'What time is it?' she asked.

'Twelve o'clock,' said Gerry, putting down the tray. 'Dr Jenkins said I was to let you sleep till twelve, then waken you, but I see you had wakened yourself.'

'Yes. Gerry, is Kate all right?'

'Well, it depends what you mean,' replied Gerry. 'Her arm is broken, and she is covered with bruises, which is what to expect if you fall downstairs in the middle of the night. However there doesn't seem to be any permanent damage. Mr Lindsay drove her to the hospital to have her arm attended to — she's back now, and — well, it's a funny thing. She's very tired, of course, but in an odd way she looks better than I've ever seen her.'

'May I see her?'

'Yes. She says you are to have your breakfast, then if you feel well enough to get up, she'd like to see you in her room.'

It rather surprised Elizabeth that Gerry did not ask her anything about what had happened last night, but it was a passing surprise, because she really had so many other things to think about. But as Gerry was leaving the room, she remembered that there was something she should say to her.

'Gerry — I'm sorry about what I said to you last night. You were quite right, I was a little beast.'

'The matter is forgotten,' Gerry assured her pleasantly. 'We're all little beasts from time to time.' But before she shut the door, she took a close look at Elizabeth, raised her eyebrows, and added, 'Funny thing — you look better than I've ever seen you, too. Well, well.'

And she went away, leaving Elizabeth to eat her breakfast and wonder how, after all that had happened, she could ever have the courage to face Kate. But she found that the courage came to her, perhaps because for the first time she was thinking more about Kate than she was about herself. She would go to Kate, she decided, and ask her to forgive her for being so nasty, and say she was sorry for all the pain and trouble she had caused her, and that she was going to be a nicer person in the future. Armed with this determination she got up and dressed, and found her way to Kate's door.

Although she had been at Robinsheugh for eleven weeks, Elizabeth had never been inside Kate's room, and when she opened the door what struck her was the tidiness of it, a tidiness not usually associated with rooms inhabited by Kate, and which for a moment confused her more than the usual jumble would have done. It was then she remembered that of course this was Thursday; everything was packed, and they should have been half-way to Oxford by now. She looked for Kate in the high, old-fashioned bed, but she was not there, and it was not until her voice said, 'Come here, Elizabeth,' that she located her in an armchair by the window, and set off across the floor towards her.

Kate was wearing her dressing-gown, and her hair was tumbling around her shoulders in even more than its usual disarray. Her right arm, in plaster, was resting in a sling, and there was a bruised, smudgy look around her eyes which made Elizabeth feel sad and guilty at the same time, for she knew that Kate had been looking like this all through the summer, and this was the first time she had allowed herself to care. Yesterday she would have started to make excuses for herself, but today she was past such dishonesty. So she did what she had come to do, and went and knelt on the floor beside Kate, and said she was sorry.

Kate did not immediately answer her. Instead she put out her free hand, and with her finger she raised Elizabeth's chin so that she could look right down into her eyes. For a moment Elizabeth was afraid to look back, because she knew now that eyes were the most important part of a person; they told you all you could ever know. And some people's eyes you ran away from, and for their eyes you would follow other people to the ends of the earth. But she knew too that this was one test she could not afford to fail, so she lifted her head, and returned the long, grave, silent look without flinching, and she knew that everything was going to be all right. At last Kate let her hand fall, and lay back suddenly in her chair, as if a great burden had been lifted away from her.

'It's all right, Elizabeth,' she said quietly. 'You don't have to worry any more. I know who you are.'

They were the sweetest words Elizabeth had ever heard. She allowed herself to put her hand on Kate's knee.

'Your arm,' she said. 'Does it hurt terribly?'

Kate was beginning to say that it didn't hurt at all, when she saw Elizabeth's face preparing to disbelieve her, and changed her mind.

'Put it this way,' she said. 'There are bearable pains, and unbearable pains. This is a very bearable pain.'

Elizabeth, more than anybody, knew exactly what she meant. She too had had her share of unbearable pains, and she could understand that the pain of a broken arm, however severe, was at least normal and understandable. She found herself sitting on the floor then, leaning against Kate's knee, with Kate's arm lightly round her shoulders. It was very pleasant. They sat in companionable silence for a few minutes, then Kate said, 'I'd like it if you would tell me the whole story, Elizabeth. Of course you don't have to if you'd rather not, but it would help me if you would.'

'Help you?'

'To understand my own experiences.'

Elizabeth turned her head, and looked up wonderingly into Kate's face.

'Did you see them too?' she asked in a whisper.

'No. At least, not until last night. I saw something then, though what it was I saw, I can scarcely begin to imagine. Before that, I heard voices, and footsteps, and music, sometimes, but mostly I just felt — that I wasn't alone.'

'You weren't,' Elizabeth assured her.

A first faint smile flickered across Kate's mouth.

'So it seems,' she agreed. 'Perhaps at your age, you can take such an experience in your stride, but at mine, and with my kind of training — well, one tends to draw an obvious, horrible conclusion.'

'You mean, that you were going mad?'

'Yes. It has been going on ever since I started coming here three years ago, but this summer — since you arrived, in fact — it has been getting worse by the hour. I had decided that I would have to consult a doctor when I got back to Oxford. It has all been very lonely and frightening.'

Elizabeth was silent for a moment, rubbing her cheek sympathetically against Kate's knee. Three years since she started coming here. Three years since the happy Kate of her childhood had begun to change into the morose, absent-minded creature she had lived with this summer, who was like a shadow of the person Elizabeth remembered. This was why. She had thought she was going mad.

'I wish I had known,' said Elizabeth, speaking her thoughts aloud. 'I'd have been nicer to you.'

'I wasn't nice to you either,' replied Kate, 'and there was less excuse for me. What I did to you was unpardonable, and I can only say I'll try to make it up to you in the future. I've known all summer that there was something wrong with you, but I kept telling myself I only thought so because there was something wrong with me, and I've been so tired — but there, I'm not going to make excuses for myself.'

'I can understand,' said Elizabeth, recollecting how Elizabeth Melville had felt too tired and ill to play with James, and how he had distressed her with his puzzled brown eyes. Perhaps because she knew what it was like to be Elizabeth Melville, it would be easier now for her to understand what it was like to be Kate. 'It isn't easy to be nice if you're feeling awful. I will tell you everything that happened, from the very beginning, when I found the looking-glass in the chest of drawers.'

And she did. She found that after all it was easy to tell Kate about the finding of the glass, and how by accident almost she had first found her way into the eighteenth-century world of the Melville family. She told her all about Grizel, and the children, about Lady Melville and Mr Cockburn, and how it felt to be Elizabeth Melville. She told how marvellous Robin had been in his youth, how he had made the whistle, and taught her Latin, and danced with her on Elizabeth Melville's birthday.

'Ah, yes, of course,' murmured Kate, remembering. 'So that

182

was what was happening. Go on, Elly, what else?'

'It was nice till then,' said Elizabeth. 'Until Elizabeth's birthday, I went because I wanted to. I was lonely, Kate, because you and Gerry were always so busy, and it was an adventure, and the babies were lovely. But after that, it stopped being fun, and I began to get frightened — Robin changed a lot, you see.'

'He did, indeed,' agreed Kate.

Elizabeth glanced up at her curiously.

'Kate, do you know all this already?'

'Oh, yes, certainly. It has been uppermost in my mind for many weeks. It's all in the letters, and in Giles Melville's diaries. I felt — but no, tell me the rest first, from your point of view.'

So Elizabeth told her the rest, from her point of view, and from Elizabeth Melville's point of view, how Robin had seemed to change from a happy schoolboy into an arrogant coxcomb, how life for Elizabeth Melville had sometimes been bitter, and hard to bear, but how she had gone on loving Robin every day of her life until she died. She did not dwell in any detail on the death of Elizabeth Melville, or the desolating experience of the Open Day at Robinsheugh, because she realised, with a new, serious feeling of responsibility, that these were the kind of pains which at the present time Kate was not really able to bear. And with some difficulty, because already she was beginning to forget how it happened, she tried to explain how she had herself come under Robin's spell, and had come to the terrible belief that he could call her at will out of her own world into his, even after her early love of him had faded, leaving nothing but a fearful fascination.

'I think perhaps it had something to do with the ring,' she said, and she explained how the ring had become invisible, although she could still feel it against her skin, and about the writing, 'QUHAIR THIS I GIVE, I WISS TO LIVE.'

'I've seen a ring like that,' said Kate suddenly. 'There's one in the Museum of Antiquities in Edinburgh.'

'Would there be more than one?'

'Oh, yes. They were quite common. They were really betrothal or engagement rings — that was what these words were really meant to signify. It didn't have anything to do with possession, in the way I think you mean. You don't think you feel anything now, do you?'

'No,' said Elizabeth. 'It's gone. It vanished last night, when you came to rescue me. He realised he could never have his wish, you see.'

183

'Yes, I see. But I didn't rescue you, you know. I tried, but it was really something you had to do for yourself. And because you had courage, in the end you rescued me, too.'

Her voice was warm and admiring, and Elizabeth blushed with pleasure, but she said regretfully, 'I didn't make a very good job of rescuing you. I wasn't quick enough. But anyway, he's gone, isn't he? He won't ever bother us again.'

'No, indeed, he never will.'

'Kate.'

'Yes?'

'What do you suppose really happened?'

Kate was silent for a while, and Elizabeth knew she was thinking very hard. Then at last she said, 'I think it must be faced that a great deal has happened here which cannot be explained, at least not with any certainty. Things have happened which at the moment our minds are not sufficiently developed to understand fully.'

'Do you mean,' asked Elizabeth slowly, 'that they could be understood if our minds were more developed?'

'Certainly they could,' said Kate firmly. 'Everything is capable of being understood, but that isn't at all the same as saying we can understand everything, is it?'

'No,' agreed Elizabeth, trying to sound serious, although underneath she was experiencing a great thrill, because she realised that Kate was not talking to her in the tone of a grown up to a child, or a teacher to a pupil, but simply as one intelligent person to another.

'All right, then. Having said that, we have a responsibility to try to understand as much as we can, and I think there are certain things we can say about your experiences, although they don't so obviously apply to mine.'

Now it was Elizabeth who was urging Kate to go on.

'In the first place,' said Kate, 'we can be quite sure of one thing. You didn't go into the eighteenth century in any bodily sense. Of course a house like Robinsheugh is heavy with a sense of the past, and in a way you could say that the past there is more real than the present. But that doesn't mean that the past returns. The eighteenth century is gone, it isn't enjoying some parallel existence with our own age — that's obvious, and therefore we must agree that what happened to you was some kind of illusion.'

But Elizabeth was not prepared to go so far, so fast.

'It didn't feel like an illusion,' she objected. 'It felt real.'

'I'm sure the best illusions do. But there are other arguments. All this coming and going you describe at the house — it's just impossible. Then you said yourself that while you were being Elizabeth Melville, and playing hide and seek upstairs with Lucy, Mrs Lindsay saw you standing in the dining-room. That's what you said, isn't it?'

'Yes.'

'And you also said that when you were in what you call the Melville world, you thought you were in Elizabeth Melville's body, didn't you?'

'I didn't to begin with, I thought she was in mine. But later, when I saw myself in the glass, it wasn't my face at all, it was hers. It was all the opposite of what I thought, Kate. I thought her mind came into my body, but it didn't. My mind went into her body.'

'Darling,' said Kate gently, 'that isn't possible. Elizabeth Melville has been dead for nearly two hundred years. Don't you see, whatever happened, it had nothing at all to do with bodies.'

Elizabeth sat frowning for a moment, trying to work this out.

'But what about the looking-glass?' she asked. 'That was real, wasn't it? And the ring? What about them?'

'I don't know,' said Kate. 'I know that Elizabeth Melville did own these things, but whether you did, I really have no way of knowing. All I would say is that no one but yourself claims to have seen them, and that neither seems to exist now. Invisible rings and vanishing looking glasses do not seem to me to be the stuff of reality, if by that you mean what is physically tangible.'

'Does that mean what can be touched?' enquired Elizabeth. In a way she wished that Kate would not use so many big words as if they were little ones, but she also knew now that if Kate was going to treat her as an equal, she would never bother to make concessions of that kind just because Elizabeth was young. If Kate were talking above her head, she would simply expect Elizabeth to crane her neck.

'It does,' replied Kate.

Elizabeth remembered that she had wondered in the past about this business of what was real and what was not, and how one knew. She also remembered a piece of green ribbon which she had thought she brought back with her from her visit to the nursery of the Melvilles, and which she had put away in a drawer for safety. It occurred to her now that when she packed her trunk yesterday, that ribbon had not been there.

'Do you suppose,' she said to Kate, 'that the glass and the ring might have been real while I was looking at them?'

Kate smiled at her, the kind of private, sharing smile that Elizabeth Melville used to exchange with Robin over *Fell's Latin Primer.*

'That,' she said, 'is an argument of philosophy which I would have thought was more often discussed by undergraduates than by first formers. I'm surprised you've even heard of it.'

'I haven't,' said Elizabeth. 'I just thought of it myself.'

'Did you, indeed?' said Kate, sounding very impressed.

'Well, but is it possible?' asked Elizabeth, who felt they were getting away from the subject.

'I've no idea. I'm an historian, not a philosopher. But I dare say you could make out an argument for it.'

As Elizabeth got to know Kate better, she would find that she enjoyed making out an argument for anything, at the drop of a hat. She suspected it now, and to recall her to the matter in hand, she said, 'So you think that what happened to me was — was only in the mind?'

'Only in the mind!' said Kate, so vehemently that Elizabeth looked up at her timidly, afraid that she had said something to offend her again, so soon. But when she saw the eager flame in Kate's eyes, she remembered that as well as sounding angry when they were frightened, people could also sound angry when they were talking about something which mattered to them more than anything else in the world. Kate saw her expression, and said more mildly, 'Elly, don't you understand yet that what happens in the mind is a thousand times more important and exciting and real than anything that happens to the body? In the end, it's the only thing that matters. People live their lives, and die, and their bodies are gone for ever — all they can leave behind them is their minds, their thoughts and ideas, to live on after them in books and diaries and letters, to influence the minds of generations they will never know. If history is about anything, that's what it's about — it isn't about the dead, it's a living, continuing thing, and we're part of it. Do you understand what I mean?'

'Yes,' said Elizabeth. 'Yes, I think I do. But people do leave other things besides their thoughts, Kate. They leave their houses and their furniture and china, and their clothes, don't they?'

'Of course they do, and these things are important too, because as well as being beautiful and rare, they help us to piece together a picture of life in the past. Even more importantly, when you look at a Georgian coffee pot, or an Elizabethan virginals, you can begin to understand something about the mind of the man who made it. But all of these are perishable things, like bodies, Elizabeth. Once an idea is set loose in the world, nothing can destroy it.'

'That could be dangerous,' said Elizabeth.

'Of course it's dangerous,' said Kate. 'I said that thought was exciting, I didn't say anything about its being safe.'

It was all confusing and bewildering, and like being under attack, with new ideas flying around her thick and fast, so that she barely had time to pick one up and examine it before the next one was thrown at her by this eager, enthusiastic creature who had scarcely spoken to her for three years. And through it all, Elizabeth felt a wonderful happiness; it was a feeling Elizabeth Melville might have known, but never before had Elizabeth Martin realised how exhilarating it could be just to think.

'All right,' she said. 'I'm with you so far. I accept that what happened to me happened in my mind — up to a point.'

'Up to what point?'

'Up to last night. Last night I didn't go into the eighteenth century, and neither did you, yet we both know what happened. I saw him, and you saw him too.

She shivered a little, and felt Kate's arm tighten about her shoulders.

'You're quite right,' Kate agreed. 'And I have to admit that this is where I get hopelessly out of my depth. I don't know how to explain what happened last night, any more than I know how to explain the peculiar sensations I've had myself in that house, because such things are as much outside my experience as they are outside yours. I only know that I am having to open my mind this morning to something against which I have been resolutely shutting it for three years. It's rather shocking, really, that one should pride oneself on one's mind, yet prefer thinking one is going crazy to admitting the possibility of ghosts.'

'Did we see a ghost last night?'

'Why, yes, I'm sure we did. What else could it possibly have been? It seems to me that for that one time, instead of your mind pushing through into the past, his mind pushed through into the present, for what purpose I really shudder to imagine. As I said, I have felt presences in the house before, and heard things, but I had never actually seen anything. But last night, for some reason — perhaps because we have thought about him so much — he

187

appeared to us in some semblance of human shape. Whether that was due to the power of his mind, or the power of ours, who can say?'

'Do ghosts have to do with the mind too, then?'

'I suppose so. I don't see what else they could have to do with. You see — although as you say, we both saw him, I had no feeling of fighting against a whole person, only against a strong and evil mind.'

'I killed him,' whispered Elizabeth, in sudden revulsion. 'I killed him, Kate.'

'No, you didn't,' said Kate quickly, drawing her in close to her side. 'Not in the sense you mean, and you must never think it. He was killed two centuries ago, and people can't die twice. You struck down a phantasm, because you realised in time that friendship for a person living matters far more than a yearning after a person dead. It had to be done, and if you had not had the courage and presence of mind to do it — well, we should certainly not be sitting here together this morning.'

Elizabeth knew that this was the truth. It was exactly what she had realised.

'I had forgotten till then,' she said shyly, 'how much I really cared for you. I'm glad I remembered in time.'

'My dear, I think everything happened just in time. When I think of the danger you have been exposed to this summer, I can't forgive myself. It appals me to think that Robin Melville's influence may really have been abroad in the house, affecting you. I can't bear to think of your coming into contact with anything so evil.'

'Was he so evil, Kate?' Elizabeth asked sadly. Even after the terrible vision of the night before, she somehow kept thinking of the Robin who had worn woollen stockings and a brown jacket, and called Lucy 'Mistress Ginger'.

'Yes, I'm afraid he was. From his childhood, even, he was violent and deceitful and cruel. As a tiny boy, his fits of temper were quite uncontrollable — he tormented animals and terrified the servants, although it was said that Grizel Elliot could always handle him.'

'She loved him,' said Elizabeth.

'Many people have loved him,' said Kate, 'and some of us at least should have known better. He was expelled from Harrow for beating a smaller boy half to death, and later he was sent down from Oxford after one term, because of a vicious attack on another undergraduate who had beaten him at cards. He spent the rest of his life idling in London and Edinburgh, a dissolute, drunken, disreputable rogue. He was killed in a brawl in an Edinburgh tavern when he was only twenty-six.'

Elizabeth could feel tears of horror and pity running down her cheeks. So that was what he had come to in the end, Robin who had danced to please his little sister, and had taught her Latin, because learning was the gold at the foot of her rainbow.

'Poor Robin,' she sighed. 'Oh, Kate, why did it have to be like that?'

'I don't know, Elly. It's a question his father asked too, over and over again. He was a brilliant boy, and he could be delightful when he chose, but he was false — like a beautiful apple with a rotten core.'

Elizabeth wiped her eyes on her sleeve.

'He wasn't all bad,' she said. 'I know he wasn't, Kate. He was kind to the little children, and he loved Elizabeth.'

'Yes, I know he did. This was the other side to his character, one which unfortunately lost ground as he got older. But it was dangerous too, because it blinded people to his wickedness — they saw his kindness and his joviality, and before they saw beyond it he had his knife at their ribs. I don't know whether this is any comfort to you, but I do believe that his love for Elizabeth was the only sincere and whole-hearted affection he ever had in the whole of his life. When she died, he blamed himself terribly, although there was never really any proof that he was the one who brought the infection into the house, and Elizabeth had been unwell for a long time. She was a very delicate child, probably tubercular, and it's unlikely that in those days she would have lived into adult life anyway. Perhaps if she had, Robin might have been different, but I doubt it. He was well on the road to ruin before she died.'

'She sometimes suspected it,' admitted Elizabeth, 'but she wouldn't let herself believe it. I wouldn't either, because, you see, I loved him too.'

'I know,' said Kate, running her long fingers sympathetically through Elizabeth's hair. 'And so did I. It must have been a rare and powerful attraction he had, to have reached out to a woman of my age after two centuries, but it did. When I read about him in his father's journals and letters, I couldn't help loving him too, in spite of all I knew about his later career.'

She paused for a moment, and looked down at Elizabeth as if

she were wondering whether she ought to tell her something very private, wondering whether she would really understand. She must have decided that she would, because she went on, 'It's one of the things I couldn't have told anyone before, and I certainly wouldn't tell anyone but you now, but I have been — haunted is not too strong a word — by Robin and Elizabeth Melville ever since I first began to read about them, which is really only this summer, because before that I was researching the earlier part of Giles's life. I always get very interested in the people I study — it's the way I am, and probably what first attracted me to history when I was young, but this wasn't like that. However strongly you may feel about the dead, they are dead, and you can't be involved with them as you are with the living. I remember once overhearing you saying to your mother that I liked people in history better than people now. What I suppose you were too young then to understand is that there is simply no comparison. The two feelings are completely different. But I have to admit that as far as Elizabeth and Robin were concerned, I did react to them as if they were living people. All the things you've told me this morning, I knew — I've lived these events in my own mind for months. I suffered over Elizabeth Melville's death as if she were my own child, and as for that boy Robin, I always seemed to see him through his father's eyes. Of course I knew what he was really like, but in my heart I could only see what Giles saw, a kindly, amusing, charming boy whose quick temper got him into trouble. Till the day he died, Giles could never face the truth about Robin, and I think I only faced it fully last night, when I came up the stair and realised that he had turned his mind on you.'

'That was when I faced it too,' agreed Elizabeth, drawing closer to Kate's knee. 'Till then, one part of my mind kept telling me he was bad, and the other part kept telling the first part to shut up. I just couldn't believe he was bad, when he had seemed so good.'

'We could be more on our guard against evil,' said Kate gently, 'if it didn't so often appear dressed up as good.'

'Kate — if you hadn't come last night — what do you suppose would have happened? Would he have killed me?'

'No, I don't think so, Elizabeth. You're too young and healthy to die of fright, and he certainly couldn't have killed you in any other way. He was only a ghost, after all. But I do think you might have had an experience so terrifying that you might not have recovered from it for a very long time. Anyway, that didn't happen, and I really don't advise you to dwell on it too much.'

'No, I shan't,' promised Elizabeth. 'I just wondered what you thought.'

'I think,' Kate continued, 'that the most hateful aspect of the whole affair — to me, at any rate — is the possibility that his mind has really been at large in that house all these weeks, and that it may have been working in you, putting thoughts into your mind — '

'Whatever makes you think that?' asked Elizabeth.

Kate was silent for a moment, then she said, 'It's the ultimate problem, of course. You must see that. It's the only thing we haven't discussed yet. How you knew — ' She broke off, and started again on another tack. 'Elizabeth, I wonder if you can tell me something. When you first started to know about the Melvilles, how did it feel? How do you think your information came to you?'

Elizabeth considered this for a moment, then, choosing her words carefully, she replied, 'I felt as if another person was feeding the thoughts in his — or her — own mind into mine.'

'That's what I thought. Who do you suppose was feeding these thoughts into your mind?'

'I don't know. Elizabeth Melville, I suppose.'

'That is what I just can't believe. Elizabeth Melville was a perfectly normal little girl who died when she was thirteen, long before her mind had reached the peak of its power and maturity. I have come to think now that all the Melville children left something of themselves behind them in the house where they had spent such a happy childhood — I heard more laughing and singing than anything else, to tell the truth — but I just don't see how Elizabeth Melville's mind could have been capable of such a feat.'

'I see. So you think it was Robin Melville?'

'I do. You see, if you had come to your knowledge of the Melvilles through reading about them, or hearing me talking a lot about them, then I'd say that imagination had a lot to do with your experience. I'd say that because you were lonely, you played a lonely child's game, and invented company for yourself in the form of children who lived long ago in a house that fascinated you. And that because you are sensitive and intelligent, your imaginings seemed real to you. But I know it isn't like that. You had never heard of the Melvilles till you came here. You certainly never read about them. Gerry wouldn't talk about them, because privately they bore her to tears, and I have never talked about them because I couldn't. So we know your knowledge didn't come from any of these sources.'

'And that's what makes you think that — it was Robin — '

'Yes, I think that in some way I can never understand, Robin Melville used his power over Elizabeth Melville's mind to get a hold on yours — I know it's astounding, but I am beginning to accept astounding things with surprising ease. What I find hard to bear is the idea that you have been exposed to something fundamentally evil, when I was supposed to be looking after you. I feel I failed you completely.'

There was silence in the room for a while, broken only by the ticking of Kate's clock, and the further-off sound of river water. It was Elizabeth who spoke first.

'Kate,' she said, 'I think you're wrong.'

'Do you?' said Kate miserably. 'I'd like to be.'

'I'm sure you are. Shall I tell you what I think?'

'Please do.'

'Well — ' Elizabeth paused, groping for the right words to express the thought which was now overwhelming her. 'All the time you've been speaking, I've been thinking how all the things which were happening to me have been — what was it you said? Uppermost in your mind for weeks. You said you'd actually lived those events in your own mind. Could it not be that my knowledge came to me out of your mind, and not out of Robin's at all? That because you were thinking about him and Elizabeth so much, and I am so close to you — ' There, it was out, and she was the one who had said it. Of course you could only feel so strongly and bitterly about someone whose closeness to you was a fact that could never be altered, no matter how much you tried to tell yourself it was not so — 'so close to you, that what was in your mind came into mine more easily than it ever could from the mind of a stranger? It's as if I knew you cared for her, and I felt you were friendlier to me when I was Elizabeth Melville than when I was myself. I didn't ever think this way at the time, but it's how it seems to me now. I've missed you terribly. And Kate — ' Elizabeth spoke kindly, as if for a moment she was grown up, and Kate the child she wanted to reassure — 'I think I was wrong in thinking Robin wanted me. I think it was always the other Elizabeth he wanted, just as she wanted him, but I was thinking with the last scrap of her mind that was still sticking on to mine.

192

So you don't have to worry about that at all.'

She was going to say more, but stopped, because Kate had suddenly put her hand over her face, and Elizabeth saw that the hand was unsteady.

'What is it, darling? she asked anxiously. 'Am I tiring you?'

Kate gave her a quick, uncertain smile.

'I don't know,' she said. 'If you are, I hope you'll tire me often. How can it be I never noticed — '

She did not finish the question, but never again in all her life did she look at Elizabeth with a vague expression in her eyes, or read at the table when she was there. She thought for a moment, then she went on, 'Yes, I'm sure you're right. It would never have occurred to me, but it is the most credible explanation. But if it's true, it means that you had all these terrible experiences because of me. I am responsible, and guilty too. I knew there was something wrong. Even Gerry knew because she spoke to me about it. And yet I did nothing.'

'There wasn't anything you could have done.'

'I could have tried.'

Elizabeth saw that the old, strained expression was returning to Kate's face, and she realised that she had had enough. This day was her wakening after three years of nightmare, she had a broken arm, and she was exhausted. So she took Kate's hand in hers, and said firmly, 'Listen, it's all over. Whatever mistakes we both made, it doesn't matter any more. And in any case, I know that what has happened has done me good, not harm. When I came here in July, I was turning into an absolutely dreadful person, vain and silly and selfish — as bad as Lucy and almost as bad as that horrid Lady Melville. I wouldn't even try to understand anyone who was different from me. Well, I'm not going to be like that any more, because I understand a bit about other people's feelings. I'm quite different now — I feel peaceful and happy and — well, older, somehow.'

And before there was time for any more to be said, Gerry arrived, carrying a tray with tea, and bossily ordering Kate back to bed.

21

No Continuing City

A week passed, and on the afternoon before they were to leave Robinsheugh to return to London, Kate and Elizabeth walked together up through the village, past the shop and the school, and climbed the steep hill-track to the little grey churchyard in the heather. It had been Elizabeth's idea, perhaps her way of proving to herself finally that the Melvilles were firmly fixed in history, and Kate agreed, because indulging Elizabeth was a habit she had reverted to very easily. Gerry had declined to accompany them, saying that she had never really shared their passion for the Melvilles, and in any case she had the Whippit Sillabubs to prepare for their farewell dinner party that evening. Elizabeth had wondered how Gerry would react to the events of a week ago, whether her curiosity would prove awkward, but it had not been like that at all. Gerry had asked no questions, and from the little she did say, it was obvious that she assumed that Elizabeth had been sleep-walking, and that Kate had fallen downstairs because she tripped in the dark. She remarked to Kate that she had been worried about Elizabeth for some time, because she was obviously romancing about the Melvilles more than was good for her; she also said that she had suspected that Kate was very worried about Elizabeth too. It suited Kate well enough to have her thus provide her own explanation, and she did not attempt to contradict her. When Elizabeth said privately to Kate that she was surprised they had not had more trouble with Gerry, Kate laughed, and said she had never expected trouble.

'What you have to understand about Gerry, and people like her,' she said, 'is that they would never even remotely imagine the kind of experience we have had, and if you told them, they would try to cure you with a spoonful of Milk of Magnesia. Gerry is a marvellous girl — she reminds me of your mother, clever and practical and a tower of strength to people like you and me. Honestly, this summer I don't know what I would have done without her. She'll take her degree, and marry Peter, and be an excellent wife and mother, but she has no curiosity or imagination whatsoever. Even when — as in your case — she was at one point on a knife-edge of seeing the truth, along came her

194

common sense and rescued her from anything so uncomfortable. To try to explain to her what really happened would be worse than a waste of time.'

So Gerry stayed at home to concoct sillabubs, and Kate and Elizabeth went walking.

It was an airy day, with watery clouds speeding over a pale, windy sky, and Elizabeth, who for so long had failed to mark the sounds and colours of the countryside, seemed to savour everything with the sharp delight of a person long blind and deaf who suddenly has had her senses restored to her. Even the brightness of autumn was fading now, but there were other pleasures, like the heavy scent of earth after rain which rose into her nostrils from the grass banks along the edges of the road, and the silver delicacy of little streams trickling down among the whinstone fragments on either side of them. Elizabeth was herself again, and she sniffed and touched and listened, so that long afterwards she was able to remember clearly the feel of that day, with its fitful sunshine and its shadows, and white gulls wheeling against the sky.

Kate, who was still weaker than she would admit, could only walk slowly, and by the time they reached the little iron gate in the churchyard wall, she was leaning on Elizabeth's shoulder in a way that seemed perfectly natural after the past happy, friendly week, when sheer relief had made them laugh uproariously at everything, and Gerry had gone around saying that she w... only sensible, grown-up person in the house. The gat... with much squeaking and groaning, and they we... open behind them. Gravestones of many age... lop-sidedly over the short, hummocky grass, ... and weathered and hammered into the ea... rain of four centuries, sheltered inadequat... few thin, crippled trees. Kate and Elizab... through them, making for the farthest c... where Mr Lindsay had told them Giles ... buried. They found it easily, a separat... a low stone parapet, containing several tombstones with names of them as familiar to Kate and Elizabeth as their own.

They had not talked much about the Melvilles since the day when they had had their long talk in Kate's room, partly because each felt it was better for the other that for a while they should talk about other things, and partly because they were finding so many other things to talk about, and planning a future in which for each of them a very important part was to be the friendship of the other. And it promised to be a delightful future for Elizabeth; Kate was going to buy a spinet for them to share, and take Elizabeth up Magdalen Tower on May Morning, and in the Christmas holidays, when Kate's arm would be mended, they were going to the theatre in London with Gerry and Peter, then on to a late supper at the most expensive restaurant Kate could afford.

'But what if Mother says, "No"?' Elizabeth had asked anxiously. She knew her mother's views on late nights.

'She won't say "No" to me,' replied Kate complacently.

So there had not been much time to talk about the Melvilles. But now, as they rested against the wall, they found that once again they were talking about them, quite naturally, as they would discuss any interesting people who had lived two hundred years ago. Kate told Elizabeth how James had gone to the High School in Edinburgh, because Giles did not want to send another son to Harrow after the sad affair of Robin's expulsion, and had been a very good scholar, though inclined to wildness and much beaten because of it; afterwards, however, he had become more sober, and had gone on to the University of Edinburgh to study Law. On his father's death in 1797, he had become Sir James Melville, and had stayed on in Edinburgh to become a Judge of the Court of Session, and a very important person indeed, before ttling down as Laird of Robinsheugh with his pretty little wife e children.

 em was called Elizabeth too,' Kate said.

 had become a minister, much to everyone's ince he was the one who never knew his ursed hares on the Sabbath, and had once put s skirt during a Sunday morning service. He ut had been a very popular and fashionable rch in Glasgow, before coming back to h his brother's family in his old home at

 urprised,' remarked Elizabeth. 'Lady Melville had a pretty low opinion of lawyers and clergymen. She didn't like Mr Cockburn, and you should have seen the expression on her face when she said that Elizabeth would be lucky to find a lawyer who would marry her.'

'Ah, yes,' said Kate, 'but to understand that, you have to understand a bit about society in those days. In the first place,

James and Alexander were younger sons, and at a time when all the property and money, as well as the title, went to the eldest son as a matter of course, younger sons had to have a profession. One for the Law, and one for the Church — that was traditional. But Lady Melville didn't want her daughters to marry younger sons, simply because they had no money. It was eldest sons she had her eye on, preferably very rich ones. She really was a tiresome woman.'

'She was worse than tiresome,' said Elizabeth soberly. 'She was absolutely beastly. She was so cruel to Elizabeth.'

'Yes, I know. Of course there was a reason for that. She was jealous.'

'Jealous?'

'Yes. You see, her marriage to Giles Melville was just of the kind I've been telling you about. It was arranged by their parents, and they were never consulted at all. Giles Melville was an excellent match — he was rich, and titled and very good-looking, but although he gave his wife wealth and position and treated her with courtesy, I don't think he ever really cared for her much at all. If she had felt the same way about him, it might not have mattered so much, but unfortunately she was deeply in love with him, so you can imagine how she felt.'

'Yes. But what had that to do with Elizabeth?'

'Everything. You see, of all his children, Giles adored Elizabeth. He thought that the sun rose and set on her. Perhaps he made it too obvious. I'm not saying that it in any way excuses Lady Melville's behaviour, but it does make it a little more understandable.'

Elizabeth could never have foreseen a day when she would feel sorry for Lady Melville, but when she thought of the misery of such a situation as hers, she did feel a certain stirring of pity in her heart.

'What happened to Lucy?' she asked.

'Ah, it was sad about Lucy,' said Kate, laughing. 'I'm sorry to have to tell you that she did not marry as well as she and her Mamma had hoped. Apparently lots of young men came a-courting, but although Miss Lucy had a long pedigree, and was a wonderful housekeeper, and her possets were the wonder of three counties, the sharpness of her tongue seems to have scared the gentlemen away. In the end, she had to make do with a fat farmer of forty-five, who carried her off to the Isle of Skye, which I suppose was even wilder then than it is now. She had fourteen

197

children and thirty-two grandchildren, and her bad temper was famous well into the reign of Queen Victoria.'

Elizabeth found this story particularly satisfying.

'What about Grizel?' she wanted to know next.

'I think I rather envy your having known Grizel,' said Kate. 'Of all the people in this story, she's one of the ones I like best. Do you know that she used to write to Giles every week, long letters about the children, telling him everything they were doing and how they were growing up? In that way she probably gave him more happiness than anyone else he ever knew, because he hated being away from the children so much. He kept all the letters — that's how I learned so much about what went on in the nursery. Normally that kind of information is very hard to come by. Really, Grizel's letters would make a book on their own.'

'Would you write it?' asked Elizabeth.

'No. I think you know I never would. But you were asking me about Grizel. She stayed on at Robinsheugh to become nurse to James's children, all twelve of them, and she had three of her own as well. She married Matthew Grimble, the steward, and I understand from Mr Lindsay that there are descendants of theirs still living on the estate. I expect she and Matthew are buried here somewhere.'

They wandered among the headstones, reading the ancient inscriptions, pointing out to each other the graves of people they had seemed to know, Mr Cockburn, Grizel and Matthew, Alexander and James, Sir Giles and Lady Melville. Finally they stopped in front of the stone Elizabeth had come to see, and read the words finely chiselled there by a hand itself long stilled. Lichen had gathered around the plain eighteenth-century lettering, but it was still perfectly legible.

Here lie the Mortal Remains of
ELIZABETH FRANCES MELVILLE
Elder Daughter of
SIR GILES MELVILLE, BART. and
THE HONBLE. ELIZABETH CLARKE
who Departed this Life
the 21st Day of December Anno Domini 1779
aged 13 Years
also of
ROBERT ADAM CLARKE MELVILLE
their Eldest Son

who Departed this Life
the 23rd Day of November Anno Domini 1789
aged 26 Years

For Here have we no Continuing City, but we Seek One to Come

Elizabeth read it several times, till she was sure she remembered it all, then she turned to Kate, who was sitting on the parapet, and said, 'It was sad about Elizabeth Melville, wasn't it, Kate?'

Kate drew her down beside her on the little wall.

'Yes, it was sad,' she agreed. 'It's always sad when people die before they have a chance to fulfil their promise. But you know, Elizabeth, if Elizabeth Melville had lived, I doubt very much whether she would ever have had the chance to fulfil hers. She certainly would not have been happy. I think there's some comfort in remembering that on the whole she had a very happy childhood, but if she had lived into adult-hood, things would have been very difficult for her. Apart from the heartbreak she would have suffered on account of Robin, there was absolutely no place in the eighteenth century for the kind of woman Elizabeth Melville would have become. The idea that a woman might want to be a scholar would be treated not even with contempt, but just with incredulity. In the end of the day, I don't think even her father would have taken it really seriously, for all that he allowed her to learn Latin. He thought it was a childish whim. She would have been obliged to marry, and have children, and manage her household, all good things in themselves, but not for her. She wanted to read books, and look at the stars, and think deep thoughts in peace and quiet, and they would never have let her. She would have been stifled, and frustrated, and never in all her life allowed to be what she really wanted to be. I think perhaps it's better to have a short life, and die with your heart full of hope, than to live long, and have your hopes ground into the dust by people who couldn't even begin to understand them.'

'For here have we no continuing city, but we seek one to come,' repeated Elizabeth quietly. 'Is that what it means, Kate?'

'I don't think that's what it originally meant, Elizabeth,' replied Kate, 'but as with many other things in the Bible, you may take it to mean what you want it to mean in different situations. I think it was a good epitaph for her, don't you?'

'Yes, I do,' agreed Elizabeth. She sat fingering a withered stalk of grass which she had picked, but she was thinking about the

Open Day at Robinsheugh. 'Kate,' she said eventually, 'you don't suppose, do you, that Elizabeth Melville suffered terrible things in her mind, because of me?'

Kate shook her head.

'My dear,' she said, 'I don't think you need ever worry about that for a moment. What happened to you happened only to you, and all the evidence is that Elizabeth Melville was a happy, normal little girl who lived for thirteen years, and died in her father's arms without ever being aware she was dying. When he wrote about it afterwards, Giles said, "Then my dear child sighed, and fell asleep." '

There was comfort in this. Still, there was a wistful note in Elizabeth's voice as she remarked, 'You'd have liked Elizabeth Melville, actually. She was very like you.'

Kate laughed, and gave her a friendly push.

'Then I probably wouldn't have liked her at all,' she said. 'What on earth makes you imagine that I'd like anyone because she was like me, you silly ass? Have you any idea what a trial I am to myself, all untidy and unbuttoned, and dropping hairpins all over the place? And have you noticed how I can never remember what day of the week it is?'

Elizabeth giggled, and admitted she had noticed it once or twice.

'Elizabeth Melville couldn't either,' she said.

'Well then,' said Kate, 'think how annoying it would be if there were two of us like that around.'

They sat for a while in the lee of the wall, enjoying a spell of sunshine, and chatting of this and that. Elizabeth told Kate how she had looked for the nursery in the twentieth-century house over and over again, but had never been able to find it.

'Does that mean that it didn't really exist at all?' she asked, for many things were now becoming blurred round their edges in her mind.

'Not at all,' Kate said. 'It certainly did exist, but it doesn't any more in a form you'd be likely to recognise. In fact you've probably been in it without recognising it. The last construction work on the house was done in 1830, and at that time the nursery room you're talking about was divided into three smaller bedrooms for the children — James's grandchildren — and the passageway from the landing was blocked up. A new door was cut from the main bedroom on that floor, and the other rooms inter-connect. I could show you, if you like.'

'It doesn't matter,' said Elizabeth. 'Actually the only other thing I'd still love to know is why Elizabeth Melville was cut out of that portrait. But I don't suppose I ever will, now.'

Kate looked shamefaced.

'Oh, dear,' she said. 'I forgot to tell you. I came across the explanation of that last week, in a letter from James to Alexander. There was nothing sinister about it at all. Apparently when the new ceiling was put into the dining-room in 1800, the room had to be stripped of all its furnishings. When the workmen were taking that painting down from the wall, they were careless, and let it slip, so that it fell across an iron candle-holder on the hearth — the kind with spikes to hold the candles. The spikes gored the canvas so badly that the whole corner had to be cut out. Of course they didn't have the techniques of restoration which we have today. James was very upset about it, naturally, under the circumstances.'

'Yes,' said Elizabeth, 'he would be. He was very fond of Elizabeth, although I don't suppose he would remember her at all clearly. He was only four when she died. Kate — '

'Yes?'

'Is there any other portrait of Elizabeth Melville?'

'I'm afraid not, Elizabeth.'

'Well, in that case,' said Elizabeth wonderingly, 'I am the only person living who really knows what she looked like. The only person in the whole world.'

But as she thought of Elizabeth Melville, with her deep brown eyes and wide, curly mouth, she knew that that memory too was fleeting, and would soon be gone.

A ragged cloud crossed the sun, and a flurry of rain made them scramble to their feet, but by the time Elizabeth had buttoned up both their waterproofs, it was dry again.

'I wonder how Gerry is getting on with the sillabubs,' said Kate, as they moved back towards the gate.

'You'll be in trouble if they don't work out,' warned Elizabeth.

'But that isn't fair,' objected Kate, 'for it will be Lady Melville's fault.'

They made their way home across the fields, the wet turf springy under their feet, thinking their own thoughts in the peace of each other's company. It was Elizabeth who noticed the rainbow first, one foot in the river, the other on the hill, the frail bridge of light which has been a symbol of hope to people ever since Noah first sent out his dove from the ark. They leaned on a gate to look at it, and Elizabeth found herself telling Kate about Mr Cockburn, and how he had told Elizabeth Melville that seeking for learning was like looking for gold at the foot of the rainbow; you might never find it, but that did not matter, because the quest was all.

'I didn't think of it then,' she continued, 'but now I remember, it's what Gerry said about you, too. She said that learning was the gold at the foot of your rainbow, and that really you didn't care about anything else.'

Kate pondered this for a moment, then, 'Of course it isn't as simple as that, Elizabeth,' she said. 'There are other things — perhaps I should say people — I care about too. But for myself, yes, it is the only thing I really want. It's like a hunger in me that nothing in the world can satisfy.'

Then Elizabeth thought again of the words from the Bible which Elizabeth Melville's father had written on her tombstone, 'For here have we no continuing city, but we seek one to come.' They were all the same, these people, Giles and Elizabeth Melville, and Kate, and Mr Cockburn, and perhaps even poor Robin when he was very young, all positive, ardent people with a secret in their hearts, all seeking a distant city which was always round the next turning of the road, a city of gold at the rainbow's end.

They watched the rainbow disappear. Elizabeth opened the gate, held it open for Kate to come through, and closed it again. They walked in silence across the next field, and crossed the bridge over the Wishwater into the drive of Robinsheugh. There Kate paused under the beech trees, and looked seriously at Elizabeth.

'And what about you, Elly?' she asked. 'What's the gold at the foot of your rainbow?'

Her voice was quite casual, but Elizabeth was not deceived. She knew that it was the most important question she would ever be asked in her life, and that on her answer the whole shape of her future might depend. But she did not even have to consider how she would answer. She too would join in the search for that city.

'The same as yours,' she said, 'and Elizabeth Melville's.' But then she glanced up rather anxiously at Kate, and added, 'Only — '

'Only what?'

'Only, you see, I don't think I'm exactly like you and Elizabeth Melville. I think some day I'll want to get married, and have babies of my own, like James and Alexander.'

Kate did not seem to think there was any difficulty about this. She smiled at Elizabeth, and said, 'Of course you will. And why on earth not? After all, I'll be relying on you to provide me with children to spoil in my old age. But for your own sake, when the time comes, try to choose someone who will understand about the rainbow. Fortunately there are plenty of them about. Things have changed a lot since Elizabeth Melville's day.'

Together they walked round the side of the soaring, secret house, and passed under the archway into the courtyard.

'I was wondering,' Kate said, as they crossed the cobbles to the door, 'whether perhaps you would like to spend the summer with me in Italy next year. I'm considering writing a Life of the Young Pretender, and I want to do some research in libraries in Rome, and probably in Milan and Florence as well. We could combine business with pleasure — you work with me in the libraries in the mornings, and in the afternoons and evenings I'll take you to the art galleries, and to the Opera.'

Elizabeth thought she was going to burst with happiness. She wanted to shout and sing, and caper round the yard. But she remembered that scholars were dignified people, so she contented herself with a few skips and hops on the doorstep, and said kindly to Kate, 'Well, I expect I had better come, hadn't I? I mean, Granny would never allow you to go as far as Italy on your own, without me to look after the tickets, and tell you what day of the week it is.'

And Kate admitted that she did very frequently lose tickets, and she said that if Elizabeth would look after them, she would be very grateful. Then they went into the kitchen to see how the sillabubs were coming along.